Praise for L

No one brings the Old West to life quite like Darlene Franklin. From its unforgettable opening scene to the sigh-inducing epilogue, *Lone Star Trail* is a skillful blend of a charming love story and a realistic portrayal of the hardships and heartbreak that marked the lives of the first German settlers in Texas.

—AMANDA CABOT, author of *Tomorrow's Garden*

With *Lone Star Trail,* Darlene Franklin deals with a time of turmoil in Texas history. The melding of various cultures didn't come easy, and she depicts this in an authentic way. She also has a real handle on the setting. I could feel the heat, taste the dust. Her three-dimensional characters leapt off the pages straight into my heart. I highly recommend this wonderful read.

—LENA NELSON DOOLEY, award-winning author of the McKenna's Daughter series and *Love Finds You in Golden, New Mexico*

Lone Star Trail tells the moving story of one man's journey from prejudice to love. Darlene Franklin sweeps the reader into the complicated relationships between two families as they learn who they are and how they can survive together. My only complaint is that the next book isn't already on my nightstand.

—REGINA JENNINGS, author of *Sixty Acres and a Bride*

Wande Fleischer searches for contentment as a German immigrant in a foreign land—Texas. Jud Morgan resents the passel of people who've crowded his territory. But he notices the lovely German woman helping out in his mother's kitchen. Both have suffered great losses; both must come to terms with the path on which God has led them.

Romance woven into an historically accurate view of the times gives this book thumbs up! This Texan thoroughly enjoyed *Lone Star Trail.*

—Eileen Key, *Cedar Creek Seasons*

Lone Star Trail is a delightful mix of German culture and Wild West spirit. Each page drew a new emotion, from tears to laughter, and ultimately a renewed excitement about my own faith. I devoured this book, like Franklin's characters devoured their homemade peach strudel.

—Elizabeth Ludwig, author and creator of *The Borrowed Book*

Darlene Franklin has created a delightful story that takes two cultures and blends them into a fine mixture that will warm your heart and satisfy your craving for a well-told story. I look forward to the rest of the series.

—Martha Rogers, author of the *Winds Across the Prairie* and Seasons of the Heart series

Loved it! *Lone Star Trail* is a fascinating look into the lives and struggles of German immigrants in Texas; a story packed full of adventure, prejudice, survival, and betrayal, yet sweetened with forgiveness, enduring love, and romance. Don't miss this first book in what promises to be an excellent series!

—MaryLu Tyndall, author of the Surrender to Destiny series

TEXAS
TRAILS

LONE STAR TRAIL

DARLENE FRANKLIN

A
MORGAN FAMILY
SERIES

MOODY PUBLISHERS
CHICAGO

Edited by Andy Scheer
Interior design: Ragont Design
Cover design: Gearbox
Cover image: Image Source Photography and iStock Photography
Author photo: Motophoto

Library of Congress Cataloging-in-Publication Data

Franklin, Darlene.
Lone star trail / Darlene Franklin.
p. cm. — (Texas trails: A Morgan Family Series)
Summary: "The six-book series about four generations of the Morgan family living, fighting, and thriving amidst a turbulent Texas history spanning from 1845 to 1896 begins with Lone Star Trail. Judson (Jud) Morgan's father died for Texas's freedom during the war for independence. So when the Society for the Protection of German Immigrants in Texas (the Verein) attempts to colonize a New Germany in his country, he takes a stand against them. After Wande Fleischer's fiance marries someone else, the young fraulein determines to make new life for herself in Texas. With the help of Jud's sister Marion, Wande learns English and becomes a trusted friend to the entire Morgan family. As much as Jud dislikes the German invasion, he can't help admiring Wande. She is sweet and cheerful as she serves the Lord and all those around her. Can the rancher put aside his prejudice to forge a new future? Through Jud and Wande, we learn the powerful lessons of forgiveness and reconciliation among a diverse community of believers." —Provided by publisher.
ISBN 978-0-8024-0583-8 (pbk.)
1. Texas—Fiction. 2. Domestic fiction. I. Title.
PS3606.R395L66 2011
813'.6—dc22

2011020230

We hope you enjoy this book from River North Fiction by Moody Publishers. Our goal is to provide high-quality, thought-provoking books and products that connect truth to your real needs and challenges. For more information on other books and products written and produced from a biblical perspective, go to www.moodypublishers.com or write to:

River North Fiction
Division of Moody Publishers
820 N. LaSalle Boulevard
Chicago, IL 60610

1 3 5 7 9 10 8 6 4 2

Printed in the United States of America

This book is dedicated to . . .

My coauthors Susan Page Davis and Vickie McDonough. You have long been my friends and writing mentors. How privileged I am to write Texas Trails with two such talented authors!

My agent, Chip MacGregor. A big thank-you for coming up with the idea for the series and inviting me to help bring it to life. Your faith made it happen.

And to Deb Keiser, Andy Scheer, and all the folks at Moody Publishers who fell in love with Texas Trails and breathed the breath of life into *Lone Star Trail.*

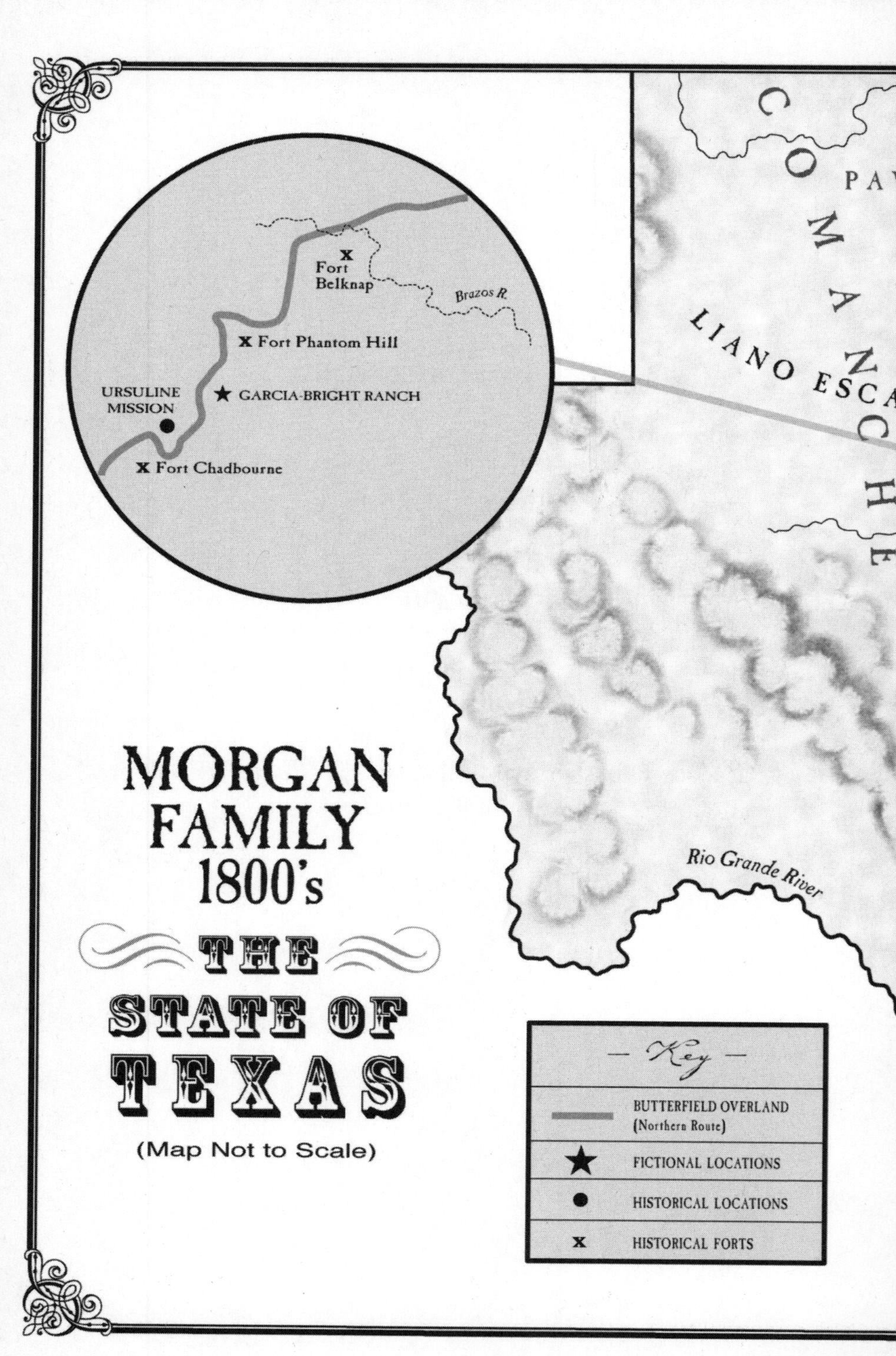
COMANCHE
PA
LIANO ESCA
Fort Belknap
Brazos R.
Fort Phantom Hill
URSULINE MISSION
GARCIA-BRIGHT RANCH
Fort Chadbourne
MORGAN FAMILY 1800's
THE STATE OF TEXAS
(Map Not to Scale)
Rio Grande River
Key
BUTTERFIELD OVERLAND (Northern Route)
FICTIONAL LOCATIONS
HISTORICAL LOCATIONS
HISTORICAL FORTS

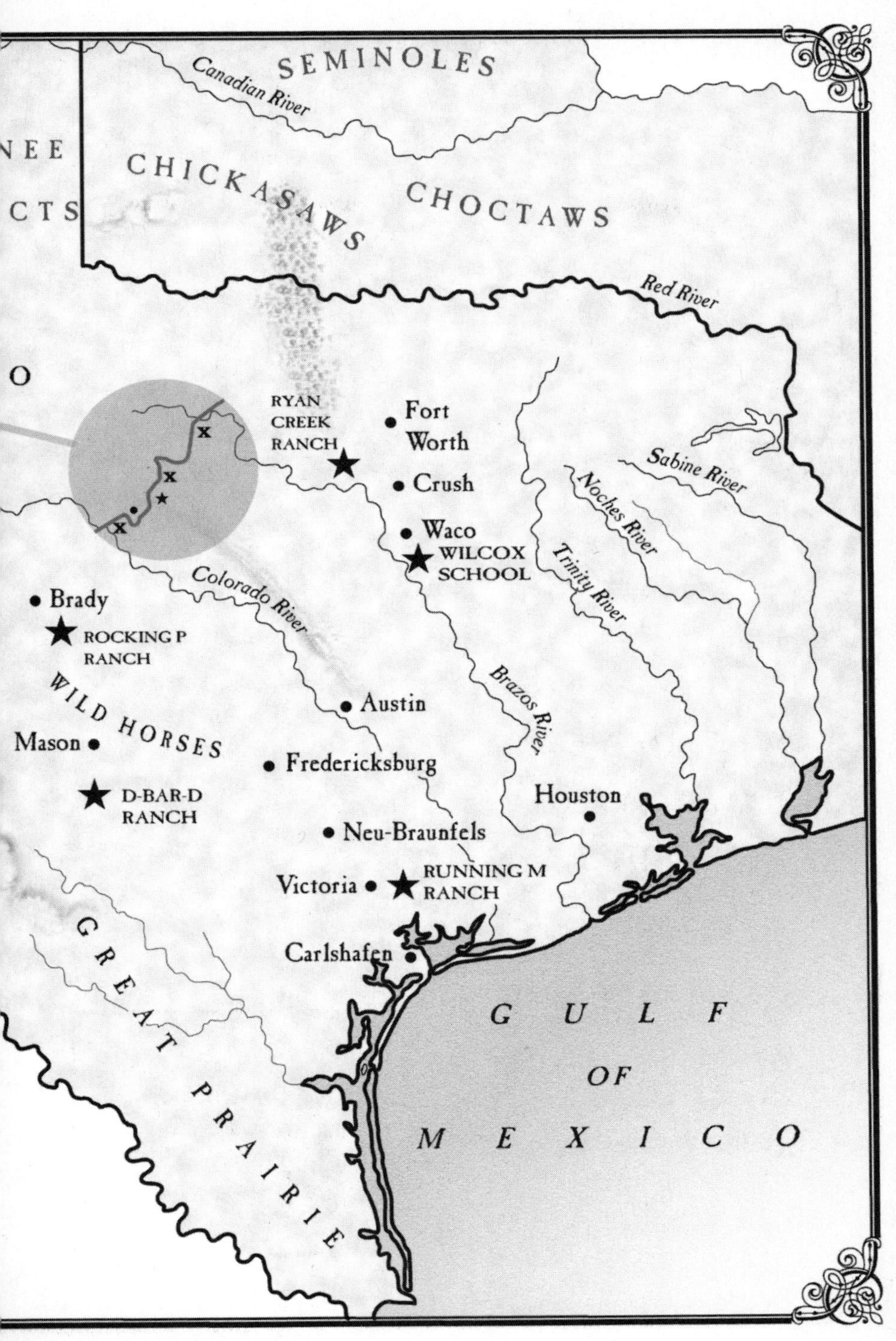

SEMINOLES
Canadian River
NEE
CHICKASAWS
CHOCTAWS
CTS
Red River
O
RYAN
CREEK
RANCH
Fort
Worth
Crush
Sabine River
Noches River
Waco
WILCOX
SCHOOL
Trinity River
Colorado River
Brady
ROCKING P
RANCH
Brazos River
WILD HORSES
Austin
Mason
Fredericksburg
D-BAR-D
RANCH
Houston
Neu-Braunfels
Victoria
RUNNING M
RANCH
Carlshafen
GREAT PRAIRIE
GULF
OF
MEXICO

PROLOGUE

RUNNING M RANCH NEAR VICTORIA, TEXAS, EARLY DECEMBER 1844

In December, shadows fell earlier with each day. On the darkest night of the month, Jud Morgan found himself searching after a stray colt. The new moon was hidden, leaving only starlight to guide him. He hoped his ranch hands, Bert and Tom, had been able to get the rest of the herd back into the paddock before evening fell. He didn't like the look of the night. A hoot that didn't quite sound like an owl's reminded him that the dark of the moon invited the Comanche to come for the ranch's prime Morgan horses.

He was leading the pesky colt back to the paddock when the crack of a broken stick made him start. Lantern light threw figures at the opposite end of the field into shadow. He stopped under the cover of a tree. He heard voices, a man and a woman's, before he could make out their shapes.

"Jud," Tom Cotton's voice boomed.

"Billie!" Jud's sister Marion called for their baby sister.

Their voices rang across the empty space. Jud rode out of the thicket. "It's me." His horse trotted to where the others waited on horseback. "What's happened to Billie?"

"Isn't she with you?" Marion's voice revealed her panic. "She came home from school with news she couldn't wait to tell you. She got permission from Ma to go out to the pasture to meet you, and I guess she followed you up into the canyon."

Jud shook his head. "She never reached me. And I'm later getting home than I expected. That colt ran halfway up the mountain before I caught him." He frowned when he thought of Billie.

The owl call. "Comanche."

Marion sucked in her breath. Tom reached for the rifle at the front of his saddle and glanced around him. In the center of the pasture, even in the dim starlight, they'd make easy targets.

"Did Billie catch up with you and Bert?" Jud asked Tom.

"Yes, when we was just starting to bring the horses in. Over that way." Tom nodded toward where Jud had left them earlier that day. "We told her you had headed for the stream. Maybe thirty minutes after you left."

The stream. It was too dark to track the Comanche, and foolish with only the two men. But Jud knew where Billie always forded the stream. "Keep an eye out for Velvet as well." Billie had claimed the dark brown, nearly black, mare as her own on her last birthday.

Jud guided Marion and Tom through the trees toward the sound of burbling water. Since Billie knew the direction Jud had headed, she would have crossed the stream here. On the far side, he jumped off JM's back to check the mud along the bank. A multitude of hoofprints, enough for seven, maybe nine, horses. Only one horse had shoes—*Velvet*. He skirted the edge of the impressions and found where the shod horse had shied and sidestepped. Not more than a yard away, he spotted Velvet's saddle, the girth cut clean through.

Marion let out a low cry, and Tom put out a hand to steady her.

Of the horse—and Billie—Jud saw no further sign.

Jud wanted to throw back his head and howl. Instead, he picked up the saddle and climbed back on his horse. How could he tell Ma that the Comanche had grabbed Billie? His gut twisted at the possibilities. *I'm doing the best I can, God. Why did You let them take my little sister?*

CARLSHAFEN, TEXAS, EARLY DECEMBER 1845

Land, blessed land. Wande Fleischer raced down the plank to the wharf, wishing she could fling herself headfirst on the ground and kiss the sand like a child. She felt like a year had passed since the ship left Antwerp, Belgium, instead of less than two months. Her eyes scanned the shore, hoping Konrad would be there to greet her. But her fiancé had not known when the ship would arrive. She carried a letter ready to mail to inform him.

Her brothers, Drud and Georg, raced past her, thrusting their arms in the air and shouting. Papa stopped by Wande's side. "We have arrived, *Liebchen*."

Wande closed her eyes and embraced the sky, welcoming the fresh air after so many months aboard ship. Laughing children—her little sister Alvie among them—ran through the sand. She opened her eyes and spotted a seagull picking at crumbs a few feet in front of her. *"Mama, Wir sind in Texas."* At last.

Mama stopped midway down the plank. Ulla had her arm around Mama's shoulders and helped her take the next step. Papa hurried to Mama's side and guided her to solid ground.

"So this is Texas?" Mama looked around the beach, as warm as summer in the ocean town her grandparents called home. She took another step and stumbled. "I think it will take me as long to regain my land legs as it took to get my sea legs." She managed a smile, but she looked a little pale. "Do we start for Neu-Braunfels now or do we spend the night here?"

"I will find out." Papa guided Mama to the pile of crates with their belongings, then headed for Herr Lang, the unofficial leader of their shipboard company. Forty families had traveled to America to join the Society for the Protection of German Immigrants in Texas—the Verein. The two men talked, Papa making angry gestures, Herr Lang shaking his head.

"We will not like the answer." Mama spoke in a voice only Wande and Ulla could hear. "But I can count on you to help everyone stay happy. You are good daughters." She patted their hands.

Papa returned, his feet making heavy marks in the damp sand. "We will have to make arrangements for a wagon. That is up to us. Until we can leave, they have tents for us." He gestured to a spot away from the beach, where Wande could see white fluttering in the gathering breeze. Overhead, storm clouds formed, and wind whipped the waves into froth. "Only a tent for protection, with a storm moving in." He shook his head.

Mama stood, her mouth in a firm line. "Come, *kinder*. Tonight we will have an adventure."

With Wande's help, Mama got the family settled in the makeshift tent and even kept them mostly dry during the rainstorm that lashed in during the night. Her frequent trips to the encampment's privy made it clear the intermittent stomach ailments she had suffered aboard ship had returned. At some point during the night, Ulla also became sick. Wande prayed for their strength and God's healing.

In the morning, Mama felt better. Papa and the boys went to ask about a wagon, and Alvie begged to join them. Wande slipped the letter to Konrad into Papa's hand. "*Bitte* mail this."

Papa glanced at the address and smiled. "I will find a way."

The sun had come out, and Wande joined Mama in spreading their damp clothing in the sunshine. But Ulla felt too ill.

After her fourth trip to the privy, Ulla stumbled into the tent and crumpled in a ball at Mama's feet. Her arms cradled her chest, and she moaned.

"*Liebchen,* what is wrong?" Mama found a pillow and placed it under Ulla's head.

"Es . . . ist . . . nichts." The pallor of Ulla's cheeks said otherwise.

Wande took Ulla's hot, dry hand. Ulla couldn't get sick, not now that they had reached the promised land.

A young woman from the neighboring tent joined them. "The bloody flux," she said. "I do not know of a family here in tent city not affected."

Ulla moaned again.

Mama stood. "I must go for a doctor."

The neighbor shook her head.

But they had to ask. Wande put her hand on Mama's arms. "I will go." She ran among the tents. "*Arzt!* We need a doctor!"

As she passed the rows of tents, she spotted a mother rocking a wailing infant. *"Fraulein!"*

Wande forced herself to slow down. *"Kann ich Ihnen helfen?"*

"My daughter is very sick. If you find the doctor, please ask him to see her."

Four more people stopped Wande before she completed her circuit of the camp. As expected, she didn't find a doctor. Behind the last row of tents, she came across a fresh grave, mourned by a mother hugging her children. Wande rushed away, afraid of what tomorrow would bring.

Back at their tent, Wande sought out the neighbor. "You know something of this bloody flux. *Was können wir tun?*"

Weariness formed deep lines around the woman's eyes. "All that I know is to keep her as comfortable as possible. Some survive, many more die." She shrugged. "I lost my baby." She turned away.

"I am so sorry." But the neighbor was no longer listening.

Wande poked her head through the flap of the tent, where Ulla lay moaning. Mama questioned her with her eyes, and Wande shook her head. "How are you, *Mutter*?"

"Don't worry about me. I am only a little tired from the ocean journey, is all."

Wande prayed her mother spoke the truth. "I will take care of everything. You stay here with Ulla and rest." First things first. Slipping back outside, she grabbed the water bucket and headed for the well. She could at least offer relief for the thirst and heat that ravaged her sister.

Ulla grew worse as they waited for Papa to return. But as Ulla weakened and hallucinated, Mama suffered only a mild fever.

Papa didn't return until long past noon. Wande briefly explained the situation. "It would be best if the rest of the family stays somewhere else." Papa shook his head. "I will stay with my wife and my daughter. But if you can find someplace for the *kinder* . . ."

Georg nodded. "I will find us a place to spend the night. Come tell me if something happens."

Day passed into night. Ulla grew more frail while Mama began to sleep peacefully. As the sun cast its first rays over the ocean, Ulla slipped into eternity.

Tears streamed down Wande's face. Her sister, the one she whispered her deepest dreams to, had died. How many more victims would Texas claim from the Fleischer family?

CHAPTER ONE

Near Victoria, Texas, December 1845

Wande Fleischer could hardly see the road in front of her through the slashing rain. Her shoes sank in the mud with each step; the hem of her dress became filthy. If the rain continued, her hair would be drenched; dirty as leaves in the fall instead of its usual bright blond. So far Texas—which was promoted by the Adelsverein back in Germany as the "land of milk and honey"—was anything but sweet. Her fingers curled into a fist that she longed to raise to the sky. But only a child would do that. Even her little sister, Alvie, the family songbird, hadn't lifted her voice since they left the plain pine box at the port of Carlshafen only three days ago.

They could have made it to Victoria in one day, but Papa decided to take it easy for his wife's sake. Wande looked forward to reaching the town, one of the oldest in all of Texas, which had an established German community. She was cheered by thoughts of a dry roof, pleasant conversation in the only language she knew, and a chance to rest her feet.

Alvie tugged at Wande's sleeve and pointed ahead to the wagon piled high with the family's belongings. *"Was ist los?"*

Mud sucked at the wheels, bringing the wagon to a standstill. The harder the two oxen pulled, the deeper the wheels slipped into the ruts. Papa had insisted they take all the crates, instead of leaving some in storage in Carlshafen. Before they had traveled a mile, the wagon groaned under the weight. The tired oxen lacked the will to pull the extra load.

Mama sat on the seat of the listing wagon. She glanced over the side and clutched the edge. Papa had insisted that as weak as she was from her recent illness, she should ride. Everyone else walked.

"Gather around." Papa climbed down and called the family together. Georg and Drud stood beside Papa, and Alvie huddled next to Wande.

"Wande, you take Georg's place beside the team. Alvie, child, go in front to lead. I need you to signal the oxen while we push the wheels. Now, wait until I tell you."

Papa placed his hands on the right wheel, while Georg and Drud braced the left. At Papa's signal, Wande called, *"Hu!"*

The boys pushed. Alvie waved her arms. The oxen strained, but the wagon did not budge.

"Again."

They moved a short distance, then slid back into the rut.

Wande yelled *"hu"* once more. The wagon budged a couple of inches before the wheels sunk to their hubs in mud. Papa rested his back against the wheel, sighed, and wiped his forehead.

In the distance, a wagon carrying three people approached from a side road. As it neared, Wande made out a tall man driving the horses. He was seated next to two women, one quite a bit older than the other, all as blond as any German, but with skin deeply tanned. Wande hoped that God had sent this man and his family to their rescue.

The younger woman gestured to the man holding the reins. She pointed out the Fleischers' plight. The man ignored her, frowning at the obstacle the Fleischers' wagon created in the road. He flicked the reins and turned the wagon while the young woman continued to plead. They rode past on the far side of the road—splattering Wande with mud.

"Dummkopf . . ." Wande mumbled to herself. She glared while the wagon headed toward the horizon. The younger woman looked back over her shoulder. Apology was written in her expression.

Papa waited until the wagon disappeared. He sighed. "Let us try again."

This time, the wagon lurched forward. An ominous crack sounded as the wagon gained momentum. It tipped. Crates and packages tumbled and broke open. Their precious bags of flour spilled across the soggy road.

"What happened?" Mama twisted to see, and the wagon's balance shifted more. She slipped sideways and teetered over the edge of the seat for a long moment before she landed on the ground, covered in rain-soaked earth in a perfect sitting position.

Alvie reached her first. Mama's face was still and white. No sound passed her lips, but Wande could tell she was in pain.

"Where does it hurt, *Liebchen*?" Papa bent next to Mama and ran his hand lightly along her legs. "Did you break any bones?"

"Nein." Mama tried to rise, only to crumple with a sigh of pain. "Perhaps I twisted my ankle a little."

Wande recognized Mama's understatement. She saw Georg stare at their wagon, frowning. She agreed: another problem for them to overcome. Mama could not walk, and the wagon they depended on had broken. In December, the sun would set early. They needed to take action.

"Do not worry, Mama," Wande said. "I will go ahead to Victoria and find someone to help."

Georg squared his shoulders and glared at his sister.

Papa shook his head. "No, daughter. Your mother needs you here—and besides, you do not know much English yet."

"But there are Germans in Victoria. You said so." She hesitated to mention her hope of finding a letter from Konrad waiting for her.

"And there are also Mexicans and *Amerikaners*. We do not know whom the good Lord will send to help us. I will go."

"I will go with you." Georg took off his hat, shook the rainwater from it, and plopped it back on his head.

"You are needed here, to defend the family. Drud will accompany me."

"Let me come, Papa." Alvie twirled in a circle swinging her skirt. "I speak English almost as well as you do."

"And you would charm everyone, I am sure. But no, little one, you will stay here. Cheer up your mama for me. Can you do that?"

Alvie looked down the road, and Wande allowed her imagination to run along. Perhaps a hot cup of coffee or even a strudel . . . little things would bring joy in this miserable land.

"Take heart!" Papa said. "I will return before you know it. We can take comfort that the winter season is less harsh here in Texas." Papa took a walking stick and gestured for Drud to join him. "Let us get going."

Papa turned to survey his family among their possessions scattered along the road—and smiled. "Back in Germany, I might have had to leave you in a snowdrift."

Wande watched as they walked toward Victoria, then she

turned to Alvie and Georg. "Let us pick up what we can." She reached for a damask tablecloth that had fallen in a puddle.

⟵ ★ ⟶

As the wagon approached Victoria, Jud Morgan was glad he was wearing a hat. Otherwise the harangue by his mother and sister would have roasted his ears.

"You should go back and help those poor people." Marion picked at the threads on her sleeve, a sure sign of her displeasure. Jud's sister couldn't kill a rabbit that was destroying their garden, let alone bypass someone in need just because they had pressing business in town.

"If we had stopped, we probably wouldn't have made it into Victoria today." Jud knew his excuse sounded weak. "You said you needed to go shopping."

"'He that loveth not his brother whom he hath seen, how can he love God whom he hath not seen?' The apostle Paul asks that question in the New Testament." Ma was at it again, quoting Bible verses.

"It's a sad thing, to pass them by when we are celebrating the birth of the God who is love."

With each word, Jud's scowl deepened.

"We'd better stop fussing at him, Ma, or else my brother might turn into a stone pillar." Marion poked his arm. "If we keep it up, he might decide to help us with the baking, and then he'll eat it all before Christmas day."

Jud put a lot of energy into keeping his scowl but didn't succeed. One corner of his mouth began to lift.

"Be careful, or I might think you're smiling." Marion leaned against him. "You do, however, need to let go of your resentment of our new neighbors."

Their arrival into town spared Jud the familiar argument. "Where do you want to go first?"

"The mercantile," Ma said. "Drop us off while you go about your business."

Several wagons crowded the streets, and he had to wait before he found a spot in front of the mercantile.

"Business is brisk today," Marion said. "People must be getting ready for Christmas."

Snatches of "O *Tannenbaum*" floated through the air, as well as shouts that weren't in English or Spanish. *The speakers must be German*. But Jud kept his irritation to himself. "I'll leave the wagon here while I see if the blacksmith can come out to the ranch after Christmas."

"You just want to have a word with your friends over there." Marion nodded at a group in front of Sally's eating place. Men drifted in and out of an ongoing game of checkers and passed around a week-old newspaper.

Jud shrugged. "A man has to keep up with what's going on in the world." Marion's laughter followed him as he joined the men on the porch.

"Hello there, Boss. I didn't expect you today." Tom Cotton, the youngest of the bunch, scooted to the side of the bench and patted the space beside him. "Take a load off."

"Thought I'd sneak in a game of checkers while my womenfolk do their Christmas shopping." Jud took a seat next to Tom and studied the game. Without asking permission, he skipped a black piece across the board and said, "King me."

"It was my turn!" Jimbo Rawlins said.

"Were you red or black?" Jud tapped the crowned playing piece.

"Black." Jimbo arched his back against the chair. "I was gonna make that move next."

A boy, still too young for long pants, scurried up the steps and stared at the checkerboard. A man stepped up behind him. Jud had learned to play by watching the men, like this boy was now. The man apologized for the intrusion, nodded to the silent group, and steered the boy across the street to the mercantile.

"That's Herr Gruber." Jimbo let out a long breath. "I met him at the saloon the other night. He was looking for beer. Couldn't believe we didn't have any." Jimbo shrugged. "But he seemed nice enough. Said *'danke'* pretty as you please and walked out."

Jud supposed that was something in the German's favor.

"Did the rest of you see this?" Tom dug a square of paper out of his pocket and flattened it on top of a barrel.

Jud leaned in. He could read only a handful of the words—*"Adelsverein,"* the word they had come to associate with the onslaught of Germans invading Texas—and even "Neu-Braunfels," the community started by Prince Carl of Braunfels in Germany.

"They're describing Texas as 'the land of milk and honey,' or so the newcomers say." Jimbo stretched his hands over a small fire blazing in a pot. "Coming in by the hundreds. A passel of them came through yesterday bound for that Neu-Braunfels."

"I can't believe they plan on building a 'New Germany' here in Texas." Tom gazed down the street as if seeking out strangers to send back where they came from.

Bile rose in Jud's throat at the thought. His father had died to make Texas free from Mexico—and now these Germans wanted to make it over in their image.

"But one thing is true, Tom," Jimbo said. "Unless you're part Indian, all our ancestors came here from Europe sometime or another. And the government leaders in Austin have been begging for settlers. Not their fault that more Germans took them up on the offer than anyone else."

"Then let them get on up to that land grant in the hill country—and leave us alone down here," Jud said. "Every time a group goes through, seems like one or two stay behind and decide they like Victoria just fine."

Some of the foreign words on the flyer were enough like English that Jud could guess at the meaning, like *"neu"* for "new" or *"frei"* for "free." But most was unintelligible. Someone was offering free land in a new Germany—*his* Texas. He crumpled the flyer and dropped it in the fire.

"You won't stop them that way." Jimbo chuckled. "Want to play a round of checkers?"

"I need to get along to the blacksmith. I'd best be going." Jud trotted down the steps, anxious to work the frustration out of his limbs. On his way to the smithy, he saw one strange face for every familiar one—all of the newcomers were speaking German. He could have been in Germany, except for the brown Texas dirt beneath his feet and the pungent odor of frijoles.

After consulting with the blacksmith, Jud returned to the mercantile. His mother and sister stood in the doorway, their backs to him, speaking to someone inside. Jud started up the steps, ready to help with the packages.

Before Jud reached his sister, she motioned for him to stop and gestured to someone coming out of the store. The burly man Jud had left stranded on the road came through the door, carrying a box full of packages and foodstuffs marked for the Running M Ranch.

CHAPTER TWO

The man saw Jud at the same moment Jud recognized him, and both stopped. He gestured to Ma as if to ask, "Is that your son?"

Jud closed the distance in one long step and grabbed the box from the stranger. "Ma, I'm here. You don't have to trouble this gentleman to help you."

"Mr. Fleischer wanted to help." Her cheerfulness dared him to say a word."They had an accident after we saw them. His wife hurt her ankle, so I offered to take his family to the ranch with us. Mrs. Grenville has already sent for the doctor."

Jud bit back a groan. Dr. Treviño was as bad as the preacher when it came to welcoming the newcomers. Between him and the two women, Jud feared the ranch would be saddled with unwelcome guests for the foreseeable future.

"Climb aboard." He nodded for the stranger to get in their wagon. Jud had already forgotten the German's name.

"I ride with the things. My son, also. Thank you, Herr Morgan."

Jud swung the box into the bed of the wagon. A young teenager Jud had not noticed jumped in and extended his hand to his father.

Doctor Treviño climbed into his saddle. "I'll take my horse, so I can come back when we're finished. Straight down the road, you say?"

"You cannot miss it. Thank you."

Jud helped Ma onto the seat of the wagon first, followed by Marion. He took his seat, said a brief prayer for patience, and flicked the reins.

Tears spilled from Alvie's eyes. Wande wanted to cry with her, but held back. Bags of precious flour and sugar had torn, spilling their contents into the mud. In their short time in Texas, Wande discovered flour was scarce, whether wheat, oat, or rye. Sugar was available but costly. Corn grew in abundance, explaining the ever-present cornbread and tortillas.

But to Wande, *bread* meant a loaf of bread, leavened with yeast, baked a crusty brown. By the looks of it, their store of wheat was cut in half.

Wande thought of Jesus' words, "I am the bread of life." He taught the crowd after He fed five thousand people with only five loaves and two fish. The bread He offered wasn't what they wanted, but it was what they needed. *Foolish girl. Crying over flour.* Wande smiled and pulled Alvie next to her. "Come now, little sprite, let's sing something for Mama."

"Please do that, *Liebchen*." Mama smiled, although pain formed lines around her mouth. "Sing to me about the cat in the snow, a cat like Mittens." She clucked and the cat approached close enough for Mama to rub her head.

Alvie giggled and began to sing. *"ABC, die Katze lief im Schnee."* ABC, the cat ran in the snow. She added the same motions she always did, illustrating the white boots the snow gave the cat and the way the cat shivered and licked its paws.

"I wonder if it ever snows in this place." Mama looked across the land that rose and fell around them like sea waves.

"Snow will surely fall before Christmas." Alvie looked into Wande's face. "It will not seem like Christmas without snow." Her voice quavered.

"There was no snow in Bethlehem when Jesus was born," Wande reminded herself as much as her sister. "We celebrate our Savior's birth, not the arrival of winter."

"And there will be presents and good things to eat." Mama shifted position and spotted a rider and horse approach.

Wande prayed again that Papa would return soon. The man on horseback slowed and dismounted. He wore a long brown frock coat and carried a black doctor's bag. His kind face put Wande at ease. He first spoke to Georg, which made her feel better about him. He was doing things the right way.

"Do you speak English?" the man said.

"Enough." Georg shrugged.

"I'm a doctor, Dr. Treviño. Herr Fleischer sent me. May I examine your mother?"

Georg stepped aside and let the man pass.

The doctor asked what was wrong, and Mama pointed to her foot. Again, the man stopped to ask "may I?" before he examined her ankle under her petticoats.

A whimper escaped Mama's lips when the doctor probed her ankle. He ran his hand over her skirt, up to her knee. When Mama didn't cry out, Wande hoped their assessment of no broken bones was correct.

"Someone else is coming." Alvie danced out of the corner of Wande's vision.

"Papa!" She ran toward the wagon.

Papa climbed out and scooped up his youngest child, but

Wande's attention was focused on the man still seated in the wagon. He was the man who had passed them earlier—leaving the Fleischers stranded.

Surely God had not chosen this man to rescue her family.

Jud took in the scene. The wagon bed was splintered like matchsticks. The mother sat propped against a tree, legs stretched in front of her as if she dared not move. A young girl hugged her father, Herr Fleischer. A slightly older version of the son who had traveled in the back of the wagon talked with Dr. Treviño. A cat ran for cover.

Jud saw all this and dismissed it as he climbed from the wagon. But his eyes paused when they reached a young woman with hair the color of corn and eyes as blue as wildflowers in springtime. Her smile disappeared when she caught his glance. She looked so beautiful, so wholesome, Jud could almost forgive the accident of her German birth.

Her gaze seemed to drift from the top of Jud's hat to the tips of his boots, leaving him feeling exposed.

Marion took a step forward. *"Hallo, Fraulein Fleischer. Mein name ist Marion Morgan."*

The blond blinked at the German words coming from the American. "Wande Fleischer."

To Jud, the name sounded like "One day," which seemed strange. *Wanda, maybe. A good American name for such a beautiful girl.*

"Sprechen sie Deutsch?" Wande asked Marion.

"Only a few words." Marion offered her hand. "But we will be friends, *freunde, ja?"*

"Freunde." Wande stared at the hand Marion had stuck in front of her, then placed her smaller palm inside Marion's.

The two women shook hands, then linked arms. "Wande,

this is my *mutter,* Frau Morgan. Ma, this is Wande Fleischer."

Wande curtsied in her mud-soaked dress.

"Don't be so formal." Ma threw her arms around the girl. "Welcome to Texas, Wande."

A gleam in her eye, Marion headed for Jud.

Torn between running for cover and holding the hand of the beautiful woman, Jud stayed rooted to the spot.

"And this bear is my *bruder,* Judson Morgan."

"Danke, Herr Morgan."

He looked into eyes as clear as a lake, wide as the sky, and deep as the ocean. "My friends call me Jud."

"Jud ist Freunde?" Wande smiled and scanned the spot on the road where he passed the Fleischers by only a few hours ago.

"Freunde Jud," he said.

Wande held out her hand, and Jud accepted it without thought. He held on a second longer than necessary.

Did he just tell Wande he was her friend? But he was determined to hate the German immigrants for taking over *his* Texas. He wouldn't make this mistake again.

He had a feeling that Fraulein Fleischer could disturb his peace in a thousand different ways.

Marion Morgan fought not to laugh as she watched the exchange between Jud and Wande. He looked like a calf separated from his mother. She had never seen that look in his eyes. As for Wande, Marion hoped her new friend could see past Jud's gruff manner. She deemed him the most loyal man in all of Texas.

Wande touched Marion's arm. *"Meine familie."* In short order, she introduced her parents and her brothers, Georg and Drud. Up close, Marion could see the differences, but they could be twins.

"Are they twins?"

Wande looked confused, and Marion searched for a word to fit. All she could come up with was the word for two. *"Zwei?"* She pointed to the boy's faces.

Comprehension dawned and Wande shook her head.

Last of all, Wande introduced her sister, Alvie. The little girl was staring into a tree, calling *"Katze, Katze."*

Marion could see a patch of black and white fur high in the branches. "Can I help?" She gestured to illustrate what she meant.

Alvie's face screwed in concentration. "I speak a little English." Her English turned out to be better than Marion's German. "Our cat is in the tree."

"So I see."

"At home, we leave her outside, and she comes back when she is ready. But here there is no home for her to return to."

"ABC, die Katze lief im Schnee." A sweet soprano melody floated through the air. Wande sang to the cat. *"Und als sie wieder raus kam."*

"She is telling Mittens to come down. The cat always comes when we sing this song." Alvie joined Wande for the second verse. Marion recognized only one word—*katze.*

The cat put one tentative paw on the tree trunk, then a second. She crawled down several feet, but stopped higher than either woman could reach.

"So German cats like to climb trees, too." Jud's voice sounded in Marion's ear and she jumped. "Let me help." He reached up with his great arms. The cat saw him and prepared to pounce higher. Jud grabbed the cat before she could leap, and she yowled as he pulled her to his chest.

That was her brother, Marion thought. A big, tall, rawboned cowboy—cradling a cat in his arms.

CHAPTER THREE

Wande didn't know what to make of this *Amerikaner*. Earlier he passed them on the road without a backward glance. Now he rescued their cat, cradling Mittens against his chest. He was so big, and the cat so small, that the scene reminded Wande of the picture of Jesus holding a lamb. The cat settled and began purring in Jud's arms.

"Do you have a box?" He pantomimed grasping a handle.

"Ja." Alvie ran to the pile of their things and returned with the cat's basket. "I let her out when we stopped here."

"I'm surprised she hasn't run away." Jud disengaged the cat's claws and secured her in the basket. Mittens yowled at the indignity. "I know you don't like being locked in, but it's for your own good." Mittens responded with a plaintive meow.

When Jud straightened, Wande saw a thin trickle of red staining his shirt. "You've been hurt!" Cat scratches could develop into bad infections, and she didn't want this man who rescued Mittens to suffer. She made a "may I?" gesture.

He looked at the scratches. "Oh, that's nothing. Your cat was just scared."

So American men weren't so different from German men. With two brothers, Wande knew about sidestepping male pride. "Alvie, bring me some water, and a clean cloth."

Then she turned to Marion. *"Bitte sag ihm, danke für unsere Katze retten."*

The *Amerikaner's* sister repeated her message in English: "Please tell him thank you for rescuing our cat."

Jud tipped his soiled brown leather hat. "And now I'll help load your things onto our wagon."

Alvie returned, water in a pot, a clean rag draped across her arm. Wande put a hand on Jud's arm. *"Nein."*

"She's not letting you go anywhere." Marion grinned and unbuttoned his shirt against his efforts to stop her. "That is nasty." Marion took the rag Alvie handed her, immersed it, then wrung it out.

Wande kept her eyes focused on Jud's face while his sister cleaned the scratches. She noticed his hazel eyes had flecks of gold. He winced a few times, but kept still. She thought he blushed, but she couldn't be sure with his sun-darkened skin. The sun here must shine sometime for him to grow so tanned.

"All done!" Wande tried not to watch as Jud secured his shirt.

He turned to leave. Wande reached out to touch his sleeve. "Herr Morgan. *Ich bedauere, daß sie verletzt wurden.*" Even if he didn't understand the words, she hoped he would catch her meaning.

He almost smiled. "I asked you to call me Jud."

"Jud." She repeated his name. Perhaps her first impression of him was not accurate. Perhaps he is more like his name—sturdy and firm, like the man standing before her. *"Ich bin froh, daß wir Freunde sind, Jud."*

⟵ ★ ⟶

Jud studied the face before him. A few hours ago he had raged against the wave of German immigrants taking over his Texas. But now he encouraged Wande to call him by his Christian name. Her awkward pronunciation—the *J* that sounded more like a *Y*—made it almost charming.

"Ma'am." Jud clapped his hat on his head and turned to the doctor. "How is Mrs. Fleischer?"

The lady answered in a stream of German, and Jud decided she must be all right. Upon a second look, he saw the same kind eyes and pleasant face he had noticed in her daughter, only faded with time.

Dr. Treviño smiled. "As you can tell, she's in fine spirits. She's sprained her ankle and needs to stay off her feet a few days. She should be ready to travel by the time they have a new wagon, as I was just explaining to Herr Fleischer." Jud noticed the older man listening intently and translating the words into German.

The man addressed Jud. "*Ja,* Frau Morgan has offered us the room at your house. Is that good with you?"

"Of . . . course." Once Ma had extended the invitation, Jud couldn't uninvite them.

"Isn't it wonderful?" Ma smiled. "We'll have company for Christmas."

The last thing Jud wanted for Christmas this year was company. Their family suffered a loss about this time a year ago—and he wanted to mourn in private.

"You needn't frown," Ma said. "We can rejoice with those who rejoice at the Savior's birth, and mourn with those who mourn." She transformed the small catch in her voice with a smile. "I learned that the Fleischers also suffered a loss this past year. God knew we needed each other this Christmas, and look at the distance they crossed to reach us."

Jud would rather take a solitary horseback ride and discuss his grief with God, but Ma would never permit that, not on a holiday. "That is something," he mumbled.

"Thank you, Herr Morgan." Mr. Fleischer clasped Jud's hand.

"Call me Jud," he said with less enthusiasm.

"My name is Meino. My sons put the boxes on your wagon. We are ready. My wife and daughters go first. *Ja*?"

A few boxes remained—they couldn't all fit in a single load. Neither could all the people. The German's plan was sensible. First Jud helped his mother onto the seat before lifting Mrs. Fleischer beside her—taking care to avoid putting stress on her ankle. Jud held out his hand to Wande. She pressed her thumb gently into the back of his hand as she stepped into the Morgans' wagon. Within minutes they were ready to go.

Marion sat in the back next to Wande. Alvie held the cat's basket tightly. "Our kitty does not like dogs," Alvie said. "Do you have dogs?"

"We have a dog, but Marmalade—that's our cat—taught him who was in charge a long time ago. He got his nose scratched too many times when he was a puppy."

Alvie looked at the basket. Mittens continued to let out desolate yowls. "She only—what is the word?" Alvie made claws out of her fingers. "When she is scared."

"Jud didn't mind," Marion shouted. "Did you, Jud?"

He shook his head.

Wande stared at the rolling countryside, not taking part in the conversation.

Perhaps, Marion thought, Wande didn't understand English well enough to join in. A few times Marion had gone to a friend's house where everyone spoke Spanish or German. She remembered the isolation when she didn't understand the stream of conversation flowing around her, though her friends did their best to include her.

Alvie and Mr. Fleischer already spoke some English. Maybe she could encourage Wande to learn. "Alvie, what was that song you were singing when Mittens climbed the tree?"

"ABC, die Katze lief im Schnee." Alvie sang in a clear soprano. "ABC, the cat ran in the snow."

"So *katze* means cat? The two words sound a lot alike."

"There are more words like that. *Garten* is garden in English; *schule* is school. I think English is easy." Alvie pointed to her sister. "But Wande thinks she does not need to learn English, at least not very much." She whispered in Marion's ear. "She expects to get married as soon as we reach Neu-Braunfels."

"She does?" Marion looked at Wande, who smiled at her. She wasn't surprised that someone as pretty and kind as Wande had a beau, but Marion had hoped . . . She had never seen Jud perk up around any of the young women of Victoria the way he responded to Wande.

Marion had romance on her mind a lot lately. She thought Tom planned to join them for supper tonight, although she wasn't sure after she had seen him in town.

They reached the turn to their house, and Marion imagined the impression it might make on strangers. She remembered the day Pa hung the sign, "Running M Ranch, est. 1834," across the entrance. The letters faded some through the years, but Marion knew they all took pride in their ranch, which was only a bit older than Texas itself. Jud, already tall by then, had helped hang the sign. Calder handed them the tools. Marion had looked on with Mama and baby Billie.

They hadn't known that would be one of their last good times altogether. Before Pa . . . before Billie . . . Marion blinked back tears. She had already cried enough to turn the Guadalupe River into salt water. She needed to laugh. "I'd like to learn the cat song. Please teach it to me."

"I'd like that. Repeat after me. *'ABC, die Katze lief im Schnee.'*"

Marion made a valiant attempt.

Alvie frowned. "I guess it's good enough. We're singing to have fun. It goes like this." She put the words to music. "Now sing with me."

Like all the Morgans, Marion loved music—even if the lyrics had foreign words. If she could learn a language by singing, it would be easy. *"ABC, die Katze lief im Schnee."*

Wande's attention wandered across the empty fields; fields she expected to see cultivated with corn and potatoes and all the wondrous crops possible in this new country. Free land, lots of free land, available to anyone. How could these *Amerikaners* let it sit there . . . doing nothing? Konrad planted a crop as soon as he settled his new piece of land. He said so—in the one letter she received from him before they left Germany.

Alvie touched her arm and spoke in German. "Sing with us, Wande. We are teaching German to Marion. She wants to learn the cat song."

Wande smiled at the American and nodded.

"I know the first line already," Marion said. "The words rhyme, which make it easy to remember. C, *Schnee*."

"The words in the second line rhyme, too. Kam and *an*."

Marion soon picked up the rhythm of the nursery rhyme.

"You must be a musician," Wande said.

"Everyone in our family likes music. We're distant relations of Justin Morgan, the man who bred the Morgan horse. Have you heard of him?"

Wande could understand more English than she could speak. She shook her head.

"We raise horses, like he did, but he was also a composer." Marion smiled. "Why do you think I am a musician?"

"You have a beautiful voice," Wande said.

Alvie giggled.

"Also, Papa says musicians hear the differences in languages better. You speak German well," Wande said.

"You're musical, too," Marion said. "I'm sure you could learn English, Wande. I can teach you, if you would like."

Wande had resisted learning. If it were up to her, she never would have left Germany.

She had fought the new language, since it represented leaving her home and everything she had loved. But both Papa and Konrad believed the stories about Texas. On the way, she continued to speak her native tongue. She traveled among Germans—and to a German husband.

But learning English to become better friends with *Amerikaners* like Marion and her family might not be so bad. Konrad would be proud if Wande arrived in Neu-Braunfels able to speak with their American neighbors.

"You speak English. I answer in German," Wande said. "We both learn. *Das ist gut*."

"That is very good." Marion smiled.

CHAPTER FOUR

Look!"

Alvie's cry drew Wande's attention. In the distance, a dozen horses galloped, a blur of chestnut and black with a silver streak. Wande's heart jumped back ten years, when she was a girl wanting a horse of her own. She had never seen so many. For that matter, she had never seen wild horses. They were breathtaking.

"They are beautiful." The same hunger Wande had known as a girl blazed in Alvie's eyes. Perhaps in Texas, she might own a horse.

"Those are our horses." Marion's hazel eyes gleamed with pride. "Morgan horses—the breed Justin Morgan developed. We raise the finest horseflesh in this area."

"You own all those horses?" Wande could scarcely believe it. Back home, only one farmer in ten was lucky enough to own a horse.

"That's only part of them." Marion laughed. "That silver one is my favorite. Most Morgans are bay or black or chestnut, so he really stands out. If one of the mares ever has a dappled foal, I'm going to talk Jud into keeping it." She grinned. "If I can."

Wande glanced at the man holding the reins. "Your brother cares for you deeply."

"But he won't let me keep a valuable colt just because I want to. He takes his responsibility as the head of the household seriously—too seriously sometimes. He's run off almost everyone who's tried to court me." She smiled, and Wande wondered if there was someone special. "Oh, there's our home."

Marion said the words with such pride, Wande expected an ornate castle. Instead a cluster of buildings, not too different from her farm back home, came into view: a fenced-in area for a kitchen garden, a barn, a chicken coop. The two-story wood-frame house was larger, however. *A home,* Wande realized, and a longing for a place of her own swept over her. *Soon,* she hoped. Perhaps Konrad had already built a place for them.

Despite her eagerness to reach Neu-Braunfels, Wande didn't regret the time she would spend on the Morgan ranch. Marion, and even Jud, had offered friendship. Wande no longer felt as lonely.

Marion scrambled from the wagon and waited for Wande to join her.

"I expect Ma will offer the extra room to your parents. You and Alvie can sleep in my room."

Wande looked to the front of the wagon, where Mama stared at the ground as if expecting a staircase to appear. "Let me help you, Mama."

Jud walked around the wagon and stopped in front of Mama, extending his arms to lift her down. Wande scrambled onto the seat beside Mama.

Mama sighed. "I am embarrassed to have a stranger carry

me. But since God has given someone to help me, I need not worry, *ja*?"

"Ja." Wande helped Mama inch forward. When she reached the side of the seat, Jud lifted her and carried her into the house. Wande hurried after them. He settled Mama on a padded chair and slid a footstool under her injured foot.

"*Ach!* Now everyone can see my foot!" But Mama's eyes twinkled, and Wande suspected she enjoyed the special treatment.

Mrs. Morgan, Marion, and Alvie came in, each carrying a valise. "Alvie said you would need these bags first," Marion said. "If you need anything else, just let Jud know." She started for the staircase. "This way, Alvie."

Alvie stopped before the stairs. "Are you all right, Mama? I want to help unload our things."

"You go on, dear." Mrs. Morgan shooed her away. "I'll fix your mother some tea while I start supper, and we'll be as right as rain." Mrs. Morgan headed to a different room where Wande glimpsed a stove. A wonderful iron stove to cook on—not an open fire.

Outside, Wande met Jud returning from the barn. She reached for the nearest box on the wagon.

"That's too heavy for a little thing like you." He took it from her and headed to the barn. "Ordinarily I'd have our hands help you unload, but we gave them a few days off for Christmas."

Too heavy? She shook her head. She had carried packages much heavier than these. To make it easier for Jud to carry the boxes, she moved a few to the edge of the wagon bed. As soon as she lined one up, Jud grabbed it, and they fell into a routine like a bucket brigade for putting out fires.

Jud moved with an easy grace, saying as little as possible. This friend might not talk much, but he took care of what needed to be done.

Was there a young Frau Morgan? Such a fine man as Jud must surely have a wife, but Wande had not seen any signs of her.

At supper, she would discover the truth.

Jud stacked the boxes in the barn as high as he dared. In the house they had an extra bedroom, the room they had added for Calder and his bride to share until they moved out. But for now Jud expected to sleep in the bunkhouse, so the Fleischer brothers could have his room. Ma insisted.

Maybe Wande's offer to help shouldn't have surprised him. For a little bit of a thing, she had enough muscles to heft those heavy boxes. He hoped Tom might return early from town, but the ranch hand intended to take full advantage of his extra day off. Jud and Wande made quick work of the crates without him.

Jud hustled back from the barn to help Wande down from the wagon, but he didn't get there in time. She was smoothing her skirt and brushing off some of the mud when he reached her side. He stood there and shoved his hands in his pockets. "I'd best be getting back for the rest of your family and your things."

"Auf Wiedersehen, freunde Jud." Her smile said thank-you.

As he climbed into the wagon, he heard her singing a melody he vaguely recognized. There hadn't been much music around the Morgan household since Billie disappeared. The melody both pained and uplifted him.

Dusk approached, so he had best hurry back to retrieve the Fleischer men and the rest of their belongings before full dark set in.

Jud scooted over his chair at the head of the table to make room for Mr. Fleischer to join him. They were about to say grace when someone knocked at the door.

Marion's face turned pink. "That must be Tom. He said he would probably be back in time for supper."

Jud went to the door. "Come on in and join the crowd." He found another chair and set it on his other side.

Tom's glance took in the crowded table, and he backed up a step. "I didn't know you were having company. I can catch a meal in town."

"Nonsense," Ma said. "We have plenty. Marion, why don't you introduce everyone while I get another table setting?"

Jud listened to Marion's tale of the afternoon, which she made sound like a grand adventure. "If we're lucky," Marion said, "the Fleischers will be with us for Christmas. Won't that be merry?"

Tom offered an uncertain smile and took his seat. "Do these folks speak English?" he murmured to Jud.

"Some." Jud turned to Mr. Fleischer. "Would you like to return thanks for our food?"

"Certainly. Alvie, what prayer would you suggest for tonight?"

"How about, *Comm, Herr Jesu, sei unser gast,* since we are guests tonight?"

"Very good." Everyone around the table bowed their heads as the Fleischers spoke a short prayer in German. The father continued in English, "Come, Lord Jesus, and be our guest, and let these gifts to us be blessed. Thank You for the Morgans and all their kindnesses to us and for this food. Amen."

Amens sounded around the table, and they began passing food. The Fleischers showed their appreciation by digging into their food heartily.

Jud caught Ma's gaze and started the platter of ham

around a second time. "Oh, thank you." Alvie took a small piece. "We have had nothing but frijoles and cornbread for days. And the frijoles are so hot, and the cornbread gets so hard. This is wonderful."

"Alvie." Mrs. Fleischer spoke with the tone of mothers everywhere, but the others laughed.

Ma had outdone herself with such a short time to prepare, but she was always ready to entertain strangers. She said they never knew when they might entertain angels unaware.

Jud glanced at Wande, who looked as pretty as an angel. Even with her pretty face—she was still German.

Marion knew that Jud meant to honor Tom by putting him at the head of the long oak trestle table, but he looked uncomfortable. Maybe he couldn't understand the Germans' pronunciation of English. Tom didn't even take a second serving of the sweet potatoes, and she had made them as a special treat for him.

Something pressed against her leg. She reached down to pet their cat. Ma used to scold Billie something fierce for feeding Marmalade from the table. Now that Billie was gone, even Ma slipped him a tidbit sometimes. Not that the cat was fussy—Marion had caught him eating everything from green beans to the frosting on a cake.

But when Marion offered a sliver of ham, she didn't hear Marmalade's usual contented rumble. Instead, she heard a soft purr, and green eyes between black ears stared up at her. It was Mittens.

Something bumped her other leg. Marmalade demanded his share.

"Is that the cat?" Ma said.

"*Both* of them. I'm afraid they'll start fighting. I'll put them outside until we finish supper." Marion scooped up a compliant Mittens with one arm, then reached for Marmalade.

Mittens yowled and jumped from her arms, her long hair bristling. She dashed under Wande's chair, and Wande grabbed her. "Outside. That is good." The cats snarled as the two women walked into the yard and set them on the ground. Mittens ran for the safety of the wagon, and Marmalade hid under a bush.

"I don't know what got into Marmalade. He's usually friendly."

Wande plucked some long black cat hairs from her arms. "Mittens should stay outside." She leaned forward. "Is the young man who is eating dinner with us your beau? He is very handsome."

Marion smiled. "He came here from Tennessee with his folks, only they died along the way. Tell me about your fiancé. Alvie says you plan to get married when you arrive in Neu-Braunfels."

A shadow passed over Wande's face. "Only if Papa gives his blessing. Konrad was to meet us, but he only sent a letter. He said we would meet in Neu-Braunfels. Papa's not happy." She sighed. "He thinks something is wrong."

CHAPTER FIVE

Wande reviewed the few lines she had scratched on the page. So much had happened in the short time since they had left Carlshafen. She had given Konrad only the highlights: the damaged wagon, Mama's injured ankle . . . the Running M Ranch. . . . But she left unspoken her deepest desires. She signed her name and sealed it.

Across from her, Marion looked up from a book. "Did that quill work well enough?"

"Ja." Wande lifted the letter.

"I'll ask Tom to take it into town today." Marion smiled shyly, as she always did when she mentioned his name.

Wande had learned that the young man lived and worked at the Running M. Since he was an orphan, he had chosen to stay with them for Christmas.

"I know you must be anxious to hear from Konrad," Marion said.

"We planned for *Weihnachten* in Neu-Braunfels." Wande

looked out at the gray winter sky. "But God wants us here with your family. And look. There's Tom."

Marion joined Wande at the window and waved. "Be right back." Her light footfalls padded down the stairs.

A few moments later, Wande saw her friend hand Tom the letter. How sweet they looked, with their heads bent close, their hands touching as they exchanged the letter. Wande's heart yearned for Konrad. How long would it take for him to receive the message? When could she expect to hear from him?

She shook her head. For today and tomorrow, she must put aside all worries and help her family celebrate the birth of the Savior. Perhaps they could make *lebkuchen* after all, and learn what special things the Morgans liked to eat.

Alvie danced through the door. "Are you going to stay in this room all day? It is Christmas Eve! Come on, let's have fun."

Wande let her little sister pull her out of the bedroom. "What are we doing, then?"

"Papa asked Mr. Morgan if he could cut down a tree."

"I did not recall seeing any evergreens." No Christmas tree at all would be better than one stripped of its leaves."

"He asked Mr. Morgan where he might find a tree that was green even in December." Alvie giggled. "Mr. Morgan grumbled, but his mother made him go."

"I heard that." Marion came in.

Since Jud was away for the morning, Wande might venture out farther. The man went hot and cold—sometimes kind and helpful, other times he looked at her with a distant expression that was almost angry.

"Don't mind my brother," Marion said. "Jud's bark is worse than his bite."

Alvie shook her head. "Mr. Morgan does not bark. And I *know* he does not bite."

"It's just an expression. It means he sounds loud and

threatening, like a dog. But he does not hurt anybody."

Wande nodded. "English is a strange language."

"Come on, girls." Mrs. Morgan called from the kitchen. "Time's a-wasting. Let's do some baking while the men are hunting for a tree."

"Lebkuchen!" Alvie shouted.

Mama sat by the table, her leg propped on a stool while Mrs. Morgan organized the work. "I'll roll out pie dough. Marion, you can whip up the filling for one pecan and one sweet potato pie."

Marion was already cracking the nuts.

"And Nadetta," Mrs. Morgan said to Mama, "what do you need for that—what did you call it—lebkuchen?"

Mama surveyed the kitchen, shaking her head. No evidence of almonds—they hadn't seen them since they set sail from Germany, nor were raisins or dates to be found.

"We cannot make *lebkuchen* without dates and almonds." Alvie frowned.

"We will make *Texas*-style lebkuchen." Mama studied the cans of fruit and preserves in front of her. "Look at all the pecans Marion has. We can use those instead of almonds. And there's a bag of dried fruit. Apples are just as moist and tasty as raisins or dates."

Wande opened the sack and sniffed. "I think these are peaches and not apples."

"And we have honey and flour and all the spices we need. Let's get busy."

What a waste of a day. Jud intended to put the finishing touches to the presents he planned to give at Christmas, in-between routine chores, of course. Horses needed to be tended and their stalls cleaned, regardless of the date on the calendar.

Tom had taken off for town, saying Miss Fleischer asked him to post a letter. Then Ma roped Jud into hunting with the Fleischers for a "Christmas tree"—whatever that was.

"Mrs. Morgan said there are trees here that stay green all year-round, *ja*?"

"There's the *huisache*, or sweet acacia. Ma's real fond of it because of the yellow flowers that bloom in the spring. I kinda hate to take one of them down."

"Then we will look for one . . . out there." Mr. Fleischer gestured to a stand of trees a short distance away.

"I think I see them!" Drud, the younger brother, called. He jogged away, dashing Jud's hopes of steering them away from where the acacias grew.

Drud reached the trees first, followed by Georg. Jud followed at a fast clip, with a panting Mr. Fleischer struggling to keep up. The boys stared into spreading branches overhead. When their father joined them, they wandered from one tree to another, studying the leaves, branches, and trunks.

"It is not what we are used to," Georg said. "Not very—green."

Jud didn't know if he could bear hearing the Germans complain about the color of his trees.

"It does not matter. As long as they are green, they remind us that our Lord came to give us eternal life." Mr. Fleischer put his hands on a young tree, only fifteen feet tall. "What do you think of this one, Georg?"

The three Fleischers stood beneath the tree, talking in German. Drud led them to another tree, but they returned to the first one the father had chosen.

"With your permission, we want to cut this one down. Then the four of us, we can carry it back to the house."

The tree was far too tall for their parlor, but they must realize that. He should either speak his doubts now or keep quiet.

"I'm not real comfortable with cutting down a tree for Christmas," Jud said. "It almost seems pagan."

All three Fleischers stared at him.

"Our Lord died on a tree," Drud said.

"But isn't putting up a tree like worshiping it?"

"Oh, no." Mr. Fleischer shook his head. "It is like a symbol that represents something else. The tree reminds us that even though Christmas is a happy time, when we celebrate the birth of our Savior, we also remember that He came to die so we might have eternal life. Are you a Christian, Herr Morgan? Do you know these things?"

Mr. Fleischer asked the question with such earnestness, Jud swallowed down his reaction to the implied insult. "Of course I'm a Christian. Go ahead and cut down your tree if it means so much to you."

The tree looked festive, Jud admitted. The Fleischers had cut several feet off the bottom, but it still dominated a corner of the parlor from floor to ceiling.

Marion and Wande were poking threaded needles through wolfberries and popcorn, making a garland for the tree. "We have never had this corn before, but it is pretty." Wande smiled. "*Sie nicht so*, Alvie?"

"Mm-hmm." Alvie popped a piece into her mouth.

"Stop that, or we will not have enough."

Mrs. Fleischer had dug a few small candleholders out of her crates and now was fastening them to branches. "They say Martin Luther was the first to put lights on the tree, to re-create the stars in the sky." She lit the candles one by one.

"The star of Bethlehem!" Alvie said.

Jud caught a whiff of honey and cinnamon from the

kitchen. He peered through the door at the pies and cakes on the countertop.

"Those are for tomorrow, Jud." Ma looked up from her cookie dough and smiled.

"Let's sing '*O Tannenbaum*,'" Alvie said.

"Of course. We must sing of the Christmas tree." Mr. Fleischer smiled at his daughter. "Come, let us hold hands." The Fleischers assembled in a circle that didn't quite make it around the tree. Wande gestured for Marion, who nodded to the rest of her family. Jud found himself between Wande and Marion.

"It's beautiful." Awe filled Marion's voice. "I think we should do this ourselves next year."

Mr. Fleischer cleared his throat. "We will sing the Christmas tree song for you."

They sang two or three verses, a beautiful harmony, of which the only words Jud remembered was the repeated phrase *"O Tannenbaum."* But he noticed tears in Wande's eyes as they sang the last verse. Mrs. Fleischer began crying.

"*Liebchen,* Ulla would not want you to cry." Mr. Fleischer embraced his wife, laying her head on his shoulder. "It is as the song says. Because of our Jesus, we know Ulla has only gone ahead of us."

Beside him, Marion sniffled. She dropped his hand and reached for a handkerchief. "Billie would love this tree."

The candles flickered, their cheery light a mockery of the somber mood that had come over the gathering. A part of Jud wanted to escape; another part of him relaxed, allowing grief to wash over his soul. Wande put her arm on his. When he saw the compassion in her eyes, he felt tears form in his own.

At length Mrs. Morgan broke the silence. "Tell us about Ulla."

Wande and Marion walked to the room they were sharing, arms around each other. Alvie skipped in front of them. After tonight, Wande felt closer than ever to her new friend.

"Tomorrow is Christmas morning!" Alvie giggled, the ten-year-old suddenly turned five again.

"Morning will not come any sooner if you stay awake." Wande kissed the tip of Alvie's nose. "You need to get ready for bed."

Alvie giggled again. "I know we will not have many presents this year. But just being here, in Texas, with new friends—that makes it a special day. I always like to think about our Lord Jesus being a tiny baby."

"I feel the same way. I remember holding you when you were just a baby. And I imagine Jesus when He was so tiny." Wande helped her sister into her nightclothes. "I told Mama that not even our Lord had such soft blond hair, such tiny hands and feet."

"I love you, Wande. *Frohe Weihnachten*. Merry Christmas. You are the best big sister ever."

Wande sat on the mattress beside Alvie, rubbing her back until at last she fell asleep. A few minutes later, Wande extinguished the lamp and lay down next to her. Marion lay in a trundle bed.

"She reminds me a lot of our Billie," Marion said. "Cheerful. A songbird."

"You said Comanche Indians took her. How awful." At least Wande's family knew that Ulla's death had been peaceful. "Is she dead?"

"Either she's dead or they've adopted her into their tribe. We tried everything we could think of, but even the Texas Rangers could learn nothing about a girl matching Billie's description."

Silence lengthened between them.

"Billie was special. She was born a little before Pa died in the war with Mexico, for our independence. Losing her was like losing Pa all over again."

"That must have been terrible." Wande couldn't imagine. "Your father, he died ten years ago?"

"Nine years," Marion said.

"And Jud took over for his father then?"

"Yes. He grew up overnight. One day he was a brother who would laugh with me and take me fishing. The next, he walked around with this long face, worried about how to keep the ranch running. He was only a couple of years older than Calder, but he took the family on his shoulders. Of course, Calder pitched in too. We all did."

How old would Jud have been nine years ago? As young as Georg? Wande shuddered. No wonder he was so serious.

"Were you close to Ulla?" Marion said.

"We were sisters. We loved each other. But Ulla was . . . delicate. She stayed inside, helped Mama, and read books. She did not even like going to *schule*."

"The trip across the ocean must have been hard on her."

"*Ja*. I did not want to come. But I did not mind the ocean crossing. Ulla never got over her *meer krankheit*—her sickness. She was weak when she arrived in Carlshafen. She caught a fever and died a few days later."

CHAPTER SIX

Tom Cotton was worse than useless around a ranch, Jud had decided, although he might make a passable farmer. But when the orphaned teen showed up at their doorstep a couple of years ago, Ma took him under her wing. The same way she took in every stray. Just like the Fleischers.

At least Tom was willing to try to do his share of the work. Now, with the budding romance between Tom and Marion, Jud would face a mutiny if he encouraged him to look elsewhere for employment. Always cheerful, Tom got by with doing things the easy way.

Now, Jud. He could almost hear Ma's voice. *Just because Tom doesn't work from can see to can't like you, don't mean he's a slacker. You should take a lesson from him, Son, and stop working so hard.*

Why didn't anyone else see that if Jud did that, the ranch would fall apart? As it was, Jud pushed himself hard, waiting for the ranch hands to return after the New Year. He didn't begrudge them the time off. But when did he ever get a break? Christmas week had come and gone. Yesterday was Sunday. New Year's was this coming Thursday, and then his regular ranch hands would be back. Maybe then . . .

The Fleischer boys headed toward Jud.

"We can help. I speak some English. Tell us what to do." The older one, Georg, grabbed a shovel. "Clean animals, *ja*?"

Was the kid offering to clean the stables? That job usually fell to whoever grabbed the short straw. "Sure. And do you know how to ride a horse?" He needed to make sure the horse herd was all right and wouldn't mind some company, even if they were Germans.

Georg shook his head and disappeared into the barn.

After Jud went inside to tell Ma his plans, he returned for his horse. Years ago, Pa named JM after the originator of the line, Justin Morgan himself. The gelding was getting old, but he remained Jud's favorite.

Georg nodded to Jud, then continued pushing clean straw to one side and tossing the dirty straw into a wheelbarrow. The kid was working hard, for no reason except it was the neighborly thing to do. "Hey, Georg, thanks. Good job."

"I am glad to *helfen*." Blue eyes like Wande's, except with a hint of green, blinked at him.

"I'll see you at supper, then."

Jud didn't make it home for supper. The stallion had herded his mares farther afield, to a greener pasture. Jud ended up spending the night beside a campfire. He hoped nothing would happen at home before he could get back.

His return to a quiet yard the next morning reassured him. Maybe Tom had taken Ma into town for provisions. They'd have company at least until after the New Year. If the Fleischers hadn't moved on before the ranch hands returned, Jud might end up sleeping with the boys in the bunkhouse. Pushed out of his own house by a bunch of Germans. He shook his head.

Jud led JM into the barn, removed his gear, and gave him a good rubdown. For the past ten years, the gelding had carried Jud everywhere he wanted to go—and some places he hadn't. "It's getting time for you to enjoy your retirement, JM. But who am I going to find that is as good as you?"

The horse nickered. Jud took a bit of apple from his knapsack and held it under JM's nose. Soft lips caressed his fingers as he accepted the treat.

"Hey, Jud. I thought that was you."

Tom opened the barn door wide, letting in a blast of blinding sunlight. Jud raised his arm against the light. "Shut the door, will you?"

"Sorry, Boss." Tom strode across the barn. "You got a letter today. Thought it might be important." He waited, as if expecting Jud to open it.

"Thanks, Tom. How have things been?"

"About the same. The Fleischers' wagon's not ready. Truth be told, I'm not sure those German fellas have the money to fix it. They expecting you to pay?"

"I'm sure that's not the case." Fleischer had insisted on feeding his oxen with his own supplies. The man—what was the fellow's name? Meino?—had asked him privately if he knew of anyone who would buy some of their things for cash. But that could mean several things. Maybe he only wanted to lighten the load before they left.

"I am going to turn into a doll if I continue to do nothing." Mama sat up in the bed she shared with Papa, while Wande and Alvie took turns reading to her. They shared conversation in German while in the sanctuary of the room Mr. and Mrs. Fleischer now called home.

"You are teaching me." Alvie looked from the slate where she was practicing division. "Papa says it is important for me to continue my lessons while we are stopped."

"I know, my little sprite." Mama's voice softened. "But I am tired of all this sitting."

"Maybe the doctor will say you can start walking again when he sees you on Friday." Wande hoped so. The continued silence from Konrad troubled her, and she was anxious to continue on to Neu-Braunfels. "If you try to walk now, you might hurt yourself again, and he might tell you to stay in bed another week."

"Wande, you sound like Mama." Alvie giggled. "Telling us what to do."

"I am practicing. Someday soon I will have children of my own to boss about."

"The longer I sit here, the more I think about Ulla." Mama gazed out the window. "I want to do more than see this tiny square of Texas. I want to smell the air and feel the earth beneath my feet. I want to find out for myself what kind of soil we have here."

"And you will, Mama. You will soon." A part of Wande welcomed Mama's complaints. They spoke of the strength she gained day by day. The family had hurried from Carlshafen, anxious to leave grief and sickness behind. This enforced stopover had done Mama good. She would be ready for whatever challenges faced them in Neu-Braunfels.

When Jud started undressing for the night, he heard paper crinkling and remembered the letter. He lit the lamp.

The postmark stopped him cold. *Neu-Braunfels*. The Fleischers knew people over there, not him.

He checked the address again: Herr Judson Morgan, Running M Ranch, Victoria. He broke the seal, unfolding the letter on top of the table next to the lamp. A smaller sheet, addressed to "Wande," was tucked inside the page addressed to him.

As he read the shaky handwriting, the words jumped off the page. Their meaning was all too clear.

Mr. Morgan,

I know you are a good man. You have taken in the Fleischers in their time of need. Now I have a favor to beg of you.

Mr. Fleischer refused to allow an official engagement between myself and Fraulein Wande. Perhaps he saw into my heart that all was not right. Wande deserves the very best. Any man married to her will be fortunate. She is hard-working, capable, and good-looking as well. She also has an unshakeable faith in God.

But our agreement was based on our long association and common goals. To my shame, I confess that on the voyage to Texas, I found my heart pursuing someone else. The short of it is, I married her as soon as we arrived at Carlshafen. We are already expecting our first child.

I sent word to Wande as soon as we landed, but the Fleischers must have left Germany before my letter reached them. Imagine my shock when I learned they were in Texas!

I have enclosed a letter for Wande, but I beg of you, as a Christian gentleman, to break the news to her as gently as you can.

Jud read it a second time. Not that he would ever marry a German girl, but how could any decent man abandon a woman like Wande?

"Coward." The word exploded from Jud's lips. Bad enough that this Konrad had betrayed Wande's trust; he didn't even have the courage to tell her in person. Jud wanted to shred the letter, as if he could destroy the news it carried. But Konrad had more to say. Jud forced himself to continue.

One more favor I must beg of you. The Fleischers expect my help in starting their farm. As you may know, the land purchased for us by the Verein is at a distance. The Fleischers may need assistance in reaching their goals. They will not ask; they are too proud. But if you could offer a job to any of them, especially to Wande, I would be most grateful. I do not wish her to go hungry because of me.

With warmest regards,
Konrad Schuster

Jud clenched the letter in his fist. Did Konrad expect the Fleischers to stay in Victoria instead of going on to where they belonged? Now that Konrad had abandoned his responsibility, he wanted Jud to take care of the problem.

Jud had always known Germans couldn't be trusted. Now he had proof.

CHAPTER SEVEN

"You should go in." Tom laced his fingers more tightly with Marion's. "Your Ma and your brother are both watching." He leaned in close to her face.

Marion's breath caught. Was Tom about to kiss her, in full view of every resident of the Running M Ranch? She felt her face lifting to meet his kiss, her eyelids fluttering shut.

Instead of lips, calloused fingers brushed her cheeks. "Sweet Marion. I'm not near good enough for a lady like you."

Marion's eyes flew open, and she gazed into Tom's dark brown ones. "You're a good man, Tom Cotton. Don't let anybody tell you different. Especially not my brother."

Jud cared about her. She knew that. Unfortunately, that meant he was overprotective and interfering. The curtain in the parlor window swayed, and Marion hoped whoever was there had stepped away.

"Shall we walk?" He offered his arm, and they strolled among the trees in the gathering dusk. They stayed close enough to the house for propriety, but far enough away for privacy.

"Your brother is the one I have to convince." Tom frowned. "He thinks I'm a lazy good-for-nothing."

"That's not true." The words came automatically. Jud had made no secret of his displeasure with Tom's work habits. "Maybe you weren't supposed to be a rancher. What did you dream of doing when you were a boy?"

"I thought I'd be a farmer, like my dad and his daddy before him. I grew up listening to the stories of how Granddaddy crossed the mountains from Virginny and started all over again in Tennessee. Later my daddy got the wandering spirit and came to Texas."

Marion gazed at the landscape of the ranch, at the beloved rills and hillocks. She couldn't imagine leaving, at least not to go far away. "Do you think you'll want to leave Victoria some day?"

"Why, Miss Marion, are you saying you'd miss me?" Tom stopped where the split-rail fence enclosed their chicken coop and took a seat. He patted the spot next to him. She gathered her skirts and sat beside her beau.

A breeze blew, and Marion drew her shawl around her shoulders. Without asking permission, Tom drew her close, warming her body with his nearness. She nestled against his shoulder.

"Here we are smack dab in the middle of the continent," Marion said. "I wonder what it's like to travel across the ocean. Ma and Pa took us to see it once, before we moved here, but I was too little to remember. Or what about going south or west into Mexico? Or to head into the United States?"

"We'll be United States citizens soon. Just a few days from now, on the twenty-ninth of December."

"I keep forgetting." Texas's battle for independence cost Marion's family so much. She couldn't quite believe they had gone and joined the United States less than ten years later.

"The other day, I heard they're going to keep flying the Texas flag as high as the United States flag—because Texas was a country all on its own before it joined the Union." Tom's arm dropped to Marion's waist, and her stomach did flip-flops. "I can tell you one thing."

"What's that?"

"There's nothing anywhere on this continent that's half as pretty as you." Tom lifted Marion's chin, and their lips met.

Jud watched the lights blink out in the main house. If Ma saw him pacing the bunkhouse, she'd worm the truth out of him. He wasn't sure he wanted to tell anybody about Konrad's letter, at least not yet.

Jud didn't need more responsibility dumped on him. With Calder away and married, and Marion infatuated with Tom, he might have a chance to do something for himself—like look for a wife. Of course if Marion did settle for Tom, Jud would have to provide something for them. He had his eye on a piece of property that could work for a small farm. Tom might make a good farmer. He might be able to grow things—Lord knew, he couldn't handle animals.

Then there was Billie . . . Jud had hoped over the winter to look more into her disappearance, not that he expected to learn much new. All their searches and offers of ransom last spring yielded nothing. Now the trail was even colder. Ma said he should accept the fact she was dead and move on. He tried. But he couldn't with reminders of his little sister everywhere around the ranch, in Victoria, and in every waking sunrise.

Something scratched at the door.

Jud scooped up the cat, which started to purr. "Yeah, I'm upset tonight." Marmalade couldn't spread any secrets, except to another cat. He smiled at the thought. But Mittens wouldn't betray his confidence, not even to Wande.

Wande again. He was brought back to Konrad's letter. So help him, Jud felt responsible for the Fleischers, no matter what he thought about Germans.

Marmalade jumped from his arms, and Jud resumed his pacing. No. He refused to accept responsibility for anyone else. He had already raised one family. If he wanted more dependents, he'd start a family of his own.

Where had that come from? Jud hadn't thought much about getting married, not that he was opposed. Now a shadowy figure of his wife emerged, someone with blonde hair and blue eyes, a lilting voice, and a ready laugh . . .

As soon as the year turned, he'd go to town and hunt out the leaders of the German community. Jud would turn responsibility for the Fleischers over to someone else.

Wande checked the English spelling as she formed the letters on a sheet of writing paper.

Dearest Oma,
Happy New Year!

Oma, that's English for Prosit Neujahr. *Can you believe I am finally learning English? My new friend Marion is a good teacher. We are staying with them while our wagon is being fixed. They are very kind to take strangers off of the road and welcome them to their home.*

Alvie sat at the table as well, painting a watercolor of their "funny Texas Christmas tree" to send to Oma. The family wouldn't send cards as they usually did at the first of the year, but Papa said they could each write something to Oma. Papa had sent a letter when they arrived in Carlshafen, but so much had happened since. A shadow fell across Wande's heart. She was glad she wasn't the one who had to tell her grandparents about Ulla's death.

Wande lifted the quill from the page. What should she write about? During the ocean voyage she had thought of her Opa. Before he married Oma and settled in Offenbach, he had been a sailor. Ulla had remained sick for the whole crossing, but after the first few days, the motion didn't bother Wande. She enjoyed walking on deck, breathing the salt air. The farther south they traveled, the warmer the days became. She almost wished their journey could last forever, except she wanted to reach Konrad.

Oma would wonder about Konrad, but Wande wouldn't write that he failed to meet them in Carlshafen. She would wait until she heard his explanation, when she would be writing as a *Frau* and not a *Fraulein*.

She could write pages about life at the Running M Ranch, but Oma might think she was more interested in Texas than her own family and their broken wagon.

So . . . that left her with what? Wande described the Texas-style spice bars they made for Christmas, and how different they tasted with pecans and peaches instead of almonds and citron.

> *We think Mittens may soon have some yellow tiger kittens. Marmalade, the Morgans' cat, has been paying her extra attention lately. I miss Ulla, but God is so good. Marion has become like a sister to me. I will miss her when we leave for Neu-Braunfels. But God will have a new family for me there. I know He will.*

Wande looked out the window. Instead of open fields, she saw the patchwork farms of Offenbach. A soft snow had settled on the roofs and fields, transforming the world into something new.

"What do you think?" Alvie showed her small watercolor to Wande, and her mind snapped back to the brown dirt and hollows of Texas.

She smiled at the painting. Two cats, one yellow, one black and white, both with pointed ears and tails like question marks, fought over a ball of yarn. Strands of white and red dotted the tree with its pale green foliage. "I will tell her about the special corn that pops," Wande said. "We need to finish the card. Maybe Dr. Treviño can take it into town after he sees Mama."

"I am almost done." Alvie added a few flourishes. "There. All finished." She handed the square sheet to Wande.

"And so am I. They can dry while we wait in the parlor."

The men came in for the midday meal. There was always a full table at noon with Papa and Drud, the three women and Alvie, plus Jud and the ranch hands: Bert, Tom, and now Georg.

Georg looked to Wande. "What does the doctor say?"

The door to their parents' bedroom opened, and Mama walked through, holding Papa's arm. "I will tell you myself."

Dr. Treviño followed, smiling. "She can move about, as long as she doesn't overdo." He agreed to stop by the post in Victoria and mail the thick letter.

"I will have to trust you, Wande, to keep your mama quiet. All she wants to do is work, work, work." Papa's eyes twinkled. "And I have good news myself. I have found a wagon to buy. We will sell a few things, and we can all fit *gut*."

Jud wasn't ready to tell the Fleischers about the letter from Konrad, not when he hadn't decided what to do about the last request. He must be the one to tell Wande the news before she read the letter. New Year's Day or not, he couldn't let the Fleischers leave—not without telling them. He listened to their excited conversation and wished he didn't have to end to their happiness.

While everyone was talking, Jud slipped out and walked to the bunkhouse. His hand hovered over the page addressed to Wande. Grabbing both letters, Jud strode back to the main house.

A cold breeze blew in when he opened the door, and he hurried to shut it. The noise level in the parlor told him their celebration of the New Year was under way. Jud cleared his throat. "About your leaving."

Wande heard him and dropped her arms from hugging Alvie. Her eyes sent a plea.

Mr. Fleischer noticed him next. "What is it? You have news for us?" The German's voice descended to a deep bass.

"I received a letter the day before yesterday. Last year in fact."

"That letter I brought you from Neu-Braunfels." Tom snapped his fingers. "I knew something was up."

Every eye in the room swung to Jud.

"I did not think you knew anyone in Neu-Braunfels," Mr. Fleischer said.

"I don't. But this letter was addressed to me." He displayed it, as if to support his claim. "It's from Konrad Schuster."

Wande's hand covered her mouth.

Jud fixed his gaze on the mantelpiece. "There's no easy way to tell you. Mr. Schuster wanted me to explain why he hasn't come to meet you. He can't—he can't marry you, Wande. *He's already married.*"

Wande collapsed into the chair nearest the window and gazed at the blank glass.

CHAPTER EIGHT

"Konrad has taken an *ehefrau*?" Wande hoped she had misunderstood the English words. "A wife?"

The looks on Marion and Mrs. Morgan's faces told her she hadn't heard wrong.

"He says he met the girl aboard ship and they married shortly after they arrived in Texas." Jud hesitated. "They are already expecting a child." He dug in his pocket. "He asked me to give you this."

Wande held out her hand, but couldn't grasp the paper. It floated to the floor. A *kind*—the child that should have been *hers*. Wande bent over, covering her face with her hands.

"There, there, *Liebchen*." Papa patted her shoulder.

Georg jumped to his feet. "If that scoundrel had come here like a man, instead of hiding away in Neu-Braunfels, I would teach him a lesson."

"Now, Georg." Papa abhorred fistfights.

"He is right," Mama said. "I kept quiet because I knew you

cared for him, Wande. But I never thought he was good enough for you."

Wande shook with tears. Mama meant well, but no one besides Konrad had seriously courted her.

Tears fell. All the tears she hadn't shed when Ulla died, and the grief she had suppressed when her beloved home in Offenbach disappeared in the distance.

Alvie sat by her feet, and Marion pulled a chair next to Wande. Alvie laid her head on her knee, and Marion placed an arm around her shoulder. Papa stood beside her like a sentry.

Surrounded by such love, Wande should have felt buoyed up. Instead, she grieved the losses, disappointments, and broken dreams that Texas had brought for her and her family.

If only she could turn back the clock—six months—a year—to the day Papa had seen the flyer from the Adelsverein. Even if she had the money to go back to Offenbach, it would do no good now. Everyone she loved had left. Even Oma and Opa had moved a few years ago, back to their first home by the sea.

When at last Wande cried her tears dry, she hiccuped and stopped. Still she hid her face behind her hands. Someone hovered in front of her, holding a glass of water.

"Do you want something to drink?" Jud, the man who had delivered the awful news, wanted to help.

Wande removed her hands from her face, realizing how red and blotchy she must look. *"Ja, danke."*

His fingers brushed hers as he handed her the glass. She drank and handed the glass to Jud, then planted her shaky legs on the floor and stood. "I will go to my *raum*."

"Wande." Mama's voice followed her. "You need to eat."

"*Nein,* I want to be alone." She spotted the letter from Konrad, where it had fallen.

Before she could bend over, Jud picked up the note and handed it to her. Taking her hand, he closed her fingers around it. Jud leaned down, his cheek against hers, and whispered, "Tear it up, if it will help you to feel better."

Wande nodded, went into the room she shared with Marion and Alvie, and shut the door. Muffled sounds intruded as the parlor emptied and the family ate their noon meal in the kitchen. Today she wished she didn't have to share the room with anyone, let alone a child and someone she hadn't even known a month ago. No, that wasn't fair. Wande knew Marion would do everything she could to make things easier for her, including giving her as much time alone as she wanted.

She curled up in a ball on the trundle bed, but she couldn't cry any more. In place of her tears, anger built. How could Konrad abandon her as soon as he set foot on the boat? His letter burned her hand. She longed to discard it, unread. No words could excuse his behavior. But neither could she toss the letter away. She propped herself against the headboard.

Dear Wande,
By now you know that I have married someone else. I cared for you, Wande. I still do, as a dear friend, although I no longer deserve that title.

I thought I loved you. But when I met Hannah, I realized that the love I felt for you was friendship, a love such as might exist between brother and sister. But what I feel for Hannah I cannot describe, except that it is the kind of love that should exist between a man and his wife. I would still have honored our agreement, but I felt that would cheat both of us. Some day you, too, will find someone who loves you this way. To my shame, I am not that man. You deserve that, and so much more.

Konrad promised some day she would meet a man who would love her for herself. But she didn't believe it, not anymore.

Not here. Not in Texas. Not after he abandoned her. She had no prospects: no home, no money, no property, and she could hardly speak English.

I know right now you will not believe me. All I can do is to commend you to the One from whom nothing can separate you. Neither height nor depth nor any other creature—not even a man as miserable as me.

Hannah joins me in my prayers for you, for your family. This Mr. Morgan sounds like a good man. I pray he will help you now that I cannot.

He got the "man as miserable as me" correct. The harsh reality of the last paragraph hit Wande like a bucket of cold water.

Now that Mama had recovered and Papa had found a wagon, they could no longer take advantage of the Morgans' hospitality. But neither could they go to Neu-Braunfels.

Where would they go?

Wande didn't come out for supper either. Jud watched as Marion closed the door to her room behind her and brought her one finger to her lips.

"I left the plate by the side of the bed. She's resting, poor thing." Marion had changed into her dressing gown. "I don't want to disturb her."

Another door opened, and Jud turned his head. Mr. Fleischer emerged, still dressed in his day clothes. "May I join you? We have plans to make."

They sat at the kitchen table. Ma poured everyone fresh cups of tea, then stirred in sugar. "We need sweetening tonight. It's been a difficult day."

Wande's father sat across from Jud, his eyes locked on some internal vision. Jud didn't know how to start the discussion. He didn't have to.

"Did you know that *Nadetta* means courage of a bear?" Meino said. "That is my *frau*. She attacks anything that threatens us. It is a good thing that Konrad is far away." He chuckled. "She is reading to Alvie now. We will keep Alvie with us tonight so Wande can sleep."

Jud sent up a prayer of thanks that Meino spoke passable English. At least they could discuss the problem without constant translation from German to English and back again.

"Meino, are you sure you want to go on to Neu-Braunfels?" Ma finished one cup of tea and poured a second. "There is a nice-sized German community right here in Victoria."

"We have land, but I hear it is far away, even from Neu-Braunfels. We hoped to meet up with Konrad before we decided what to do next." Meino shrugged. "But perhaps God wants us to stay right here, where we had the accident."

Something in Jud's expression must have betrayed his ambivalence.

"Not here on your ranch," Meino said. "But perhaps there is a little *haus* we can rent."

Jud pushed back his chair. "On Sunday, let's talk with the preacher. He'll know who can help."

Wande's life had been uprooted in just a few days: the wagon accident, the Morgans' hospitality, Christmas with new friends, now New Year's Day and Konrad's betrayal. After reading the letter on Friday, Saturday passed in a blur. Since she still didn't feel well, she stayed home from church on Sunday.

Papa sought out a German Lutheran church in town. He came home wreathed in smiles. "Tomorrow morning, we will all go to Victoria. There is someone I think you should meet." He smiled so widely that for the briefest moment, Wande hoped Konrad had appeared in Victoria after all, ready to take her before the preacher and get married.

Just as fast, her memory asserted itself. For Papa's sake, she assumed a pleasant expression.

Monday morning, she dressed in her Sunday best and took extra care with her hair. She wanted to look her best to greet the start of their future. Since she could not return to Offenbach, she would embrace Texas with a smile on her face—if not in her heart.

Papa took them to a half-timbered structure in town, one with a wooden cross rising from the steeple. A simple sign read *"Lutherische Kirche St. John."* Their home congregation in Germany bore the same name, and homesickness wrenched Wande's heart.

A man wearing a clerical collar appeared at the door. "*Willkommen*! Welcome to Victoria! I am Pastor Bader."

Wande blinked back the tears at the familiar German greeting.

"Herr Fleischer, how good to see you again." The pastor greeted each member of the family in German. "And now this must be *Fraulein Wande, ja?*"

When Pastor Bader clasped Wande's hand, some of the missing joy returned. She felt God's love reaching out to her, caressing her spirit like a gentle breeze.

"We are going just next door." He led them to a compact house next to the church. It was built like the church, an unexpected mixture of styles from the old world and the new. "This was built for a parsonage. But I am only a single man and have no need for so much space." He smiled—a smile as full of sunshine as the day's sky—and opened the door.

Light flooded the open space. "When so many of the Verein

started coming through Victoria, I decided to move into a smaller place and use the parsonage as a guesthouse."

Mama sighed , and Wande could imagine the pictures running through her mind—of Papa's favorite chair sitting there and the table Drud had made over there . . .

"God's timing is perfect. Our last guests moved out right before Christmas, into their new home. Now you have need of a place to stay. We hope you will accept this house as your home until God moves you elsewhere."

Alvie raced from room to room. "We have a bedroom to ourselves, Wande!"

The familiar aroma of sauerkraut wafted from the kitchen. A pleasant woman with a wrinkled round face stepped from the kitchen. "There you are! When Pastor Bader told us a new family was moving in, I knew you must be hungry for some real German food, *ja*?"

Wande's heart danced. Maybe she could feel at home in Texas, after all.

CHAPTER NINE

Make up your mind, Morgan. Since the Fleischers left with the last of their belongings, Jud had moped around the yard. He'd fixed a rail that didn't need fixing, cleared out his gear from the bunkhouse, straightened for the returning hands—not that they cared. Maybe he should offer to help the Fleischers settle in, except one of the men had failed to return from Christmas break, leaving the ranch shorthanded.

Ma came out on the porch to ring the bell. "Come on in for supper. Tom's already inside."

Jud bounded up the steps, scraped his boots, and took off his hat. The quiet of the parlor hit him like a north wind. Every day for two weeks, he couldn't wait for the Fleischers to leave. The house couldn't fit two families; he'd had to give up his room and sleep in the bunkhouse with only Tom for company.

Not only had people filled the house, so had their chatter. All they did was talk, talk, talk, in that . . . language. When Jud was in the room, Meino and Alvie would speak English. Their attempt left Jud feeling like an intruder in his own home.

But since their departure, less than a week ago, the house felt empty, too big for the three of them—four if he counted Tom. He felt a pang of loneliness for Calder, off in Tumbleweed with his bride. Come to think of it, Jud felt the same way when Calder left. He couldn't wait to shed the responsibility, and then he missed him as soon as he disappeared over the horizon.

They had all expected Marion's turn to come next. Instead, Billie disappeared one day, never to be seen again. He shook his head in an attempt to rid himself of the grief that accompanied thoughts of his little sister.

Laughter spilled from the kitchen, and for a minute, Jud thought he heard Wande. No, it couldn't be Wande, so Marion must be laughing at something Tom said. A moment later, she poked her head out the kitchen door. "Come on, brother. Your food's getting cold."

Jud stopped listening to the ghosts in the parlor and joined them in the kitchen. It was dreary in spite of the warmth from the stove and the colorful plates set out. How empty the table looked with only one person on each side. He sat at the head as usual, Marion to his right and Tom to his left. Ma's place was at the far end, next to the stove.

"I've got us some nice chickpea soup with cornbread." Ma stirred the pot one last time. "It's been simmering nicely. I'll bring it to the table so we can all serve ourselves."

"Ma, wait, let me—"

Ma wrapped a towel around the pot handle and lifted it. The towel slipped and the iron pot's contents sloshed onto Ma's face, the boiling soup splashing her arms, dress, and legs. She screamed, slipped, and fell in the thick puddle of scalding soup.

Jud grabbed a pitcher of water from the table and poured it over Ma. "Tom, go to town for Doc Treviño." When he didn't jump into action, Jud shouted, "Now!" Ma's eyes had closed, and she gave a low moan.

Jud lifted Ma from the floor. "Open the door!" Marion ran ahead of him, into the parlor and onto the porch, holding the door open. He headed for the horse's watering trough in the front yard.

Marion reached it first and skimmed hay and debris from the surface of the water, before Jud plunged Ma into the trough. Water covered her from her feet to her neck.

A red blotch ran from her right ear down her cheek and neck, but Jud didn't dare plunge her face beneath the water. "Sis, run. Get towels."

Marion flew into the house and out again, carrying an armful. She submerged one in the water and laid it on Ma's face. She groaned.

"Ideally this water'd be lukewarm and clean, but this is better than nothing." Marion wrung out a second towel and dabbed the rest of Ma's face. "I think Ma has some carbolic acid on the top shelf of her wardrobe. Mix a bit of it with some water."

Jud nodded. Marion had learned a lot of home remedies from Ma. She knew best what to do. Who knew if Tom would find the doctor at home; he might not make it to the ranch for hours. By then, infection could set in.

"Ma keeps some cotton in her sewing chest," she said. "Soak that in the carbolic solution."

"How long does she need to soak out here?" Jud rubbed his arms. "It's a mite chilly. That can't be good, on top of the burn."

"I don't know." Marion lifted the towel from Ma's cheek. A small piece of flesh tore, and she groaned. Marion made a clicking sound. "I'll go change her bed so she's got clean sheets.

And I'll make up the carbolic solution. You keep changing the towel on her cheek every couple of minutes."

Jud felt like Marion must have had enough time to change all the beds in the house before she called, "It's ready." She dashed down the steps. "I'll hold her head up while you get her body." She cupped Ma's head in her hands.

Jud plunged his arms into the cold water and hoped they hadn't left her in it too long. He didn't know if she was unconscious from the fall or the agony of her burns. He threaded one arm under her shoulders and the other beneath her knees and lifted her from the trough.

Ma thrashed in Jud's arms. He gritted his teeth and got to her room quicker than he ever had in his life. He lay his mother on the bed, her reddened skin and pea-green soaked dress a sickening contrast to the clean white sheets. He brushed his hand against his eyes, closer to tears than he had been since . . . the Comanches snatched Billie.

"You go on out now and see if you can get the carbolic solution ready. I didn't have time." Marion nodded to the bottle on the top shelf of the wardrobe. She laid a gentle hand on his shoulder. "I'll call you after I've undressed her."

Lord, spare my mother. The words repeated themselves in Jud's brain.

"Look, Wande." Alvie stopped fluffing the pillows on the parlor chairs long enough to look out the window. "Tom from the ranch is riding by."

Wande paused her dusting to peek out the window. "I do not see him."

"His horse flew by. Do you think something is wrong?"

"Something is wrong at the ranch?" Mama stepped into the parlor. "Has someone been hurt?"

"Alvie thought she saw Tom."

"It *was* Tom."

Wande slipped out the front door and stared in the direction Tom would have taken, wishing he had stopped to say hello. She wanted a greeting from Marion—or even Jud. It had been only a few days, but it seemed an age since she spoke with them.

In the distance she heard shouts, something about Dr. Treviño.

Mama joined her. "Do you see him?"

Wande pointed. "Someone has been hurt. He is asking for the doctor."

"The doctor is not in town. He was going to see me today, but he sent word that he's attending a birthing."

Wande called inside, "Drud?"

The hammering in her parents' bedroom ceased, and her brother came out. *"Ja?"*

"Tom Cotton from the ranch came into town looking for the doctor. We think someone at the ranch has been hurt. I need you to run and ask what happened."

He nodded and took off down the street, his long legs eating up the distance.

Wande's mind ran in circles. Who had been injured? Mrs. Morgan? Marion? Jud? Wande's heart skipped a beat. "One of us must go help." She went inside and searched among the things still in crates for Mama's supply of medicines.

"What are you doing, daughter?" Mama asked the question, but when Wande raised her eyes, she looked into the gaze of her father.

She lifted her chin. "If someone has been hurt at the ranch, I am going to help."

Her parents exchanged one of those glances. "It is not good for you to go alone, *Liebchen*."

"Papa, do not you see? Now is our opportunity to repay their hospitality."

"But . . ."

"You know I am right. And Mama can't go. The doctor told her to take it easy. The boys would be useless. They know nothing of healing. I know a little. I can help. *Ja?*"

"She is right," Mama said. "But one of the boys should go with her. Drud?"

"No, Georg. Jud said he might have a job for Georg if he wanted one." Papa hugged Wande. "I am glad to see you thinking of something besides that Konrad. Go, with my blessings. Send word of what you find."

Drud returned a few minutes later with Tom.

"You wanted to see me?" Tom didn't even dismount. "I need to get back to the ranch."

"Someone is hurt?" Papa said.

"Mrs. Morgan burned herself, bad. And Doc Treviño is out of town."

Relief swept over Wande, and she chided herself. A burn. How painful. She regretted injury to any of them.

"I am sorry to hear it." Papa shook his head. "Yes, you must hurry. Tell them my Wande and Georg are coming to help. They will take the wagon as soon as they can. The doctor will come here, to see Mrs. Fleischer. We will get word to him as soon as we can."

By the time Wande and Georg arrived, the sun was beginning to fade. The ranch seemed deserted until Tom ran out of the house, waving his arms. "There you are. Marion said for you to come right in."

Georg helped Wande from the wagon. "I will take care of the animals. Tell Jud I will do the chores so he can stay with his mother."

Wande patted her brother on the back. *"Danke!"* She took

a firm hold of her valise and entered the house.

Odors she had never smelled before assaulted her from the kitchen. Onion, garlic, chicken, tomato, and other unknown spices . . . a faint odor of something burned. Her stomach churned, and she hurried up the stairs to Mrs. Morgan's bedroom.

Marion hugged Wande. "Thank you for coming." Jud looked up briefly, then returned his gaze to the quiet figure on the bed.

"How is she?" Wande took a seat opposite him. A sweet, tarry odor filled her nostrils from the dressing of carbolic acid on the burns.

"I've been better." Mrs. Morgan spoke through lips almost gummed together. "Thank you for coming, dear."

"May I?" Wande touched the sheet. Jud turned his head, and she lifted the covers. Mrs. Morgan was swathed in cotton from neck to waist.

"It's not as bad as we first thought. Her upper body got the worst of it." Marion bent over and checked the dressing. "We'll have to change these soon, before they start sticking to her skin."

Mrs. Morgan groaned. "I know that's best, but . . . I can't believe I let the soup spill all over me."

A shadow fell across the bed as Jud stood. "I'll leave you to it." He shuddered, as his muscles relaxed from sitting so long. "I've got some chores. I'll finish as soon as I can."

Wande followed him into the hallway. "Georg is doing the chores. If he misses something, tell him. He learns quickly."

"Tom said Georg might come."

Mrs. Morgan moaned, and Jud jumped. He gestured for Wande to follow him into the parlor.

"I was going to come see your family as soon as I could get away. One of my ranch hands didn't come back from Christmas, and I wondered if Georg would like a job." He paused, his nose wrinkling at the odor from the kitchen. "And now with this . . . Marion's going to need some help around the house until Ma gets better. Do you want the job?"

CHAPTER TEN

A refusal sputtered in Wande's throat as she stared at Jud. She had returned to the ranch because it was the right thing to do—the Christian thing. She didn't want or expect payment. But only last night her family talked about ways to bring in more money for food and clothing. Now God placed an opportunity in front of her.

"I would stay for nothing." Wande wanted him to understand. "But if you wish to pay me, I will not refuse."

"That's settled, then." Jud nodded. "I'll go talk with Georg about his duties."

Duties—such an ugly word for the neighborly thing to do. At least Jud hadn't refused their help. Later she would clean the kitchen and fix a bite to eat . . . she suspected no one had eaten since morning . . . but she would check with Marion first.

They met at the bottom of the staircase. "What do you need, Marion?" Wande gestured to the kitchen. "Warm water?"

"Yes. But be careful walking in the kitchen. We don't want

you to fall and hurt yourself." Marion's nose wrinkled at the smell, and she ran a hand across her forehead. "I need to clean up in there. I hope the doctor can get here soon."

"Papa will watch for him. I bring the water when it is warm and pray the doctor returns soon." She waited until the pot of water had warmed before pouring it into a basin. She was lifting it when Jud came in.

"Let me do that." The way he raced to her side, Wande wondered if she had done something wrong. He felt the sides of the container, and his shoulders relaxed. "I don't want two people burned in this house today."

"Be careful of the floor." While the water was heating, Wande cleaned the worst of the spill, but in places the floor was still slick.

He looked down. "You cleaned up in here. Thanks."

"It was nothing." Wande walked ahead of him to open doors. In Mrs. Morgan's bedroom, she caught sight of angry red welts banding the right half of Mrs. Morgan's torso.

Marion met him at the door. "The water is ready. Good. I want to get fresh bandages on."

Jud lowered his eyes. "Let me know when you're done."

Jud didn't return as soon as Marion expected. She heard a low murmur of voices from the kitchen and smelled cornbread. Her stomach grumbled. She hadn't eaten anything since she had eggs and bacon for breakfast shortly after sunrise.

Ma couldn't eat, but she probably should drink as much water as Marion could give her. "I'll be right back, Ma." In the kitchen she found Wande preparing supper with Jud, Tom, and Georg waiting at the table.

"Is Mrs. Morgan any better?" Wande turned over the ham steak she was browning in a skillet.

Marion shook her head. "But when I smelled the food cooking, I realized she should drink water." She reached for a glass from the cabinet.

"Sit down and have a bite." Jud grabbed a pitcher. "I'll take care of this. Should Ma eat something?"

"No." Marion and Wande responded at the same time.

A faint smile played on Jud's lips.

Wande piled a plate with sweet potatoes, cornbread, and ham and laid it in front of Marion. "Eat. You won't *helfen* your mama if you wear yourself out." She placed a mug of tea in front of her. "There is no milk. Georg says the cow is dry."

At the mention of his name, Georg nodded at Marion, then returned his attention to his food.

"Until she births the calf." Marion spoke between bites. "Not too long now."

Wande had put different spices in the sweet potatoes, and it gave them an unfamiliar zing. Marion noticed that Tom picked at his potatoes, but wolfed down extra helpings of ham and cornbread. He liked his food plain.

Someone rapped on the door, and Tom sprang to answer it. "Doc Treviño."

When Marion saw the lines of exhaustion on the doctor's face, she felt bad that she'd called him out yet again.

"Where's the patient?" The cheerfulness of his voice belied his expression.

"Up the stairs, first door on the right." Marion left her chair after spooning down a last bite of food. Jud was right, supper had refreshed her. As they climbed the stairs with the doctor, she outlined the care they had given. "I've changed the dressings three times, but I'm about to run out of clean bandages."

"Mention that to Fraulein Fleischer. I'm sure she'll wash some out for you."

"Wande has been wonderful. I can't believe she came back

here when she heard what had happened." Marion smiled until she heard a moan that sent her racing for the bedroom. She burst in. "What's wrong?"

"Doc. You're here." Jud's voice radiated relief. "She's in a lot of pain."

"Don't talk about pain to a woman who's birthed four children." Ma's attempt at humor fell flat as she spoke through clenched teeth, sweat dotting her brow. "I was fine until this son of mine insisted I drink water. I told him it felt like gravel forcing its way down my throat, but he wouldn't listen."

"He's right. You do need water. Burns suck all the moisture out of you. Mr. Morgan, you may wish to leave while I examine your mother."

Marion took his place at Ma's side. When the doctor lifted the dressings, Ma flinched but didn't make a sound.

"You've done a good job with keeping the dressings from sticking to the burns. Continue doing that. All we can do in cases like this is to make Mrs. Morgan as comfortable as possible and wait for her skin to grow back." He poured a reddish-brown liquid into a spoon.

"Is that laudanum?" Ma shook her head.

"Yes. Don't fuss. It will help you rest more easily."

When he'd finished his examination, he took Marion into the hall. He gave her the laudanum and explained the dosage. "It's important to follow the directions exactly. It's a dangerous drug if used inappropriately."

Marion blinked. "I'll be careful with it."

"As long as you follow precautions, you'll be fine. She'll need something for the pain." The doctor shifted his medical bag to his left hand. "I'm glad Fraulein Fleischer and her brother have returned. I don't want to come back and discover two new patients—you and your brother. Make sure you get enough rest."

"Yes, sir." But Marion did not know how.

⟵ ★ ⟶

The days fell into a pattern, one that left Jud with little to do in taking care of his mother.

Two days had passed since she spilled the soup and burned herself. Whenever it came time to change her bandages—like now—one of the women shooed him out of the room. He could only stand by and listen to her moans. The laudanum dulled the edge of the pain, but didn't take it away.

The door to Ma's room opened, and Wande slipped out, carrying a basket of dirty bandages. She gave no sign of seeing Jud where he stood at the top of the stairs. She braced her back against the door and sagged. She rested, her eyes drifting closed.

Jud climbed the top stair and crossed the landing. "Here. Let me help you with that."

Her eyes flew open. "*Nein, danke* . . . I am fine."

"Nonsense. All this time, you and Marion have been doing all the work. How can I help?" He grabbed the basket, heavy from the damp bandages. "What do you do with these?"

A weary smile crossed her lips. "Wash them, bleach them, dry them. Marion uses more bandages than a baby does *windeln*." She colored as if she had said something inappropriate.

An antiseptic smell rose from the basket, and Jud wished he could plug his nose. "I can't say I have much experience with laundry."

Wande sniggered behind her hand.

"But I'm willing to learn. I can't take care of Ma's personal needs, but I can handle soap and water." When he reached the bottom stair, he plunked the basket on the floor. "If you'll show me how . . ."

She directed him to drop the soiled bandages into a tub of warm water, tucked beside the stove. Then she showed him the process of scrubbing, boiling, rinsing, and drying. "Do you want to scrub or iron?"

"Why bother with ironing?" Jud shook his head. "Ma won't care if they're wrinkled."

"Ironing removes dampness and *helfen* to warm them."

Wande brushed a strand of hair from her forehead, and he saw her palms—red, almost blistered, with patches that were raw. "Your hands! Did you burn yourself?"

She tucked her arms at her sides, out of sight. "*Nein,* it is nothing. It is because of so much laundry."

"Let me see."

Reluctantly she held out her hands.

"This happens when you scrub the bandages?"

She nodded.

"Then I'm doing the scrubbing today." Surely his calloused hands could handle it.

She hesitated, then pointed by the stove. "Bring that tub outside."

He bent over, surprised at the weight. How had a tiny woman like Wande managed it? He staggered outside.

After she demonstrated the use of the soap and the washboard, she unpinned the clean bandages from the clotheslines. Arms piled high with strips of cloth, she stopped where he leaned over the washboard.

After less than five minutes, his hands were already complaining.

"Danke."

He grunted and paused. "How much are we paying you?"

She colored, and he remembered they had never discussed salary. "Now that I see how hard it is to do the laundry, I might double your salary."

She shifted the load in her arms and headed for the door. "Twice null is still null; or is math different in America?" She disappeared inside before he could respond.

About the time Jud was scrubbing the last cloth, Wande came to the porch and rang the bell. He looked overhead, not believing it could be dinnertime already, but the sun confirmed it. Tom trotted in from the pasture, and Georg came out of the barn.

Wande made keeping up with meals and laundry seem effortless. Ma and Marion did the laundry every week, of course, but not every day, as Wande had to do to keep the supply of clean bandages they needed.

After they had eaten, Wande jumped up to wash the dishes.

"Stop. Sit down." Jud's arms felt like deadweights. "We need to discuss the terms of your employment."

Her lips straightened, but she took a seat. "I *helfen* because I want to."

CHAPTER ELEVEN

Jud shook his head. Wande couldn't be as selfless as she claimed. No one was. No German was. He wouldn't tell her that the man who had jilted her so cruelly had asked him to give her a job. Or that her presence in his house disturbed his peace of mind.

"You've done more than be neighborly and bring a few meals. You've come in and taken over running the household, for a week. That's *work*."

She sighed. "I told you I would work for free."

"But you also said you wouldn't refuse pay if I insisted. And I do insist. You also need time off."

"But your mother . . ."

"We'll survive without you for an afternoon. The ranch hands take Saturday afternoon and evening off. Georg will be going into town to spend the night with your family. I want you to go with him. You'll come back on Sunday night."

Jud knew he was being high-handed, but he didn't dare negotiate with Wande. If he tried, he was in danger of agreeing to something, even if it wasn't in the best interest of either one of them.

"Very well. I will go home on Saturday and Sunday. I want to go to the *kirche*."

He looked into her eyes, and the longing there made him ache. Wande was only eighteen or nineteen, in a strange land—and with her hopes for future happiness dashed. Of course she would want to make friends with those of her own kind.

He pushed aside his desire to protect her, refusing to let it take root. Let her look for comfort among her own kind. She was German, an interloper—not a Texan, but one of a swarm of newcomers who wanted to take over Texas for their fatherland.

Wande forced herself to finish one last bundle of laundry before she left on Saturday. Despite her protests, the opportunity to see Mama and Papa broke down her reservations. She fingered the coins Jud gave her at dinner. Her first pay. It felt good, solid. The first wages she had ever earned. She would lay it in front of Papa with a flourish.

An hour before sundown, Georg appeared at the door, scrubbed clean and changed into his freshest clothes. She studied him. Since their arrival in Texas, he had grown taller and his chest was filling out. Her baby brother was becoming a man. "If you keep growing, we will need to make you new clothes."

He blushed. "Pastor Bader said the Verein will hold a meeting tonight. They talk about the different societies we can join. I hope Papa will let me—us—go."

Societies—Wande liked the idea of meeting other Germans in Victoria. She had spent most of her time on the ranch. "If they have one about farming methods that will work on this soil, Papa will want to go. You should, too."

By his expression, she knew Georg had other interests in

mind—maybe the chance to meet a pretty girl.

"But I am sure there is time for more than society talk tonight. We will learn, and we will meet new people, *ja?*" After a week of straining to understand every word in this strange language, English, she welcomed the chance to speak German. Even if only for a night, she could pretend she had never left Offenbach, and that she could still expect to marry Konrad.

"*Ja.* I will meet a pretty fraulein and you will meet a handsome gentleman, and we will have a wonderful time."

Wande caught sight of a golden head of hair, the afternoon sun creating an almost angelic halo. *Jud.*

But she didn't want an *Amerikaner*—any *Amerikaner*—particularly one who couldn't even pronounce her name. God would bring her a good, German man, someone like Papa, kind and wise.

The door opened and Tom came in, all spit and polish. "Are you folks ready? Since y'all are headed into town, I thought I would go along for the ride."

Wande's thoughts skittered to Marion and her infatuation with him. Tonight Tom dressed like a man hoping to make an impression on a woman.

"We are ready." A few minutes later, they climbed into the wagon, with Georg driving. Wande studied the countryside, already becoming familiar. That tree reminded her of a thundercloud; this dip in the road almost jolted her out of her seat; there was the tree where Mittens had climbed to the top . . . and Jud coaxed her down. She smiled at the memory.

The road seemed level, but she knew the land didn't lie completely flat. If it did, she would already see the town buildings. They must be climbing a small rise. When they reached the crest, the town of Victoria stretched before them. She could see the steeple of St. John's *kirche*, and her heart raced in anticipation of seeing her family.

As Georg promised, the German community held a meeting that night to introduce recent newcomers to German society in the area. Wande couldn't believe the diversity of interests represented among the tables set up in the church hall.

Papa and Georg headed for the farm booth as soon as they saw it, though Wande caught Georg peeking at a few pretty girls.

Wande went her own way, identifying the different societies represented. So far she had seen groups devoted to shooting, singing, literature, and even gymnastics. She hoped to find a group devoted to the study of English, but so far she heard only German flowing around her.

She paused in front of the music booth.

"Do you like to sing, *fraulein*?" A petite brunette inquired with an accent that indicated she came from Swabia. Her voice suggested a soprano range. "I am Johanna Schmidt. I help my mother with the chorale."

"I do like to sing, and so does my sister. How old do you have to be to join?"

"The adult chorale is for anyone over sixteen."

Wande shook her head. "Alvie is only ten."

"We have a group for the children also. They meet at the *kirche* on Monday afternoons." She smiled. "I work with the children. They are sweet. But you. Do you wish to join the adult chorale?"

"When do they meet?" Wande hesitated, thinking of her work responsibilities.

"We meet after church on Sunday afternoons. Many of our members live on farms and come into town on Sundays only."

Of course. "Then I would like to join. Will you meet tomorrow?"

"Yes." Johanna's eyes brightened as someone passed by. She waved. "Ertha! Come and meet . . ."

Wande turned and saw a girl with hair as red as poppies, a wide smile on her freckled face.

Wande introduced herself.

"Wande Fleischer. Where have I heard that name?" Recognition dawned in Johanna's eyes at the same time Ertha spoke.

"You are the girl Konrad Schuster jilted."

Wande wished she could melt into the floor.

Marion scanned the sanctuary, hoping to spot Tom. Bless Mrs. Walford for coming to the house early this morning and insisting Marion and Jud take a break and go to church.

Last night, Tom said he was going into town to see friends, and they had engaged in a small argument. He pointed out that he had a right to a life outside of the Running M.

Sometimes she wondered if Jud was right. The way Tom spent money, he might never save enough to get his own place. And whom did he go to see on Saturday nights? He insisted he just got together with some cowpokes.

The door opened again, and Marion turned to see who entered. It wasn't Tom, but someone she never expected to see in her church—Wande Fleischer, alone.

A deacon greeted Wande while Marion nudged Jud. "Look who came to our church today." The expression on Jud's face flashed between surprise, annoyance, and pleasure. Marion took a step in Wande's direction and waved. Wande nodded to the deacon and waited for Marion, a smile replacing her uncertainty.

Marion wondered why Wande had joined them for worship instead of attending a German-speaking congregation, but she would save her questions for later. She joined arms with her friend and turned to the deacon. "Mr. Brown, I'd like to introduce you to Wande Fleischer. She's new to Victoria."

Brown's face registered the German name, but he welcomed her warmly. "We're so glad you came to worship the Lord with us today, Miss Fleischer."

The pianist began playing the doxology, and Marion and Wande slipped into a pew beside Jud. He nodded to Wande as the congregation rose to sing the words of praise.

The service, so familiar to Marion, felt different when seen through a stranger's eyes and ears. Wande didn't join in the singing but stood, eyes closed, absorbing the music.

The pastor arose. "Now let's recite the Apostles' Creed together." Marion reached for a tattered copy of the Book of Prayer in the rack in front of her and showed it to Wande.

The congregation began reciting the familiar words. "I believe in God, the Father almighty, creator of heaven and earth . . ."

Wande's finger followed the text, and recognition lit her face. Marion heard her join them in a whisper, her words in German. *"Und an Jesus Christus . . ."*

A few minutes later, the choir leader called the congregation to introduce visitors. He looked straight at Marion and Jud. "Mr. Morgan, would you introduce your guest to our folks?"

Jud rumbled to his feet. "This is . . ." He looked at Wande, as if uncertain how to introduce her. "I could tell you a long story, but I won't bore you. This here is Wande Fleischer. She and her family spent their Christmas with us, and we're proud to have her visiting church with us today."

Smiles and clapping greeted his announcement, and Wande's face turned rosy. When the pastor gave the Scripture passage, Marion showed her the reference, and Wande turned pages in her German Bible, following the verses as he read.

Marion loved her church, but never more so than that

morning. When the service ended, nearly every member came forward to introduce themselves. Sprinkled among the greetings she heard a handful of *guten tags*. Marion saw some of the worry fall from Wande's face.

"May I escort you home, Miss Fleischer?" Jud spoke as if escorting a lovely girl—other than herself, of course—home from church were an everyday occasion.

"*Ja*. That is good." Wande hummed to herself as they walked out of the church. Marion placed the tune: "A Mighty Fortress Is Our God."

"Did you enjoy our service?" Jud said.

Marion hung back to let them talk together.

"I am so glad I came. I know God sent His Son for the whole world, but until today I had never seen it." Wande paused and looked both ways on Victoria's main street. "I feel better about Texas now that I know you love the same God we Germans do."

CHAPTER TWELVE

The church service had renewed Wande's spirit. God's love reached as far as Texas. She had known it—in her head. But today, among God's people at the Morgans' church, she came to feel it in her heart.

Her problems still existed. She lost her fiancé. She was the subject of gossip among German girls her own age—the reason she sought out a different congregation than the *kirche* next door to her parents' house. Her family still had no way to get to the land promised them by the Verein. But the weight of those obstacles diminished in the light of God's love.

All I can do is to commend you to the One from whom nothing can separate you. Konrad's parting words, which once seemed to mock her, now provided a ray of hope. He had given her the best benediction he could after the way he abandoned her. At the time, his words tasted bitter, as disappointing as Isaac's leftover words to Esau after Jacob stole the blessing. But truly, what better gift could Konrad offer than God's love?

A comforting stupor surrounded Wande as she walked from the church. When she took notice of her surroundings, she realized she was only a short distance from her house. She slowed. "I am sorry. You were kind to walk me home, and I was lost in thought."

Jud chuckled. "That's all right. You've been humming and singing and almost skipping along. Made me right happy to watch you."

"Can you come in for a few minutes? Mama will want to ask how Mrs. Morgan is doing."

"We don't want to intrude," Marion said.

"Let us return your hospitality. I know you want to get home soon. It will just be a moment." Wande opened the door and drank in the scent of *hasenpfeffer*. Yesterday Drud caught a rabbit, and Mama fixed the flavorful peppered hare for their Sunday dinner. Wande gestured for Marion and Jud to enter, hoping they would see the home as she did, filled with reminders of a faraway place. "Mama! Papa! Look who has come to visit."

Alvie bounced out of the room she shared with Wande, the cat in her arms. "Marion! Mr. Morgan!"

"Is it just my imagination, or is Mittens getting fat?" Jud spoke in a low voice to Wande and winked.

Wande giggled. "Do you want one of the yellow kittens?"

The family gathered from the different rooms, and they chattered as if they hadn't seen each other for months. Papa led in a prayer for Mrs. Morgan.

"Won't you join us for dinner?" Mama asked.

"Another time," Marion said. "Our neighbor, Mrs. Walford, offered to stay with Ma this morning, and we've already kept her too long."

"We will be back before sundown," Wande said. As she watched the Morgans climb into their wagon, she remembered she planned to leave the Fleischers' wagon in town for the family. She and Georg needed to finish their noon meal quickly and start walking.

Papa had other ideas. After the meal, when Wande stood to help Mama clear the table, her parents exchanged a look. "Your father wishes to have a few words with you." Mama shooed her from the kitchen.

Wande held her breath. Mama might be the bear of the family, but everyone knew Papa ruled. "Have a few words with you" had come to mean a reprimand. She glanced at Georg, but he merely shrugged.

God loves you. Capturing that thought in her heart, Wande straightened her back and followed Papa to the parlor.

"*Nein,* daughter, you have no need to look like a frightened deer. You are not in trouble."

Wande offered an uncertain smile and settled in the familiar Biedermeier chair—solid, comfortable, fashioned out of a light ash wood. The same seat had held her through conversations with her father since she was old enough to understand the difference between right and wrong.

Papa took a pipe from the shelf but didn't light it. He almost never used tobacco, but holding it seemed to give him comfort. "Something troubled you last night. Because you are a grown woman, we allowed you to go to the church of your choosing this morning." He smiled. "And it was good for you, *ja?*"

"Ja." Wande hugged that comfortable feeling close to her again. *I will not be afraid. God loves me.*

"But now the time has come for us to talk of these bad things. Of what Konrad has done, what people are saying, and what you wish to do."

These talks with Papa—when he wasn't reprimanding her but rather talking about a difficult situation—were the worst of all. *God loves me,* she repeated to herself. "You and Mama were right about Konrad after all."

"We did not wish to be, *Liebchen*. We hoped he loved you as we love each other. As God wishes a man to love his wife."

"I know," Wande said. "But it is past. I cannot undo his marriage. I would not want him now, even if he wasn't married."

Papa tapped the pipe on the arm of the chair. "Do you still want to be married?"

That question stopped Wande. She feared she might crumple into a ball. "Who will want to marry me, Papa? I have nothing to offer, and everyone here knows my history."

"Ah, *Liebchen*." Papa laid the pipe aside and leaned forward, hands on his knees. "God has the most special man for you. Never doubt that. Someone better than you can imagine." He smiled. "God is providing for our needs—we have all found good jobs. Even your Mama has already been given piecework. When the right time comes, He will provide for the needs of your heart as well."

"Oh, Papa." Tears welled in Wande's eyes. "I will be happy, as long as I can be with you."

"No, *Liebchen*." Papa rose and embraced his daughter. "God's plan is for man and woman to leave their father and mother. He knows the day, the hour, the *second*."

"But until then . . ." Papa let her go and looked into her eyes. "You are our beloved daughter and you always have a place in our home. Until you are ready to leave it."

Marion tiptoed out of her mother's bedroom. Now that Ma had begun to improve, she felt comfortable leaving her for short periods. Evenings, after Jud insisted everyone stop working, had become her favorite time of day. Marion held Wande to her promise to learn English. Sometimes Georg joined them, but not now. Tonight, the lesson was on the letters of the English alphabet.

"You like to sing." Marion smiled. "We have a song that teaches the alphabet." Marion pulled out the chart she had made of upper- and lowercase letters.

"Those look familiar." Wande pointed. "Only we have more letters. Ä between *A* and *B*. Ö after O. A few others." She recited the alphabet, beginning *"Ah, ay, bay, say."*

"Ah, bay, say?" Marion kept her face straight. "In English, we use the 'ee' sound for letters. "Aye, bee, cee." She sang the alphabet song and got Wande to repeat it, but stopped before "kay."

"Jay." The J in Wande's mouth come out like a Y. "That letter is *'yot'* in German."

"*Ja,* I know." Marion teased. "Feel your tongue. Press it against the roof of your mouth. 'Jay.'"

After a couple dozen tries, Wande succeeded in an approximation of *J.* "So your brother's name is Jood." She smiled.

"Did I hear my name?" Jud came in from the kitchen, where he had put the latest bandages in to soak. "Only in English it's 'Jud.'"

"Jood." Wande repeated, nodding.

Marion looked at Jud and they both laughed. "Better."

The next part of the alphabet song went better than Marion expected. "El, em, en, oh, pay," Wande sang.

"Pee," Marion corrected. "In English, we call the letter 'pee.'"

"Pee." Wande sang the alphabet song all the way through a couple of times.

"That is enough for tonight. Tomorrow we start using the McGuffey Readers," Marion said. "I can't wait."

Wande groaned.

The door opened and Tom entered. "Marion, care to join me for a walk?"

“Come in! We were just finishing.” Marion sighed. “But I need to go sit with Ma.”

“I will sit with her. Take time with your *junger mann,*” Wande said. “I will sing the alphabet song. Mrs. Morgan can laugh at me.”

Marion looked at the clock and up the stairs at the door to Ma’s room. She should go take care of her mother.

“Go ahead with Tom.” Jud waved her away. “Ma will be all right until you get back.” Turning mock-serious, he wagged his finger at Tom. “But don’t stay out too long.”

Tom grinned as he helped Marion into her coat. “Are you ready, ma’am?”

“Don’t ‘ma’am’ me like I was an old woman.” She smiled up at him. He was looking-glass handsome, as tall as Jud, with dark hair that tended to grow ragged. She touched it where it edged over his collar. “Remind me to cut that for you sometime.”

He muttered something and swept her out onto the porch and down the steps to the cover of the acacia trees. He faced her, holding her hands like delicate strands of silk. “You’re a sight for sore eyes.”

“It’s just me, silly. You see me every day.”

“Not enough. Never enough.” He bent close as if to kiss her, but she stopped him with a finger.

“What do you mean?”

He blew breath through his teeth. “I’ve hardly seen you since your Ma was hurt.”

“What did you expect? My mother is ill.” Surely Tom wasn’t complaining about her taking care of her mother.

“You still find time to teach English to those . . . Germans.” Tom ground the word through his teeth and averted his eyes.

Marion dropped her finger from Tom’s chest. “You resent my friendship with Wande because she’s *German*?”

“Ah, Marion-gal, it’s not that.” Tom lifted her chin so he

could look into her eyes. "I'd resent anybody who took away any of my time with you. I just want to be with you. For the rest of my life."

This time, when he bent to kiss her, she didn't push him away.

Jud watched the two figures embrace under the acacia trees. He resisted the temptation to break them apart; that might make Marion dig in her heels. The time had come to face the fact that his sister had grown up.

Unlike his other sister. Billie would never have a chance to grow up. Anger against the Comanches bubbled inside him. Sometimes he felt like the world had ranged itself against Texas, but he couldn't hold that against Tom. He'd lost his parents in pursuit of the Texas dream.

Jud glanced at the clock. He'd give them fifteen minutes—then he'd go out and split the lovers apart for the night.

He had just dropped the last of the day's bandages into the water when he heard laughter on the porch. A brief pause followed before the door opened. Jud waited a few seconds before coming out of the kitchen.

Marion's face was flushed, and they held hands as boldly as a married couple. They *had* been kissing. Jud counted to ten, telling himself to get hold of his anger.

"Jud!" Marion giggled. "We didn't think you'd still be up." She dropped Tom's hand, but they stood so close their fingertips still touched.

"Jud." Tom straightened his shoulders and pulled himself to his full height, which still left him not much taller than Jud's shoulder. "Or perhaps I should say 'Mr. Morgan.'" He dug his hands in his pockets, then took them out again. "Marion and I have been talking . . ."

"You've been doing *more* than talking," Jud said.

"No, sir. That is, yes, sir. What I'm trying to say is that I'd like to ask for your sister's hand in marriage."

CHAPTER THIRTEEN

Marion looked at Jud, gold darting through her hazel eyes in expectation.

"I suppose the lady is willing?" Jud said.

Marion blushed and nodded.

"Why don't you go on upstairs while I have a talk with Tom."

Marion looked at him, questions swimming in her eyes.

"Don't worry," he said. "I won't hurt him . . . much."

She managed a laugh that was half a worried cough. "Good night." The dazzling smile she sent Tom expressed her feelings better than any words.

The two men watched her climb the stairs. In the space of those few steps, Jud traced Marion's journey from the gangly twelve-year-old she had been when Pa died, through her chatterbox years of girlhood, to the woman she had become. From the way Tom looked at her, it was clear he saw no girl, but a woman ready to take to wife.

"Let's go outside." Jud jerked his head in toward the door, and Tom followed.

Jud wanted to bang the two lovers' heads together. They were so young. Younger even than Calder was when he married. Calder acted like an old man compared to Tom. This kid had never found his own feet to stand on.

The two men headed toward the corral, passing by the acacia trees. Jud spoke in as mild a tone as he could muster. "From here on, I want you to stay on the porch when you're talking to my sister." He nodded toward the trees.

"Yes, sir." The rush of red into Tom's cheeks made it clear he understood.

"How do you intend to support a wife? Where do you plan to live?"

"I thought we could live at the house until I save enough money to get us a place of our own."

"How much money do you have saved?"

"Not enough." Tom hung his head.

"How much?"

"Five dollars."

The news was worse than Jud feared. "You know you'll have extra expenses when you get married. And even more, once babies start coming. And generally, the cost of things goes up, not down. Especially with more people moving here all the time."

"More Germans, you mean."

Jud shrugged. "I'm just saying, the longer you wait, the more it will cost you."

"I know. I just . . ."

"You're in love and you want to get married. I understand. But you need to understand that Marion is my sister. And it's my responsibility to see that you can provide for her." He started walking, and Tom trotted behind.

"Are you saying I can't marry her?"

Jud stopped where he could look across the pastureland. Only vague shapes were visible under the half moon, but his imagination pictured the two herds that roamed the hills. Truth was, Ma and Pa didn't have much more than Tom when they arrived in Victoria. Just their love for each other, and two of the finest Morgan horses on this side of the Mississippi—that and three growing children. But they worked hard and saved. By the time little Billie was born, they'd been able to buy their own land.

"Tell you what." Jud turned his attention back to Tom. "My sister seems to love you, although I'm not sure why. But I won't let her marry a broke cowboy. I especially don't want her married to someone working for someone else, even if it is family."

Tom's face fell with each sentence.

Jud took pity on him. "But if you're willing . . ."

"Yes?" Tom's eagerness said a lot.

"I'll raise your pay by four bits a week, only I'll keep back fifty cents and hold it for you and Marion. If you can figure out how to put more into savings, give me any extra. And we'll both keep our eyes out for some land you can afford."

"Yes, sir! Thank you, sir!" Tom pumped his hand. "I'll prove myself worthy of Marion, you'll see."

"It's Jud." He clamped his hand on the shoulder of his future brother-in-law and squeezed, then strolled to the house.

Wande rubbed salve into her hands. Now that she no longer scrubbed bandages several times a day, they were starting to heal. Three weeks had passed since Mrs. Morgan's accident. She had recovered enough to join in simple tasks in the kitchen, though neither Marion nor Jud would let their mother near the stove.

Now they were shaping biscuits, a change from the usual cornbread—twenty round shapes, barely enough for supper with three men at the table. "Should we make more?" Wande said.

"Mix some more dough, sure. But I have something else in mind." Mrs. Morgan stood, grimacing where her right side brushed the table. Wande kept her mouth closed. Mrs. Morgan didn't welcome pity, and the doctor had urged her to move about as much as she felt able.

Mrs. Morgan disappeared into the pantry and returned with a sack of dried peaches. "How about some peach cobbler? Make a few more biscuits but use the rest of the dough for the cobbler."

"Cobbler? Is that like a strudel?" One thing Wande had noticed, whether German or American, everyone loved sweets.

"Why don't we find out?" Mrs. Morgan gestured to the pantry. "Do you have the ingredients you need to make a strudel?"

"We usually use apples, but I could try peaches." Wande thought they had everything else, but went into the pantry to check. She didn't find currants, but she could drop a few more raisins into the mixture. Gathering the ingredients in her apron, she brought them to the kitchen. "First I need to make phyllo dough, more like your pie crust than biscuits." She molded the flour ingredients into a ball and started kneading it.

"Vinegar? I never would have thought of it." Mrs. Morgan sprinkled cinnamon and sugar over the dried peaches before adding a bit of water and dots of butter.

"It is the way my mother has always made it."

Mrs. Morgan had the cobbler ready to go into the oven by the time Wande finished kneading the dough. "Let me do that." Wande pushed the baking pan into the oven. "Should the biscuits go in yet?" Mrs. Morgan shook her head.

Wande placed the phyllo ball in the cold cellar while she worked on the filling: an end of a loaf of bread, crumbled; three handfuls of dried peaches; a handful of raisins; all sprinkled with the same cinnamon and sugar Mrs. Morgan had used for the cobbler. By the time she had finished rolling the dough and forming the strudel, Mrs. Morgan was hovering over the oven, removing the cobbler. Soup bubbled on the stove.

"Mrs. Morgan! I am supposed to cook. I am so sorry."

She waved away her concerns. "You were busy making us a special treat. And I needed to cook. We have a saying here, about getting back on the horse. When something bad happens, you have to go back and do it again, so you don't get scared. I *have* to cook, Wande. I can't let this silly old stove make me afraid."

"You will let Jud carry the soup to the table." Wande removed the biscuits from the baking sheet and used it again for the strudel.

"Of course." Mrs. Morgan winked. "Jud must be allowed to take care of me."

"It smells good in here." A grinning Jud came in. His coat was open at the neck, his golden hair windblown. He smelled of fresh air and sunshine.

"We want the men to judge our peach dessert contest." Mrs. Morgan grinned at Wande.

"I'll be happy to oblige." Jud rubbed his belly. "Whatever that is, it smells mighty good."

Marion and Tom came in together. "Oh, Wande, you'll have to see him. He's adorable!" She had gone to see the new calf, born a month earlier than the normal birthing season.

"Now we'll have milk and cream and butter again." Mrs. Morgan's eyes lit up.

"Is the soup ready?" Jud sniffed. "Vegetable. My favorite."

Wande set the table while Marion and Tom cleaned up. Jud

carried the pot to the table and set it in the middle before sitting down to return thanks.

Georg joined them. "Do I smell strudel?"

Wande nodded. "But I had to use peaches. There is also peach cobbler."

The six of them made short work of the soup and biscuits. Wande was relieved that her strudel had browned by the time they finished.

Mrs. Morgan stood and clapped her hands. "And now, today, for your special enjoyment, we are having a peach baking contest. I have made peach cobbler. Wande, why don't you tell us about your dish."

"We call it strudel. I don't know how to describe it. You will try it?"

"Of course they will." Mrs. Morgan cut a small piece of each and placed it on their plates. "You are welcome to seconds."

Wande tried the cobbler first. "This is very good."

Jud cut into the strudel first. He brought the fork to his mouth, bit into it, then dived for a second bite. "This is delicious."

Wande tried not to giggle at the sight of the drop of filling caught on his chin.

"Tom, wait until you try this," Marion said.

Tom ate the cobbler first. When he had finished the last crumb, he said, "I'll want seconds, for sure." Then he stared at the strudel like some alien creature. He looked apologetically at Wande. "I've never been much for trying anything new."

"That's true." Marion had finished her strudel and was enjoying her cobbler. "We couldn't get him to eat frijoles for weeks. But you must try this, Tom. It's like a peach pie with a crust on all four sides. Only better." She shared a smile with Wande.

With four pairs of eyes staring at him, Tom gave in and dug

his fork into the strudel. "It's good." With his second bite, a frown crossed his face. "I'd like it better without the raisins."

"Alvie says the same thing. I used to feel the same way, when I was younger." Wande paused. Had she just called him childish?

"I used to think oatmeal raisin cookies were good if you left out the raisins." Marion giggled. "But I like the raisins in this. It makes it special."

"How about you, Georg?" Wande wanted him to praise Mrs. Morgan's baking.

"Peaches are good, however you eat them. I like the cobbler and the strudel."

"And you, Jud?" Mrs. Morgan's eyes bore into her son.

He smacked his lips. "I'll never pass up a chance for one of Ma's cobblers." He hesitated. "But this strudel is something mighty special. Mighty good indeed."

Wande blushed.

⟵ ★ ⟶

Ma and Wande might think they had hidden the truth, but Jud knew Ma had fixed the meal. That bit of chili powder Ma always used to season her soup gave it away. Wande didn't use the spice so foreign to her.

In the weeks since Ma's accident, Wande had become indispensable. Each morning, Jud left with her cheery singing of one Martin Luther's many hymns ringing in his ears. He returned at suppertime to her happy chatter. Ma was a mother hen, always ready to take an extra chick under her wing, but she and Wande shared something special.

In the evenings, Marion continued her English lessons with the two Germans. Wande picked up the language with amazing speed, although his name still came out "Yood" more often than "Jud." Georg lagged behind, although he had no problem caring for the animals.

But once Ma was well again . . . they had no reason to keep Wande around the house.

And that thought made Jud sad.

CHAPTER FOURTEEN

"What makes you so happy this morning?"

Marion hesitated in the middle of changing the dressing on the last of Ma's burns. All but a couple of patches had healed. "Are you in pain? I can get you some laudanum." She had stopped taking the medicine except at night.

"No. But you're all smiles and singing as brightly as Wande usually does." Ma winced as Marion lifted off the last bandage, tearing a tiny pinch of skin. "Could it be because today is Valentine's Day?"

"Oh, Ma. It's just another day." Marion blushed when she thought of the card she had labored over. She hoped Tom would like it, and not think it too feminine. Since the holiday fell on a Saturday, she hoped they could go into town to celebrate.

"Knock knock. May I come in?"

She heard Tom's voice and smiled. "Give us a minute." She placed the fresh bandage over the burn, and Ma pulled down her blouse. "All right, you can come in."

"Happy Valentine's Day." Tom ducked into the room, holding a bouquet of purple wildflowers, from the lavender and white petals of the Carolina Anemone to the rich colors of the Wine Cup.

"Tom, they're beautiful. Look, Ma."

Ma sniffed the flowers and sighed. "Use my glass to hold them. It's time I got a clean one." She poured water into it from the pitcher, and Marion arranged the posies.

"I'll bring this right down to the table." Marion lifted her face and kissed Tom on the cheek. "Thank you." She traipsed down the stairs with Tom in tow.

"I have something for you too." Marion kept her gaze from the parlor, where her card lay in a drawer. "But you'll have to wait."

"Then you'll want to bring it with you." Tom grinned. "Since it's my half day, I'm going to take us to town tonight."

Marion took a second look at him. He had not only scrubbed his face and shaved, but he had also washed his hair and spruced up for the occasion. "Look at you. I'm still wearing my everyday dress."

"You look fine to me. But if you want to change, we have time. Wear that pretty yellow dress with the purple sprigs. Then you can pin a flower to your dress and it will match." The way his eyes gleamed when he looked at her made her blush.

She headed for the stairs . . . and ran into Jud's broad chest.

"Where are you going in such a hurry?" Jud looked from Marion to Tom, and his jaw clenched. "Let me guess. Valentine's Day."

"The day for young lovers." Marion swirled around. "Tom brought me the flowers on the table. Isn't it romantic?" She dashed to the table and selected a Stork's Bill bloom before heading upstairs. Though she hadn't worn the "pretty yellow dress" since last summer, Tom remembered it. She would take it out of storage and wear it with a wrap. She ran a brush through her golden hair, parted it in the middle, and made two braids. She reached behind to hook the braids in a coil at the back of her neck. She tucked the flower behind her ear and headed downstairs.

She paused at the top of the landing. Raised voices came from below.

"—save the money you're going to spend today on dinner?"

"—have the money."

"—never save enough to marry my sister."

Marion's hand went to her throat.

Wande came out of her room, her valise in hand, ready to ride into town with Georg.

Marion put her finger to her lips.

The men's voices had risen enough that Marion could hear each word.

"Valentine's Day is only one day out of the year," Tom said. "And it's my day off. I'm going to town with your sister."

Tom didn't often stand up to Jud like that. Marion felt a surge of pride.

"And I have a question for you," Tom said. "If you're so keen on saving money, why is Wande still working here? Your ma is doing her housework again. There's not enough work here to keep three women busy."

Wande gasped, loud enough that Ma called out from the bedroom. "What's wrong?"

Jud heard the gasp and lifted his eyes to see Wande at the head of the stairs, as pale as a quarter moon. Their gazes locked on each other. Then she turned and went back to her bedroom.

Jud saw the smirk on Tom's face and wanted to bash it with his fist. "I'll deal with you later." He turned his back on Tom and looked up the stairs. Part of him wanted to run after her. But that was foolishness.

Jud grabbed his hat from the coat rack. "If anyone asks, tell 'em I've gone to the barn." He didn't know if Tom was listening. He didn't care.

Within the family, "going to the barn" had become Jud's code for "I need some time alone." When the house buzzed with too much noise from his family, he'd escape to the barn and talk things over with JM. At least the horse always listened. Sometimes Jud would escape to the hayloft and sit where the sounds were muted.

Marmalade ran between Jud's legs, meowing. Jud didn't know how many problems he had talked over with the animals—and with God.

He opened the door and gazed into the barn's dark interior. He heard someone moving about, although it should be empty. Tom and Georg worked only a half day.

It was Georg. He was talking to the new calf in the silly talk he heard Marion use sometimes when she petted Marmalade. *"Gute kuh."*

Jud cleared his throat. "I thought you'd be gone by now."

"I am waiting for Wande, then we can leave."

Jud's mind flashed back to the look on Wande's face. "I'm not sure how soon that will be."

"I can wait. I like this cow and her calf. She gives good milk. Already she grows so big." Georg spread his hands wide. "Soon we will buy two cows. Mr. Grenville at the store says he will buy our extra cream and butter. Mama is going to make cheese, too—to sell later."

Tom could learn a lesson from the Fleischers. All of them except Alvie had found work, already saving enough money to buy one cow. But would they have enough for a second if Wande wasn't working?

"But our cow won't be as good as this *mutter* here." Georg scratched a spot on the cow's nose. He had a feel for not only the cows, but also the horses.

"How much are you willing to pay for the cows?"

"Papa said he heard of a man who offered for a cow 1,000 acres of the land from the Verein. But that was a long time ago. Here Papa is talking with a farmer who wants nine dollars for a cow and her calf."

Jud scratched his chin. He had four cows, the other three still pregnant. They supplied the ranch with more than enough milk and butter. They kept the steers mostly to raise beef for their own use. "I'll sell you this one for the same price, as soon as one of our others gives birth and starts producing milk again."

The delight on Georg's face rivaled the candles they lit on that ridiculous Christmas tree. "I will have to ask Papa, *ja*? But I am sure he will be pleased." He looked at the floor. "I will tell you a secret. I have named them."

Jud laughed. "I do that myself. So what is this little heifer's name?"

"She is Karlina. She is strong." He pointed to where the calf butted her mother's side. "She is looking for her food, but later, she will be a good, strong *kuh*."

Jud extended his hand to Georg and they shook. "I'll consider it a done deal, then—as soon as you talk with your father."

"It will not be long before you have another calf." Georg pointed to the cow in the next stall. "Heidi will give birth soon. Maybe even tonight."

Jud went into the stall and checked the cow. Alice—Jud's name for her—mooed low, in pain, and her sides heaved. Georg was right; her labor had started. Jud scratched his head. "So old

John Bull got to you, too. Or else you're a month early."

The door opened, admitting a shaft of sunlight. Jud saw Wande silhouetted in the doorway, holding two valises. She walked toward them, dragging her feet.

"Wande, good news." Georg bounded toward her. "Jud says we can buy this cow."

Wande looked at Jud, more reserve in her expression than he had seen since their first meeting. "Thank you, Mr. Morgan, but we do not need your charity."

"You've got both your bags, Wande. Why?"

She lifted her chin. "Since Mrs. Morgan has recovered, I will not come back on Monday."

Her glare dared him to disagree.

CHAPTER FIFTEEN

"Come, Georg. Let us leave this place." Wande trembled with the effort it took to stand still. She felt equal parts anger and humiliation.

Her brother patted the cow's neck, the one Jud wanted to "sell" to them. "I have decided to stay here. Heidi will give birth tonight. I want to help her." He nodded at the next stall. Jud ran his hands along the cow's sides while staring at Wande openmouthed.

She clutched a satchel in each hand and turned her back on them before speaking. "Then I will go into town with Tom and Marion."

"But what is wrong?"

Wande heard the confusion in Georg's voice. "Ask Mr. Morgan to explain." She took a step toward the door.

"Wande, wait."

Wande glanced at Jud's dark face, then searched for the wagon, expecting to find it in front of the house with the horses hitched. But it was still beside the barn. Why was nothing going right on this day? She waited, gathering her courage to go back into the barn to fetch the horses, when she heard Marion's soft laughter and the neighing of a horse.

Marion and Tom sat together in the ranch's carriage, a two-person conveyance that gleamed from a fresh cleaning. Marion wore a yellow dress more suitable for summer than for February, a purple flower tucked behind her right ear. She smiled, a young woman in love. Wande remembered her friend's chatter about Valentine's Day, when couples celebrated their love for each other. Tom and Marion's plans must not include taking either Wande or Georg into town.

The carriage slowed, and Marion leaned out the side. "Tom is taking me to dinner in town." She glanced at the bags in Wande's hands. "Please don't leave until I get back."

Tom's face told Wande nothing, and she wondered if she had misplaced her anger. Tom had accused her of not doing her share of the work—not Jud. She should listen to Jud's side of the story. "Very well. I will stay tonight and go with you to church tomorrow."

Wande forced a smile and waved as Tom and Marion left. She would stay one more night, but she could not think of anything that would make her stay a day longer. She would return home, back to Mama and Papa, Drud, Alvie, and . . . her empty room. This day when *Amerikaners* celebrated love mocked her. Konrad also deserved some of her anger.

The sun hung low, reminding her not to let it go down on her anger. She shook herself and headed back to the house. She would not let anger rule her world, but neither would she remain in a position that humiliated her and brought shame to her family.

"Jud, is that you?" Mrs. Morgan said after Wande climbed the stairs to her room.

Wande took stock of her appearance in the mirror. Her

cheeks had paled, and shadows darkened her eyes. She splashed water on her face, added an ecru lace collar to her dress, and practiced a smile. "Peace and love, not anger, Lord. May they see You in me." She left the room. "It is I, Frau Morgan."

"Oh, good. You left in such a hurry, I was worried."

Wande hung back at the top of the stairs, but Mrs. Morgan motioned to her from the parlor. "Come down, we need to talk."

Wande joined Mrs. Morgan at the bottom of the stairs.

"Come in the kitchen and sit a spell with me. I've brewed some fresh coffee." Mrs. Morgan took care to balance the pot before she moved it, but someone would have to know about the accident to notice. Only a small, angry puckering on the right side of her face evidenced the injury she had endured. She grimaced as she sat down, deepening the lines on her face.

"You are in pain. Let me pour the coffee." Wande jumped up to get the mugs from the cabinet.

"Don't be silly. Doc Treviño would leave more laudanum if the pain bothered me that much, but it's nothing I can't handle with the Lord's help." She paused as Wande poured coffee into the mugs. "And your help, too, of course."

Wande's hand trembled, and she spilled a few drops on the table. "Look at the mess I made."

She went to the pantry for a towel and set it on the table; then to the icebox for a pint of cream; then she got up again to grab cookies.

"Sit down, Wande."

Wande relented , feeling much as she did when Papa called her into the parlor for one of his little talks. After she poured some cream into her cup and took a sip, she dared to look into Mrs. Morgan's calm blue eyes.

"What happened to get you so upset?"

Wande did not voice the answer that sprang to her mind—*ask your son*. Mrs. Morgan had not heard the hurtful words. "I overheard Jud and Tom argue. They were in the parlor when I was in my room, and I could not help but hear their voices."

"What about? I can't believe they were arguing about you."

"Something about Tom spending too much money." Wande's cheeks warmed, but Mrs. Morgan only nodded.

"And . . . and Tom asked why I still work here now that you are well."

Mrs. Morgan sank against the chair back. "Oh dear. No wonder you are so upset. What a dreadful thing to say."

Did she feel as uneasy about Tom as Mama and Papa had felt about Konrad?

"And what did Jud say?"

Now Wande's face burned. "I did not stay to listen. I shut the door so I could not hear and packed my bags to leave."

"But you are still here."

Wande explained the events that led to her remaining one more night. "I do not know what I should do. I do not wish to accept money that I have not earned."

"Oh, Wande." Mrs. Morgan leaned forward and took one of her hands. "You make my life so much happier, in ways that have nothing to do with work."

"I do not understand." The strangeness of the English language put Wande at a disadvantage.

"You remind me of what it means to be young and new to this country. When we moved to Texas, it was still a part of Mexico—foreign to us. There were times I could barely find enough food to put on the table. I don't know how we would have survived if not for the help of our neighbors—our *Mexican* neighbors—who provided beans and cornmeal and an occasional chicken." Her eyes gazed into a distant past. "We tried not to let the children know how desperate we were. And times were hard after Bill died, but Jud was too proud to accept any help."

Now Wande nodded. Jud was like men everywhere, *Amerikaner* or German.

"But Jud is pleased—as I am—that now we can help others. And God wants us to do that, doesn't He?"

Wande fought with herself. "It still does not seem right to take money that I do not earn."

"If you didn't do a lick of housework, you'd still make a difference by bringing joy into this house. You have suffered the loss of a sister, and yet you find contentment in every task. Please stay, Wande."

"I will think about it, *ja*. And discuss the matter with my Papa tomorrow."

"That is all I can ask." Mrs. Morgan drank the last of her coffee. "And now, let's cook some supper before Jud and Georg barge in, looking for something to eat."

What had happened to the two men in Marion's life to cause such an argument? She glanced at her betrothed. He looked so calm, so in control, so *handsome*. She couldn't believe he had started the argument. A year ago, with the loss of Billie still so overwhelming, she never would have expected to find such happiness on this Valentine's Day.

During those months, Tom had supported Marion and the entire family. Jud might not acknowledge it, but Tom had kept the ranch operating when Jud left to look for Billie. He even took over when Jud was present in body but not in spirit. That was when she began to fall in love with him. The memory brought a smile. Billie would be pleased.

Tom noticed. "What's got you smiling?"

"You." She spoke without thought, then felt heat rush to her cheeks. "Us. How happy I am."

He threw back his head and laughed. "Then I'll make it my

business to keep that smile on your face, 'cause you're mighty pretty."

"Oh, you." Then she added, "If you want to keep me smiling, make up with my brother. And Wande. I can't believe what you said."

His back stiffened. "Jud said I was wasting money by taking the prettiest girl in all of Victoria out to dinner. I just pointed out I wasn't the only one willing to spend an extra penny or two on a woman."

"You hurt her feelings—and got Jud madder than a hornets' nest." If Marion were five years younger, she would have pouted.

"Ah, Marion, I'll make it up with Jud, I promise. And he's not going to let that pretty young woman go anywhere; you can count on that—even if she is German. Haven't you seen the way he looks at her?"

Marion bristled.

"I ought to know, 'cause that's the way I feel when I look at you. And look, there's Victoria, all lit up, waiting for us to arrive."

Marion couldn't stay angry with Tom. She fingered the valentine she had tucked into her reticule and wondered what surprises Tom had in store for her. "That's good to know. For a little while I thought you might have something against the Fleischers, and they're good people." She lifted her chin. "Alvie asked my help with her entry for the school essay contest. The theme this year is 'Why I love the United States,' in celebration of becoming the twenty-eighth state."

Tom flicked the reins. "Let's not talk about it anymore. I don't want any unpleasantness to make a mess of things tonight."

He was right. Valentine's Day was meant for lovers. She turned her most brilliant smile on Tom. "I love you."

Tom slackened his hold on the reins, and the horses stopped. He bent his face to hers and kissed her—while the carriage was stopped in the middle of the road.

CHAPTER SIXTEEN

Jud wanted to clear things up with Wande, but she was avoiding him. After church he, his mother, and Marion stopped by the Fleischer house for a visit. Jud closeted himself with her father. Ma visited with Mrs. Fleischer, and Marion found a corner to work with Alvie on a school project.

Jud settled into an oak chair that spoke of quality and comfort. "I wanted to speak with you about an unfortunate incident that happened last night."

The older man leaned forward. "Is there something wrong with the work Georg is doing?"

"No, he's doing excellent work. One of our cows gave birth last night, and he helped both the mother and the calf."

"Then it must be my Wande." Fleischer's voice dropped to a softer register. "She is fine?"

"I need your help, sir."

Fleischer's eyes widened. "You wish to court *meine tochter?*"

Heat rushed to Jud's face. "Nothing like that." He realized

how unflattering that must sound. “Not that she won’t make someone a fine wife.” When Mr. Fleischer still didn’t respond, Jud stopped.

Fleischer took a moment to compose himself. “Then what is the problem?”

“She thinks we don’t want her at the ranch anymore.”

Jud heard the door, but it was too late, Wande stood in the doorway, watching the two men.

Wande strode into the parlor and sat in the remaining Biedermeier chair. “I cannot believe you would repeat such awful things to my papa.”

“Wande, Herr Morgan and I are having a private conversation.” A month ago, the look on Papa’s face would have sent her out the door.

“About me. I deserve to hear his accusations in person.”

“Perhaps Wande should hear what I have to say.” Jud’s cheeks looked as red as hers felt.

“As you wish.” Papa put his forefinger to his chin, assuming his listening pose. “Please continue.”

“I had a disagreement with Tom Cotton, Marion’s fiancé.” Jud shifted in the chair. “I don’t wish to speak ill of him, but . . . he has a problem with the way he handles money.”

“Then your concern is understandable, but what does it have to do with my Wande?”

Jud looked at Wande, his eyes asking her to help him tell the tale.

“Tom said that Jud was wasting money paying me, since his mother has recovered.”

Papa leaned back. “Is this true?”

Jud turned his hands over. “That’s more or less what Tom said, yes.”

"It is true, Papa. Frau Morgan is much improved. She and Marion can do the work. I have less and less to do each day." Wande made herself stay still in the chair. "I never wanted money for helping Mrs. Morgan, and I will not accept money where I am not needed—*or wanted.*" Surely Papa would agree.

Jud watched Wande walk down the aisle to join her family at the front of the reception hall that doubled as a classroom. The school was holding an award ceremony, and Marion convinced him to attend.

Wande traveled with them to the event. Why Jud had argued so hard with Mr. Fleischer for Wande's return to the ranch, he couldn't say. All he knew was that Ma wanted her back, and so did Marion.

"I'm so glad you agreed to bring me today. I hope Alvie will win. She wrote a beautiful essay." Marion leaned toward him, trying to see around the hat of the lady in front of her.

Jud stood and offered Marion his seat. "But you corrected it for her." Didn't Marion's assistance give Alvie an unfair advantage?

"I only helped her figure out how to use the dictionary, and pointed out her grammar mistakes. Nothing her mother wouldn't do, if Mrs. Fleischer spoke better English."

But she doesn't, Jud wanted to say. But he wouldn't voice that opinion, not in front of Wande.

"Quiet." Ma reprimanded them as if they were still schoolchildren themselves. "Miss Potson is about to announce the winners for each class."

Jud cringed. Miss Potson had often rapped his knuckles when he studied in her classroom, and she hadn't changed much over the years. Her blonde hair hid the gray well, much like Ma's, and her face always looked pinched beneath her glasses.

"I'm pleased to see such a good attendance." The teacher's voice carried to every corner of the room. "Our theme for this year is 'Why I Love the United States.' We here in Victoria are proud to now be a part of the United States of America. Please join me in singing 'America.' "

The audience stood to sing. Halfway through the second line, "land where my fathers died," Jud choked up. He stared at the flag, with twenty-eight stars nestled in the field of blue, then his gaze traveled to the other flag with a lone white star—Texas.

A few more exercises preceded the announcement of the winners. The children recited the twenty-eight states in the order of their entry into the United States, until at last they shouted "Texas." Cheers erupted from the audience. Miss Potson presented the winners from each class, including Alvie in the fourth grade. After each name, the audience applauded.

The ceremony lasted forever—not like two years ago, when they waited with Billie to see if her name was called. She wrote the winning fourth-grade essay about the Alamo that also won the grand prize. *Billie*. Jud swallowed hard.

About the time Jud felt he could no longer sit still, Miss Potson reached the high point of the assembly. "Now I will read the essay that won third prize." The essay spoke of first being a Mexican citizen, then a Texan, and how he liked being a part of the United States best of all. The audience clapped in appreciation for Jorge Treviño, the doctor's son. Second place went to an older girl Jud didn't know, but he saw satisfied smiles around him.

"And now I will present the winning essay, written by our newest student. She came to our school after Christmas, but I believe you will like what she has to say."

After Christmas. Bells went off in Jud's head.

"When we left Offenbach last year, I did not know if I would like this new country of America. I did not like it at all when my sister got sick with the fever and died as soon as we landed in Carlshafen . . ."

Marion beamed. Jud didn't need to hear the announcement to know that Alvie Fleischer had won the prize.

The country his father had died for—the country his sister had taken such pride in—now taken over by a slip of a German girl who couldn't even write English without help. She was no more American than the Comanche who had stolen his sister's life.

Jud ground his teeth, unsure if he wanted to curse or cry.

Tears clouded Wande's vision. The *Amerikaner* school had chosen Alvie's essay as the best. Texas had become home, and Germany began to fade into the past.

Papa blinked several times, and Mama couldn't contain her smile. "We will hold a big party to celebrate and invite all our friends."

Papa nodded, and Wande's mind raced ahead. Mama would fix every delicacy she could manage with the ingredients available, and Wande would add some of the recipes she had learned from Mrs. Morgan. What wonderful food they would enjoy—sauerkraut and frijoles, strudel and cobbler—a mix of old and new.

Miss Potson called Alvie to the front, where she accepted her award in front of the American flag, so proud with its red and white stripes and a starlit night. Wande wished she could preserve this moment. She would count this night as the first time she felt American, though she still stumbled with her English and had traveled only twenty miles from the ocean.

Everyone pressed forward to congratulate them, a few

familiar faces , but most unknown. Wande knew several from chorale and the Morgans' church. Mama and Papa knew both teachers and many members of the *kirche*. Wande spotted Marion and Mrs. Morgan, but Jud headed out the door with Tom. Wande lifted her chin. She wouldn't let his behavior trouble her, not on this night.

When Marion reached them, she threw her arms around Alvie. "I'm so proud of you. I knew it was something special when I read it, and I'm so glad the school board agrees."

Miss Thurston—the other teacher—hovered behind the Morgans. "So did I. You have learned more about English in the past few months than most of my students learn all year." She smiled. "You should be very proud of your daughter, Mr. and Mrs. Fleischer."

"Yes." Mama managed the English word. The look on her face needed no translation. "We are proud. We are having a party on Saturday afternoon. All of Alvie's teachers must come. We want all our new friends to celebrate with us."

"I will be there, and I imagine Miss Potson would like to come as well."

"Everyone is welcome. We will go to the concert by the chorale society in the evening."

"You must stay to hear them, Mrs. Morgan. I attended their last concert, and they do a lovely job." Miss Thurston said her good-bye and left the building.

Mama turned to the two Morgan women. "Where is Herr Morgan? I saw him with you."

Marion exchanged a look with her mother. "He wants to get home as soon as possible. He asked me to say Wande should stay home with her family through Sunday afternoon. That she earned an extra day off." Marion's smile took some of the sting from the words.

"That is good," Mama said. "Will you come next Saturday? You can go to the concert and stay the night with us."

"It's a long trip . . ." Mrs. Morgan said. "I will have to ask Jud about that. But it's a wonderful idea." Mrs. Morgan clapped her hands. "We are celebrating, too. My son Calder with his wife, Emily, and their young son are coming for a visit next week."

"We won't hold you up any longer. We want to give everyone a chance to wish you well." Marion glanced at the line of people behind her. "We'll see you on Saturday."

"We have been invited to a celebration with the Fleischers on Saturday." Mrs. Morgan settled herself on the seat of the wagon, next to Jud.

Marion held her breath.

"That's my night off." Tom shrugged. "I made other plans."

"With me, I hope." Marion wouldn't let him escape. "We'll go to the party."

"We all will." Mrs. Morgan nodded, signaling the matter was settled.

Jud flicked the reins, and the horses made the slow turn to head out of town.

CHAPTER SEVENTEEN

Wande hesitated at the church door. Inside she could hear the pianist warming up, running through familiar pieces by Bach and Schumann. She longed to enter, to join the chorale, to let the balm of song ease the pain of Konrad's abandonment.

But Konrad's behavior was also why Wande hesitated. Everyone in Victoria knew the story—after that girl Ertha had blurted out the news.

"Go. Do not let the careless words of one person keep you from what you enjoy." Papa had practically pushed Wande out the door. She was at the rehearsal for the chorale society at his urging. She had promised, so she took a deep breath and placed her hand on the doorknob.

Soft chatter made Wande turn her head. The two girls she had met at the chorale booth were coming: Johanna, who had seemed nice enough, and Ertha, the blabbermouth.

Before Wande could react, Johanna waved. "Wande. I am so glad you decided to join us."

Wande nodded and went inside. The less she spoke with these two, the better.

"Wait." Ertha frowned, and she ran up to Wande. "I want to apologize for what I said on the day we met. I could tell my words upset you." The afternoon sun created a halo around Ertha's red hair. "I spoke without thinking. I do that too often, my mama says."

Wande wanted to turn her back, but that was not the Christian thing to do. And hadn't she spoken out of turn at least once? Everyone did. "I accept your apology."

Ertha slipped her hand through Wande's elbow. "I do hope you'll sit with me. You must be a soprano, with your lovely voice."

Wande smiled. "Yes, I do sing soprano."

Johanna joined her on the other side.

"Wonderful," Ertha said. "Then we can share our music folder while *Herr Musik Dirigent* prepares us for the concert. I want to be your friend, if you will let me."

Johanna also smiled.

Wande looked at Ertha. "We can be *freunde*, yes." She allowed the two girls to lead her to the waiting choir.

Marion hummed, the way she always did when Calder visited. Unlike Jud, Calder injected an element of humor into even the worst of times. His arrival with his family, a week earlier than expected, changed the mood at the Morgan ranch.

"You're sure you don't mind going to the party at the Fleischers'?" Ma asked Calder for the third time in five minutes.

"We are all eager to meet the family we've heard so much about. They're all Marion ever writes about, except for Tom, of course." Calder winked at her. "Have you set a date?"

"Not yet." Marion winked back. "But we will." She poked

her head into the parlor and raised her voice. "As soon as Jud says it's okay."

Calder raised an eyebrow.

"He's making Tom save all this money before he'll let us announce our engagement."

"I'll see if I can get him to change his mind." Calder scooped up his son, Riley, who had snatched one of his granny's cookies. "You'd like to go to a party today, wouldn't you, scout?"

"Will they have cake?"

"They might have strudel and spice bars instead, but they taste good," Marion said. "We've enjoyed some good food while Wande's been cooking for us."

"If it's as good as you say, I'll have to get the recipe," Emily said. "But do you suppose she can write the instructions in English?"

Marion laughed. "We'll figure it out."

Jud came in, followed by Tom. "Are you ladies ready to go?" Her brother wore his best Sunday clothes even if a scowl threatened to take over his face. Tom looked downright handsome, if uncomfortable in his fancy duds. After days on the road, Calder had settled for his cleanest pair of pants.

Marion matched Tom's finery in "that pretty yellow dress with the purple sprigs." She had loaned Emily her best winter dress.

"Shall we?" Calder offered Emily his arm. Riley raced ahead out the door. Tom escorted Marion to the wagon, and she felt as fancy as a queen on her way to a royal ball. Dinner and a concert—she hadn't had this much fun for almost longer than she could remember.

Not since Billie had disappeared.

Jud decided to make the best of the day. He had promised Ma.

"Shame on you, Judson Morgan, for getting yourself in a knot about Alvie Fleischer winning the prize. The Bible says to rejoice with those who rejoice, and that's what we're going to do."

What else could he say when his mother quoted the Bible at him? Nothing except, "Yes, ma'am, I'll do my best."

When Calder and Emily showed up a week early, he thought he might get a reprieve. But no, they wanted to go to town and catch up with old friends. Maybe Jud could pass the time watching his nephew. The last time he had seen Riley, he wasn't even crawling. Now he had turned into a walking, talking, tiny human being. He reminded Jud of how much fun Billie was when she was small. *Oh, Billie.*

By the time they arrived, several wagons had already gathered on the church grounds. Jud found a spot in the sunshine and helped the ladies climb down.

"Walk with me, Jud." Ma looked nice in a spring dress she had brought out of mothballs. "I don't want to be the only Morgan without a man to escort me."

The others had already gone ahead to the guesthouse next to the church where the Fleischers lived. "It would be my honor, Mrs. Morgan."

"I hope I won't be the only Mrs. Morgan in our house for too much longer." Ma patted his arm.

They arrived at the house before Jud could chew on what his mother had said. Wall-to-wall people spoke in a babble of German, Spanish, and even some English.

"Mrs. Morgan, Jud, you came!" Alvie darted between Marion and Tom and met them at the door.

Ma leveled a look at Jud. He understood the message.

"Congratulations on winning the contest." There, he had said it. That should satisfy Ma.

"Marion showed me the essay Billie wrote when she won the contest. You must miss her a lot." Alvie's face turned solemn. "I miss Ulla, too. I wish I could show her my prize." She gestured at the ribbon pinned to a wreath on the wall.

Ma smiled at Alvie. "Where shall I put my pie?"

"Over here, next to Wande's." Alvie led them to a table laden with dishes giving off strange yet enticing aromas. Among the German dishes Jud spotted a platter of fried chicken, a bowl of beans, and a pan of cornbread.

"Chicken? Beans? Cornbread?" Jud grinned at Alvie. "Who cooked all this?"

"I did." Wande joined them, her cheeks pink. "I tried to remember everything you taught me, Mrs. Morgan."

"I'm sure you did fine. Now, where do we start?"

Jud picked up a plate and surveyed the table. The first dish held that looked like shredded cabbage, but smelled unlike anything he had ever tasted.

"That is sauerkraut. It is very good." Wande's blue eyes urged him to sample it.

"Be brave," Ma whispered in Jud's ear. "Remember how much you enjoyed her strudel."

Jud took a spoonful, then continued around the table, taking a small amount from each dish. Wande stayed so close, he couldn't bypass anything without her knowledge. He filled his plate before he reached the fried chicken. He pushed the servings closer together and took a couple of thighs and two spoonfuls of beans, as well as a hefty chunk of cornbread.

"It is good I cooked American food today." The laugh lines around Wande's eyes told him she didn't take offense. "You must tell me what you think."

When she looked at him like that, he forgot her German name and remembered only how kind and sweet she was. He would eat every bite—even if it tasted like rotten apples.

She cut herself a small piece of cornbread and placed it on a napkin. "I didn't want to take the first piece."

Ma had chosen with greater discretion, serving herself a generous helping of the sauerkraut and a meat Wande called *wurst* that resembled sausage. She added a slice of bread and butter. "I can't resist the bread. It's a rare treat in these parts. And I'll take some of your beans. They smell heavenly."

Wande led them outside, where planks had been set up for extra seats. Jud closed his eyes.

He heard Wande's voice. "Pastor Bader blessed the food before you arrived—but God will not mind hearing your thanks as well."

Jud wouldn't admit that he was praying for courage to try all the new dishes. He said "amen" out loud. Dipping his spoon into the sauerkraut, he broke off a piece of cornbread to follow, just in case. The cabbage tasted different—spicy—but good.

Next to him, Wande choked and spit a bite of cornbread onto her napkin. "This tastes terrible. Nothing like your delicious cornbread, Mrs. Morgan. What did I do wrong?"

Jud placed the cornbread back on his plate.

"It can't be that bad." Ma reached for the piece he had abandoned. "May I?"

"Go ahead." Let Ma pass judgment on Wande's cooking.

She chewed a small bite and managed to swallow it, but put the remainder back on the plate. "You may have used too much baking powder or maybe baking soda. It's a mistake we all make at some time—confusing teaspoons with tablespoons, I expect."

"I should have used the small spoon?" Wande moaned. "I could not remember. I thought it was good to use more of the powder for baking. But I ruined it." She brought her hand to her mouth. "Let me remove it from the table."

"I'll do it for you." Ma winked. "I'll pretend it was my mistake." She stood and went inside.

Jud took a tentative bite of chicken, then a second hearty taste. He gestured with the bone. "This is delicious."

Tiny wrinkles appeared on the bridge of Wande's nose. Jud resisted the urge to laugh. He knew she wouldn't appreciate the humor of the situation.

Ma reappeared with Calder and Emily. "Wande, I'd like you to meet my son Calder." She completed the introductions.

Calder was juggling his plate in one hand and Riley with his other arm. "Pleased to meet you, Miss Fleischer. Ma and Marion have told us so much about you." He wiggled his eyebrows at Jud. "And Jud, well, sometimes his silence is louder than anything the womenfolk say. He thinks a powerful lot of you."

Jud would gladly have strangled his brother. Instead, he said, "Both Wande and her brother Georg have been a godsend this year."

Wande smiled and cocked her head before accepting Calder's handshake. "I am pleased to meet you, Mr. Morgan."

"Calder, please."

"Calder. And—Emily?"

"Very pleased to meet you, I'm sure."

"Uncle Jud, can you play with me? You promised." Riley squirmed in his father's arms and reached for Jud.

"May I go and play with you," Emily prompted.

"You want to come too, Mommy?"

Wande laughed and spoke to Riley. "I also have trouble understanding when I should say 'can' and when to say 'may.'"

"You do?" He opened up wide blue eyes so like Calder's.

"Play time, little man."

"Yay!" Riley almost leaped from his father's arms to the floor. As Jud chased him, he called over his shoulder, "See you at the concert?"

"I'll be there."

⟵ ★ ⟶

"But where will you put us all?" Marion asked the question that Wande was debating. "You didn't expect Calder and his family when you invited us to spend the night."

"If we must, we will sleep on the floor," Wande said. "We have enough bedding."

"You can't do that," Marion said.

Wande laughed. "We did it on our way to Victoria. And on the ship, we did not have beds for everyone. We took turns sleeping on the floor. We will be fine."

"It was *fun*." Alvie buttoned the white blouse she would wear at the concert. The party guests had stayed so long that Wande and Alvie excused themselves to change. Both the adult and the children's chorales would perform, as well as an orchestra.

With Bach and Beethoven, Weber and Schumann on the program, Wande would bask for the evening in the words and melodies of her homeland. Only the lure of the music she'd learned in childhood had convinced her to join the German Chorale Society—after the things Ertha had said when they first met.

Except for a tendency to say whatever entered her mind, Ertha was a kind, friendly soul. At the chorale, she had taken Wande under her wing, and they even shared a music folder.

More than Christian love prompted Wande's reconciliation with Ertha. It was a practical necessity. She watched Georg return from his afternoon stroll with his sweetheart—Ertha Schumann. Their families expected them to marry before the end of the year.

CHAPTER EIGHTEEN

"Why not let them get married this year?" Calder sat across from Jud in his bedroom. "I don't know what Marion sees in Tom either, but her mind's made up. You don't want her eloping." He threw his arms across the back of the chair. "You told me I was too young to get married, and Emily and I have done all right."

Jud scowled. "She wouldn't dare." He was glad he could talk things over with Calder. Everywhere he looked, he saw reminders of their shared childhood. The mark on the windowsill made during one of their fights, a box that held their collection of tin soldiers. Calder might want to take those for Riley. "At least you knew the value of a dollar. Tom doesn't. And I don't want to see Marion hurt."

Calder leaned forward. "You can't protect her forever. She's going to make mistakes. We all do. But don't you think she's old enough to decide for herself?"

"She's old enough, but—"

"What does Ma say?" Humor twinkled in Calder's eyes.

"That she and Pa were younger than Marion and Tom when they got married." The reminder stuck in his craw. "Can you come back for a fall wedding?"

"Sure, after the harvest. Emily would jump at the chance to see her family again." Calder hopped out of the chair and clapped Jud on the back. "You've made the right decision."

That afternoon, Jud sequestered himself in the ranch office and took out the account books. To Tom's credit, he hadn't once asked for any of the money Jud had set aside for him. Then again, he hadn't added anything to it. He spent his pay almost as soon as Jud gave it to him. At least Marion had a little more sense.

Calder had probably already told Marion about his decision. But Jud wanted to do more to provide for Marion financially. If Tom put a dollar a week into savings between now and harvesttime, he should have almost enough to purchase some land. If he didn't have quite enough, Jud would help him.

Acreage disappeared almost as soon as it came up for sale, gobbled up by the new settlers—German settlers. Jud shook his head. He couldn't do anything about that. But he knew about some land that the public hadn't heard about yet.

Jud saddled JM and rode to the northern boundary of his property. He let the horse drink before he turned the gelding in the direction of his nearest neighbors. He found Eli Walford in the field nearest his house, plowing in preparation for spring planting. Waving to Jud, he left the ox and plow and walked to the fence to greet him.

"Good to see you, Morgan. Tell you what, I'm about done for the day. Come on in the house and let the wife fix you up proper."

A few minutes later, Jud had settled on their couch, drinking coffee and eating a slice of peach pie. The small room felt cozy—the Walfords only had one son, and he had moved to Louisiana a few years ago.

They exchanged obligatory greetings: Had Ma recovered from the burn? How was Calder? And what about his son? Then Walford asked, "What brings you to our part of the world today?"

"I heard tell you're thinking of moving."

The couple exchanged looks. "We haven't announced it, but we're pretty set on it. I'm getting too old to enjoy working the land sunup to sundown, and the missus wants to be near her grandchildren. And our John, he says we have a home with him whenever we want to come."

Jud nodded. "What will you do with the farm when you move—if you move?"

"I'd like to sell it, to the right party. I don't expect John to come back here." Walford set down his coffee cup to indicate the start of negotiations. "Why? You wanting to expand?"

"Maybe. An investment—for my sister. She's got her heart set on getting married this fall, after harvest."

"That's wonderful news." Mrs. Walford cut him an extra slice of pie. "I've had my suspicions, seeing how the two of them look at each other." She hesitated. "She is marrying young Tom Cotton, isn't she?"

"He's the one."

"I'm so happy for her. For all of you. You deserve some happiness, after what happened last year and all." Mrs. Walford walked to a cedar chest in the corner. She opened it and pulled out a set of linens. "Give these to her for me, will you—for her hope chest? I kept them in case I ever had a daughter. I'd love for Marion to have these."

Jud couldn't refuse his neighbor's hospitality. "I'm sure she'll appreciate your gift." He laid the linens on the couch next to him. "How much are you thinking of asking for the farm?"

"I don't know as how a couple just starting out could afford this place," Walford said. "You have the buildings—and I built them solid, to last you know. And the fields are cleared and fenced in. A lot of work."

Jud understood the steps of the negotiator's dance. Build up the value to drive up the price. "But this house is small."

"A good size for a man and his wife just starting out." Walford cleared his throat.

Jud suspected it was a sore point for the Walfords, since they had only one child. The fact the land was already developed was a definite advantage, so Jud didn't fight him hard. They agreed on a price that would require Jud to invest his savings as well as Tom's. If Jud's father was alive, he would have done the same thing.

"So we're in agreement?" Jud offered his hand to Walford.

Walford stroked his chin. "Unless we decide to move on earlier." He shook Jud's hand.

Jud left the farm encouraged. The solution he'd found would provide for his sister and give Tom the tools he needed to take care of his family. After that, Jud would have to leave them in the Lord's hands.

Wande studied the table. Something was wrong. She had set too many place settings for supper. *Dummkopf*. Already the house echoed with the absence of Calder and his family. They had enlivened the house in a dozen different ways.

Wande decided to fry all the bacon she had cut off the slab. Any leftovers could go into sandwiches. Within a year, after Tom and Marion married, they would need two fewer places at the table. No wonder Jud seemed so lonely at times. He had lost his father to war, his sister to the Comanches, and his other sister and brother to marriage. Time had passed him by, with no spouse or children to lighten his days.

Though she was not yet twenty, Wande felt an old maid. Wedding plans that used to center on her and Konrad now featured Georg and Ertha. As if she would never get married. She frowned.

The bacon sizzled, and she pushed it to one side before adding spoonfuls of batter. She would know how to cook every kind of dish, American and German, and not have a family to cook for. She sniffled. She would not feel sorry for herself, not with so much work to do.

Work, the cure for feeling sad.

As Wande flipped the corn cakes, Jud came in from the barn, whistling.

"The cows gave good milk today. I brought in enough for breakfast and set the rest in the cold spring." He poured himself a glass and drank it, leaving a white mustache around his mouth. He wiped it off with his hand and sniffed the air. "Smells good."

"They should be good. I used the right amount of baking powder this time."

He laughed. "I'm sure you did. But I smell something else. Something . . . with cinnamon?"

"*Ach*, I hope they have not burned." She pulled a pan of coffee cake from the oven.

"What's the occasion?" He grabbed a piece of bacon and took a bite.

"It is spring. A time to celebrate new life, is it not?" She shook her head. "Although it does not feel like we had winter. No snow, only that terrible ice storm."

"Ma says your blood thins after a while. She says it was colder back in Tennessee, but I was too young to remember."

"This *kaffe kuchen* would be better with blueberries in it." She wrinkled her nose, debating whether to ask Jud her question. "I would like to plant a garden next to the house."

"Did someone say garden?" Mrs. Morgan came in the kitchen. "You have fixed us a feast! You must let me wash the dishes."

Wande looked at the pile of dishes she had used, taller than usual. "But there is a lot of work."

"Not as much as when Calder was here. Did I hear you say you want to plant a garden? I generally have a small patch, although I didn't last year." She shook her head. "There's a lot of things I neglected last year."

"I would like to make the garden bigger," Wande said. "Enough to plant some vegetables from home and maybe sell some at the market."

Jud darted a look at her, but Mrs. Morgan clapped her hands. "What a wonderful idea. Mr. Grenville at the store says he gets requests from people every year, looking for fresh produce when they're traveling through."

"That is what we heard." Wande nodded. She slid the bacon onto a serving plate together with the corn cakes and added a final batch to the frying pan. "I will experiment. We do not know what will grow here in Texas. Papa says the soil is different. And the weather, it is different." She laughed. "We would never start a garden in March at home."

Jud scowled.

Wande wished she could take back that word. Texas must be home now.

CHAPTER NINETEEN

Jud didn't know what to make of Wande's plan to grow a market garden. No, he couldn't say her plans would take away from her time at the house. She had ample time to take care of her duties—and to grow some vegetables.

Early the next morning, he found a secluded spot by the entrance to the barn and watched her break up the ground. She rubbed her hands against her skirt, and he wondered about blisters. Maybe she still had some of that rub she gave him when he helped with the laundry.

Jud also didn't know what he thought of her plan to run a market stall in town. Some men in town would be happy to harass a beautiful, young German woman, taking advantage of her struggles with English. Women might too, they'd just be nicer about it. But then, men didn't usually do the shopping. He'd keep on eye on her while Ma and Marion did their weekly shopping.

He chuckled. *Jud Morgan, champion of a German immi-*

grant. A year ago he would have laughed at the thought. But Wande wasn't just any immigrant.

"A sight for sore eyes, ain't she?"

Jud jumped at Tom's voice. From him, the words sounded improper. Jud gritted his teeth. Why had he let someone catch him watching Wande?

"Have you and Marion set your date for sure? Calder will want to know."

Tom tilted his head. "Thought she already told you. The second Saturday of November. That should give him plenty of time to get here after harvest and before bad weather sets in."

He did know that.

"Want to make it a double wedding?" Tom grinned—and ducked the punch Jud wanted to throw at him.

"No."

"Just asking. Say, I was talking to Walford the other day when I was riding the fence, and he congratulated me on my upcoming nuptials." Tom smiled, and Jud caught a glimpse of what drew his sister to him—a heedless cheerfulness that charmed Marion as much as it irritated Jud.

"I might have mentioned it," Jud said. "I doubt there's a person in all of Texas who hasn't heard the news by now, between Marion and Ma. I've only told the horses." He heard a soft nicker. Apple, a chestnut mare who had given birth to a filly with a distinctive silver streak, wanted his attention. Jud needed to get to work instead of dawdling around staring at Wande. He headed down the stalls.

"And Mr. Walford. You told him." Tom followed. "He said something about some land you might be buying?" Tom's grin grew wider. "For me and Marion?"

Jud turned in his direction. "What did he say?" Jud did not want Walford to tell Tom for fear he might want to stop saving from his paycheck. Jud walked to the last stall, where Apple waited with her filly.

"Just that you was planning on buying his farm for a wedding gift." Tom dug in his pocket for a dried apple. The mare took it and whinnied. Tom laughed. "No wonder you named this one Apple."

"Billie named her." It still hurt to think of his sister.

"Billie was something else, all right." Tom knelt to look at the filly. "What are you going to name this one?"

Jud made a decision on the spot. "Do you want to name her?" The gesture would please Marion.

"She sure is a pretty little thing." Tom patted her rump. "Maid Marion. What else?"

"Very well. Maid Marion it is." Since Jud had already cleaned the stall, he just added a few oats to the feed bag. "A new mother needs some pampering." He scratched the mare between her ears.

"Is it true about the land?" Tom walked to the next stall. It held a slightly older colt about ready to leave the confines of the barn.

"I'll be adding some of my own money as a kind of dowry to your savings to buy the land. Yes."

"I appreciate it."

Wande yanked a weed from around the potatoes she hoped would flourish in her garden. The squash plants were progressing well, but she hadn't realized her dream of fresh green vegetables for *Gründonnerstag,* the Thursday before Easter.

The lack of fresh vegetables hadn't stopped Mama from preparing the traditional all-green meal in Offenbach—and it didn't stop her in Victoria. When Mrs. Morgan heard about the custom of a meal consisting entirely of green foods, she let her creativity go to work. The Morgans and Fleischers would enjoy a feast tonight. As a joke, Tom had suggested frog legs, but Mrs. Morgan sent him out to the fishing hole to catch some—she said they should count, since they started out green.

Wande shook her head at the thought. She had never eaten such a thing. Mrs. Morgan would also fry some green tomatoes. It appeared that Texans fried everything.

Wande pulled a few more weeds before she went to the pump to clean her hands. Clean hands were essential for coloring eggs. They had eaten scrambled eggs the last two mornings so they would have one hollow shell for each member in their families, as well as a couple more in case of accidents—an even dozen. This morning's eggs waited for their afternoon activities. Wande missed doing the familiar rituals with Mama and Alvie, but she looked forward to sharing the special memory from her homeland with her friends.

She went up to her room to retrieve the tree branches she had collected for an Easter egg tree. Buds had already formed on the branch she had placed in a vase of water. They made the tree so much more festive. Humming "Christ Jesus Lay in Death's Strong Bands," a song of the resurrection, she brought the branches to the kitchen.

Marion peeled onions at the table, handing her mother the peels. "More green food. I'm going to be tired of eggs before Easter week is out." Marion's tears turned her laugh into a hiccup. "Or you could stir some spinach in with the eggs when you scramble them, then they'd turn green."

"I prefer the taste of, how do you say it, hard-boiled? So the yellow and the white are cooked through." Wande laid the branches on the counter by the eggshells that had been drying the past couple of days. She checked several. *Perfect.*

Mrs. Morgan dumped the onion peels into spinach juice and set the pot on the stove to boil. She joined Wande at the counter. "I declare, I've never seen anything like what you did with these. Poking a hole in each end and blowing the insides out."

"It is easy." Wande shrugged. "We do not like to waste the eggs. And now they are ready to decorate for the Easter egg tree."

"So that's what you have all those branches for. I was wondering." Marion glanced at the vase. "Look, it's budding."

"In Offenbach, we used birch branches. I am glad this acacia worked also." Wande placed two eggs in her left hand, then shook her head. "A platter will be better."

Marion went to the dish cabinet and brought a platter. They arranged the shells on it and carried it to the table.

"The juice is boiling. Should I put today's eggs in?"

"Put them in the net bag first, then cook them for ten minutes." Wande waited until Mrs. Morgan joined them at the table to explain the next step. "Think of things that remind you of *Ostern*—how do you say? Easter?" She licked her lips and picked up a stick of colored wax. "I will write *Frohe Ostern*."

"Happy Easter?" Marion said.

Wande nodded.

"But how do you fit all of that on an egg?" Marion shook her head. "I'll keep mine simple. I will draw an empty cross."

"And I'll write 'Joy.' That's nice and short." Mrs. Morgan held an egg gently in her left hand and made the first stroke. "It glides right over."

"It is not hard once you learn how." Wande debated what to draw next, deciding on an angel. "He is not here: for He is risen, as He said. Come, see the place where the Lord lay."

"He is risen." Mrs. Morgan repeated.

"He is risen indeed," Marion responded. "Do you say that in German churches? Our pastor says that is how early Christians greeted each other."

Wande shook her head and concentrated on the angel's shoulder.

When the eggs finished boiling, they had turned a lovely green. Mrs. Morgan took them from the net and placed them in a bowl to cool. "Why green food?"

"Mama says it is because green is the color of life, the new life Jesus came to give us." Wande inspected the eggs in the bowl. "They look good. I wonder why we eat green food on Thursday, instead of the day of the resurrection." When she remembered the lamb dishes they ate on *Ostern*, she decided she didn't care.

"Now I suppose we'll use Ma's wool and those twigs to make hangers for the eggs," Marion said.

"One more thing." Wande went to the pantry and found a slab of salt pork. "We will rub the shells so they shine. Then they are ready to hang."

Jud and the ranch hands finished their chores early, as Ma requested. She wanted them to enjoy a special holiday meal with the Fleischers—something about green food.

Georg and Tom headed for the bunkhouse to get ready. Jud hitched the wagon and went inside.

"We were just finishing up." Ma grinned as he entered the kitchen. "Take a look at our Easter tree."

Jud couldn't help but notice it. A branch stood in a vase of water, a few buds appearing on the ends. About a dozen eggs hung from several branches. He leaned in closer. Make that egg shells. They shone like oiled hair and had some kind of design on them.

"Go ahead and touch them. They're not as fragile as they look." Marion pointed to one with a cross. "I did that one."

Jud examined one, then another. Different words and

pictures, all related in some way to Easter, glowed on the surface of the eggshells. *"Frohe Ostern?"*

"Happy Easter—in German," Marion said.

Jud grunted. Of course. First a Christmas tree and now an Easter tree. The uneasiness he'd felt in December returned. "Wande, I suppose you want me to carry this out to the wagon and find a place where it won't be harmed."

Humor glinted in Wande's eyes. "*Nein*. This tree stays here. I am sure Mama has made one with Alvie." She handed him a bowl covered with a towel. He peeked—green eggs. That didn't seem so strange; Ma had dyed Easter eggs with them a few times.

Jud had to ask. "Why an Easter tree?"

"Does it matter?" Marion removed the pan of frog legs from the oven and wrapped it in several layers to keep warm. "It's pretty."

"I am worshiping while I make the eggs. I am thinking about Jesus and that He died and came back to life again." Wande touched the branches. "And our Lord died on a tree for our sins, did He not?"

Symbols. Perhaps most traditions involved symbols.

"Come on, folks, let's get going. We don't want to be late." Ma hustled them out to the waiting wagon. Jud helped Ma onto the front seat and turned to Marion.

"Let Wande ride up front with you today," Marion said. "I'll sit with Tom in back."

Jud lifted Wande, as light as one of those empty eggshells, and set her on the seat next to the driver's spot. He jumped up next to her, conscious of her presence less than a handbreadth away.

"Marion told me of one of your Easter customs." She smiled. "He is risen."

"He is risen indeed."

CHAPTER TWENTY

Marion turned this way and that in front of her mirror. Ma had outdone herself with the dress for her engagement party—soft buttercream calico with flowers the color of the bluebonnets springing up across the ranch. She stared over her shoulder, studying the effect of the skirt, the fullest she had ever worn.

"Tom will think you are beautiful." Wande's fingers touched Marion's lower back. "You missed a few buttons."

"We should have made it with the closing in the front. Like yours." Marion smiled at her friend. "You are beautiful yourself. The young men of Victoria—German, American, and Mexican—will line up to speak with you." Wande's face turned pink, which enhanced the soft mauve of her dress. "Let's stop fussing with our dresses, and see if we can manage a few spaniel curls." She removed the curling tongs from the brazier where they had been heating.

"My hair does not take curl. Ulla used to try. She could

make herself look an angel." Wande's voice held a wistful note. "But your hair, I think it will curl."

"It does. And I'm sure you won't burn it, the way Billie did one time." Marion settled in the chair in front of the mirror and pulled a couple of tendrils loose on each side. "I want these to curl down the side of my face."

Wande nodded. "Like a sausage."

Marion giggled. "I think I like the description of a spaniel better. That's a kind of dog."

A few minutes later, brown curls dangled past her hazel eyes. Forehead a little too low, nose a little too round, ears that tended to stick out. She considered herself very ordinary, but Tom liked her appearance, and that's what mattered. Someone knocked at the front door, and voices floated up the stairs. "Guests are arriving." A wave passed through her stomach like a wind stirring grass.

Marion resisted one last look at the mirror. "Let's go downstairs."

"Wait a minute." Wande threw her arms around Marion. "I wanted to say congratulations first."

Marion looked into her friend's eyes, clear and bright as the sky on this late April day, and gratitude overwhelmed her. When Wande arrived in Texas, she expected to be married by spring, living in her own home on the land promised by the German society. Instead, she worked for the Morgans and waited and watched while Marion and Tom, then her own brother, Georg, announced their engagements.

"You are a dear to say so." Marion returned Wande's hug. "And I'm sure your day will come."

Wande blinked. "If God so wills." She took a step back. "Let us go downstairs before Tom comes to look for you."

When Marion and Tom set the date for the wedding, Ma started planning an engagement party, two weeks after Easter.

The three women turned the house upside-down with a vigorous spring cleaning. Then they spent two days baking cakes, pies, and strudel, not to mention cooking as much beef as you could eat with cornbread and sweet potatoes. Everyone would be so full, they would not want to touch food on Sunday. Marion warned Tom against adding anything extra to the gallons of tea they prepared. Wande had never seen so much to drink, sitting in as many jars as the prophet's widow brought to Elisha to fill with oil. If they did run out of tea, there was coffee to be made and water to pump.

The house looked as good as it smelled. Mrs. Morgan insisted Wande make two more Easter trees to hang with eggshells dyed green, red, and yellow. Together with the wildflowers Wande helped Marion pick, the colors brought the house to life.

Mrs. Morgan greeted the schoolteachers, Miss Potson and Miss Thurston, as well as Pastor Bader. Marion saw no sign of Jud, Tom, and Georg.

"Do you want me to go to the bunkhouse?" Wande said.

The front door opened again and she heard men's voices. Jud and Tom came in first, followed by Jud's friend Jimbo Rawlins, and Grenville the grocer with his son. "It's true. I guarantee it," young Grenville said. "President Polk asked Congress to declare war on Mexico this morning, on account of them Mexicans not knowing where the border is."

A man coughed, and Marion spotted Dr. Treviño. "Perhaps the Mexicans think the same thing about the Americans."

A silence fell across the group. No one wanted to offend the doctor.

Marion rushed down the stairs. "What's this about a war?"

"It's true, all right," Jimbo said. "The president finally had enough."

"I'm joining up on Monday." The younger Grenville pushed his shoulders back and stood straight. "Me and some buddies of mine." He looked at the men around him, as if expecting them to volunteer.

"I may go with you," Jimbo said. "I was too young to fight back when Texas won her independence, but it sounds like we didn't give Mexico a bad enough beatin' and they're back for more."

All the other men, except for Jud and Mr. Grenville, looked at the floor. The grocer put his hand on his son's shoulder. "I'm proud of Bill, here, but the rest of us are either too old or have important roles to fill right here in Victoria. I expect Jud will provide the cavalry with some of the finest mounts on either side of the Rio Grande."

Jud raised an eyebrow and shrugged. Tom squirmed, and Marion decided to interrupt before he committed himself to something rash.

Ma moved at the same time. "That's enough talk about a war. We're here to celebrate a happy occasion."

Ma steered Tom to Marion's side. His eyes widened. "That dress is near as pretty as you are." He reached out and brushed the curl at her cheek, making Marion glad they had taken the time with the tongs. He brought her hand to his lips.

Chuckles rippled through the crowd, and heat burned through part of Marion's reserve.

"It is indeed a happy day when God brings a man and a woman together." Pastor Bader extended his hand. "A day I am still praying for God to make happen for me." Chuckles deepened into laughter, as he must have intended, and he shook Tom's hand. Marion decided she liked the German minister.

"And *Fraulein Fleischer. Hallo.* You and Miss Morgan are the prettiest flowers in the garden."

So the preacher had a flair for the ladies, Marion noted. Perhaps he was interested in Wande. He held her hand a second longer than customary.

⟵ ★ ⟶

Jud was no coward, but he had no desire to go to war. He was glad Mr. Grenville mentioned the cavalry's need for good horses. He could do his part without running off to fight.

Though Jud had few ties to keep him at home, he felt the need to stay. He would like to leave a little piece of himself behind when he died, something more than the ranch. A son or a daughter . . . a wife. He glanced at Wande as she greeted her family. She wore her new dress, made in the more American style like Marion's, and her hair shone like spring sunshine.

"Take her for a walk in the bluebonnets," Marion whispered in his ear.

"When did you creep up on me?" Jud said. "Give a fellow some warning." Again he'd been caught studying Wande.

"Quiet down." Marion kept her voice low. "I noticed because I have love on my mind. And I can't think of anyone else I would rather add to our family." She nudged him. "Go. Invite her for a walk."

"You're not going to leave me alone until I do, are you?"

"No."

"Then I think I will ask Wande if she wants some fresh air."

While Jud talked with Marion, Wande had disappeared. She had probably headed for the kitchen, drawn by her duty. No, that wasn't entirely fair. She'd want to help even if she wasn't paid, and Ma would shoo her away.

He wormed his way through the crowd. Everyone was talking with at least one other person. The usual mix of languages reigned, and for once he didn't mind. Georg and Ertha huddled in one corner, exchanging glances. They were counting the days until they could announce their wedding. Georg's father insisted he wait until he reached his eighteenth birthday, later this summer. Seventeen and in love. Jud shook his head. Sixteen when his father died, he had hardly begun to notice girls before he took over as head of the family. In one corner, Alvie chattered with several girls her own age, and the two teachers watched them from a distance.

Everyone had somebody to talk with . . . except him. And Wande. Perhaps that explained her escape. He moved a little faster and pushed into the kitchen.

"Yud." Her smile told him that any perceived loneliness was just his imagination.

He had grown used to her substituting Y for J in his name. From Wande's lips, *Yud* sounded charming.

"I will pour you and Pastor Bader some tea and another pitcher to the table." She poured a glass half full. "We just brought this in from the cold cellar."

"The weather is rather warm today." The pastor's words came out as a croak. Jud took a long drink.

"I keep telling her to get outside and enjoy this beautiful day, but she insists on staying here to help me. You tell her, Jud." Ma appeared from the cold cellar with another jug of tea—and noticed Pastor Bader so near to Wande.

"I came to the kitchen to invite Wande to take a stroll," the pastor said.

"That's a . . . wonderful idea." Ma looked from Jud to the pastor. "Wande, go on, you and the pastor get out of here. I'll take care of the tea." Ma took the glass from Jud to refill it—a good thing, since his hand was trembling.

Pastor Bader offered Wande his arm and led her toward the back door—a way outside that didn't lead past the gauntlet of the front door. "Shall we go find some bluebonnets?"

She looked up at him and smiled. "They are very pretty. And fresh air will be good."

Through the kitchen window, Jud could only watch them leave.

CHAPTER TWENTY-ONE

War, war. That was all anyone wanted to talk about when Wande went to town to sell vegetables in the market. A week ago she harvested the first squash, then she and Alvie spent the past two Saturday mornings at the market selling butter, cream, and fresh squash. They arrived early and took the prime location, next to the Grenville store. Drud stayed close by when he wasn't busy talking with his friends. About the war.

Wande tuned in to their conversation. Drud thought it would be heroic to join the army, though he was barely fifteen. That would break their parents' hearts. The armies had gathered at a town called Palo Alto, right here in Texas. She wondered how close that was to Victoria.

"Texas is a big place," Alvie said. "Bigger even than Germany. We are miles and miles away from this *Rio del Norte* everybody keeps talking about." She rearranged their squash. "I told Mama the same thing. She asks Papa, why did we come to America if they were going to start a war. She has been very upset." She bent over. "I found a penny! Can I buy a lemon drop? Please, please, please?"

"Go ahead."

Two *Amerikaners* approached the stall, and Wande completed the sale, even with the strange American coins, in English. They bought butter and cream.

"You're doing a brisk business." Jud strolled up, his hat pulled low and a smile lighting his features.

"Your cow gives rich milk. People like her cream."

"And your squash."

"The squash God's rain and sunshine helped grow." She smiled. Another woman came up, German this time, delighted to find fresh squash.

"Will you have more vegetables? White potatoes?" Frau Decker asked in German. Her eyes gleamed.

"I have planted sweet potatoes, corn, and tomatoes—and other things my *Amerikaner* friends tell me will grow well."

Frau Decker fixed her with her stare.

"*Ja*, I have planted white potatoes, but I do not think they grow here." Wande shrugged. "I will be here every week this summer with whatever I can harvest."

"I hope you succeed." They bartered about the price, and when Frau Decker left, Wande felt she had gained a permanent customer.

"What was that all about? She looked like she was mighty disappointed." Jud's gaze followed Frau Decker.

"She wanted to know if I will have white potatoes. I told her I do not know if they will grow." Wande sighed. "We miss white potatoes. And yeast bread." Papa wanted to grow several varieties of wheat, but he couldn't start until they had a farm of their own. Next year, she promised herself.

Alvie danced back to the stall, her mouth working around

a lemon drop. She held out a second one to Wande. "Mr. Grenville gave me two. He is nice."

Wande rubbed her sister's head. "You keep it."

"Thank you." Alvie stuck it in her mouth.

Business slowed, and Wande passed the time chatting with Jud. She rearranged the remaining squash. The butter had already sold. Mama strolled down the far end of the market, bartering with Frau Schmidt for some beets. Wande's mouth watered. *Rübensuppe,* beet soup, sounded wonderful.

A tall, pencil-thin man sprinted down the street.

Jud came to attention. "That's Bernie Caruthers, with the newspaper they're starting up. He must have news of the war." He stiffened. "And he's headed this way."

Caruthers ignored everyone's questions. Jud called, "What news of the war?" But Caruthers bolted past him and up the steps into the store.

"He brings bad news?" Wande said.

Jud frowned. "I expect so."

"Mr. Grenville, Mrs. Grenville." Wande moved toward the store, but Jud put out a hand to stop her.

The street that only moments earlier buzzed with bartering silenced as Caruthers entered the store. A scream tore through the air. Children whimpered, women put their hands over their hearts, and men's faces tightened. They waited as one—the fate of young Bill Grenville a portent for the fate of every mother's boy. The vendors and shoppers formed a circle in front of the store.

Mr. Caruthers came out and shook his head.

Pastor Bader stepped forward. "What is the news, Herr Caruthers?"

"A few of you ladies might want to go in to support Mrs. Grenville."

Wande reached the stairs first. Muffled sobs came from

inside. Mr. Grenville held his wife, the same grief and unity Wande had seen between her parents when Ulla died—the look of parents who had lost a child.

"I am so sorry," Wande whispered. She wasn't sure if they had heard her.

Mrs. Walford, the Morgans' neighbor, rushed in next. "Oh, it's so awful." The room filled with tearful women as the town mourned the loss of a son.

Independence Day, Marion reasoned, came at a perfect time this year. The people of Victoria needed a reason to celebrate. Somber spirits prevailed as they prepared to celebrate their first Independence Day since Texas joined the Union. Instead of red, white, and blue, several families wore mourning black. Two more local men had fallen in the war with Mexico, and they'd heard rumors about a cholera outbreak.

The mayor declared that Victoria would celebrate the holiday in American style. They would set off one firework for every state in the Union: twenty-eight in all. The day began with a parade, veterans of the War for Independence from Mexico marching alongside a few men who had fought in 1812. One rugged oldster who claimed to have been a drummer boy in the Continental Army led the way, his hands rapping a steady beat even as his steps faltered.

"Oh, Wande, have you ever seen anything like it?" Marion stood on tiptoes, straining to see over the hat of the man in front of her.

"What is so special about this Fourth of July?" Wande waved a fan at her glistening brow.

The heat didn't bother Marion much. Ma said your blood thinned after you lived in Texas awhile. Marion would probably freeze if she ever went to Germany.

"It is the day the members of the Continental Congress adopted the Declaration of Independence from England." Alvie waved a flag she had sewn. "Miss Potson says it is the birthday of the United States."

More and more, Alvie acted like she was born in Texas. She had suggested a picnic to enjoy the fireworks. Ma liked the idea, and Mrs. Fleischer carried a basket full of fascinating foods. Marion giggled.

"What is it, sweetheart?" Tom tucked her arm through his.

"Ma and Mrs. Fleischer are holding a contest to see who can provide the most food. How lucky we all are."

"You won't catch me eating any of the *bratwurst*—or whatever they call it." At least Tom smiled when he said it.

"And here's our own birthday boy." Marion smiled as Georg and Ertha moved their way. "Maybe we'll hear an official announcement today." She beckoned to the couple to join them along the parade route.

Alvie wriggled her way to the front. The other Morgans and Fleischers stayed put. Marion's thoughts turned to romance, as they often did these days, and she noticed the pairings. Tom never left her side. Georg laid a protective arm on Ertha's shoulder. Mr. Fleischer leaned over his wife, pointing to the elderly "drummer boy" in the parade. Ma sat on a stool the Fleischers provided.

That left Jud and Wande. They stood several inches apart, not looking at each other, showing none of the gestures Marion and Tom exchanged. But Marion saw little signs. Wande leaned forward, probably looking for Alvie. Jud's eyes roamed the crowd, his head barely moving, and then he stopped. He said something only Wande could hear, and she relaxed.

The soldiers marched onto the church lawn, the drum cadence sounding its last beat. The crowd followed, sweeping Marion and the others along with it.

“Let me carry that for you.” Jud fell into step beside Wande.

“Danke.”

The basket smelled of that German sausage the Fleischers favored, as well as the ever-present sauerkraut. He bet they also had some peach strudel or something like it. Wande wore the pretty mauve dress she made for Marion and Tom’s engagement party—the night Wande went in search of bluebonnets with Pastor Bader. Today she had pulled her hair back with blue ribbon. The midsummer sun shone on the crown of her head, creating a pale golden halo.

“So this is how you celebrate your Independence Day? With your soldiers marching and with picnics?”

“And music. Your German band is quite good. Very stirring. And fireworks—don’t forget the fireworks after dark.”

Wande shook her head. “We do not have an Independence Day in Germany. But many times we hear long speeches on special days.”

“There will be speeches. But don’t worry. You can eat while folks are talking.” He stepped toward a stand of acacia trees that would provide some shade. Ma had already spread a blanket. Mrs. Fleischer added a quilt so there was plenty of room for everyone. Jud handed her the basket. Wande tucked her legs under her.

Soon both families took their places, as well as Ertha’s family, the Schumanns, and Pastor Bader. Once all sixteen people had filled their plates and the mothers settled the children, Mr. Schumann tapped a spoon against his jar of tea. “Today we have many reasons to celebrate. It is the first Independence Day that Texas has been part of the United States.”

The children cheered and Alvie waved her flag.

"It is also the birthday of Georg Fleischer. He has reached his majority today."

"Happy birthday!" Tom shouted.

"And today it is my great privilege to announce that my daughter Ertha is betrothed to Mr. Georg Fleischer."

Everyone cheered, and people around them glanced in their direction.

Mr. Fleischer stood and brushed a few strands of grass from his trousers. "I also have an announcement to make. Pastor Bader will be happy to hear we will no longer make the parsonage our home."

Jud's eyes sought out Wande, but she had turned her head.

"God has been good to us. He has given us work, and He has provided for our needs. We have decided to stay here in Victoria."

Jud relaxed.

"By God's goodness, we have saved enough money to buy land of our own. We will be your neighbors, Mrs. Morgan. We will return to where we first met you in this wonderful new country. We are buying the Walford farm."

CHAPTER TWENTY-TWO

Anger, mixed with surprise, surged through Jud. The Walfords had sold their land—land they promised to Jud—to Germans. And they had bought it with his money, money Jud had paid to Wande and Georg.

"How wonderful." Ma clapped her hands. "I'm so glad you will be our new neighbors." Pastor Bader and others offered their congratulations—everyone except Tom, who looked as upset as Jud felt.

The bratwurst turned to sawdust in Jud's mouth. He pushed the plate aside and poured himself more tea. After gulping it down, he excused himself. He wouldn't embarrass Ma, but he would hunt down his neighbor. Walford should be somewhere at the picnic; Jud saw him watching the parade.

Jud wished JM was there so he could ride hard and fast until he had a handle on his anger. Instead, he walked the perimeter of the crowd until he found the Walfords eating by themselves. He balled his hands into fists, and then released them. Pa had said it took a brave man to settle disputes without a fistfight, and he wanted to honor his father's memory.

Walford looked up. "Why, good day, Jud." His wife's smile faded when she saw Jud.

"Mr. Fleischer just told us the news." Jud forced himself to use an even tone.

"Have some peach pie. It's too much for us," Mrs. Walford said.

"I thought we had an agreement."

"Well, you said you wanted to buy it come fall. But with this cholera starting to plague the town, we want to get out of here as soon as possible." Walford stood face-to-face with Jud.

"You should have come to me. That's what neighbors do."

"Pastor Bader knew we were moving right away, and he passed the news on to Mr. Fleischer. They came over to talk yesterday and handed over the money."

"It seemed like God planned it that way," Mrs. Walford said.

What was done was done, and Jud could do nothing to change it. "Just tell me one thing. Did you mention my interest in the land to Fleischer and Bader, before you sold it away?"

The look the couple exchanged told Jud the truth. "I may have mentioned another party was interested in buying the land."

Fleischer had known . . . and the pastor had known . . . and they contrived to buy the land anyway. Jud had known he couldn't trust a German, but let his defenses slip. That would not happen again.

"Where did my brother disappear to?" Marion handed an almost empty bowl of sauerkraut to Wande. "He's been gone a long time."

Wande did not want to admit she wondered the same thing. He had left while everyone else was congratulating Papa. "He should be back soon. He said there would be speeches and music." She pointed to the bandstand. "And the brass band will play soon."

"They are pretty good." Marion held her hands in front as if holding a trombone and puffed out her cheeks while moving the slide.

Wande frowned at the small amount of sauerkraut left. Not enough to save to take home, but she couldn't eat another bite. Perhaps she could coax Georg to finish it—if she could separate him from Ertha long enough. At the moment, the couple walked among friends, accepting their good wishes.

Wande pushed down her disappointment. Last summer, she thought she would have married by now. Today, during the parade, she had welcomed Jud's companionship. Now he had disappeared, and she didn't know where or why. She tucked the remaining dishes into the picnic basket and stood holding the quilt.

Brushing off the crumbs and flapping the quilt, she glanced around the lawn. With all the people gathered, she could not see very far. She turned in a circle, scanning the crowd for Jud. At last, she spotted him, talking with a group from town. He had sought out the company of other men. The way dear Papa talked with Mr. Schumann and Pastor Bader while Mama and Mrs. Schumann watched Alvie and the younger Schumann children at play. Only the affianced couples, Georg and Ertha and Marion and Tom, stayed glued to each other's sides. Wande had no claim on Jud's attention.

But he had talked as if they would share the day's activities: the music, the fireworks, and even the speeches in a language she still struggled to understand. Something changed when Papa announced they had purchased the land next to the

Running M. Jud had walked away as if all the bees in a hive were chasing him.

"Wande, please help me bring everything back to the house." Her mother held a basket.

"Coming, Mama." They carried the leftovers from the three families to the parsonage.

"It will not be so easy to clean up once we move out of town." Mama smiled. Wande knew how she relished having a place of their own again.

By the time they returned to the grounds, people had moved close to the bandstand. The mayor welcomed the crowd and began a long speech. He listed a lot of names—some *Amerikaner*, some Mexican—it sounded like he was telling the history of the town. Alvie sat with her elbows propped on her knees, as if she expected to take a test on the information. Wande stopped trying to follow. Alvie would repeat the story, with many embellishments, as many times as she could get her family to listen. Full of good food, Wande's eyelids drifted shut until the concert began. No one could sleep through a brass band, especially when it was good music. They played a variety, some of the songs Wande had learned as a child.

After the band, the man who had beat the drum in the parade came forward with a slightly younger man—holding what looked like a miniature flute. High notes pierced the air with a lively tune, and Wande's foot tapped to the drum's steady rhythm.

By the time the music ended, Wande's mood had lifted, although Jud had never returned. A few families left when the sun set, but most waited for the fireworks. "Do you think they will begin soon?" Mama said.

Wande shook her head. "Marion said they wait until it is fully dark."

"Then let us return to the house and bring back water. I am thirsty."

Wande jumped to her feet and helped Mama stand. At the house, they both drank their fill and took care of necessities before returning. The first rocket went off with a splash of red larger than any firework Wande had ever seen.

Georg hurtled toward them, heedless of the colors filling the sky. "Mama, come quick. Drud is sick."

"*Nein*. Do not call the doctor. It is only the food I ate." Drud leaned over the side of the bed to be sick. Wande had placed a bucket there. A foul odor arose from the bed, and Wande knew her brother had soiled himself. Grimacing, he pulled his knees toward his chest. "Oh, my legs!"

She pressed a cool hand on his forehead and poured him a glass of water. "Here. Drink some."

He groaned. "It will only come up again."

"All the more reason you need to drink it."

"For you, *Schwester*."

She lifted his head and helped him drink. Drud, quiet Drud, never asked for anything for himself but only gave and gave some more for the sake of the family. Wande prayed that something he ate caused the illness, but she didn't see how. They had all eaten the same dishes, but only Drud was sick. A soured dish brought less fear than the dreaded word being whispered from Carlshafen to Victoria and beyond—*cholera*. Another bout of vomiting interrupted her silent prayers. She held his head and offered him more water.

"I will ask Mama and Papa to come help you with your bedding." He didn't respond, his lips quietly moving in the fashion of the *Vaterunser*, the Lord's Prayer.

As she stood, he opened his eyes. "Wande, promise me you'll pray for me."

"Of course. I haven't stopped." She took his hand.

He closed his eyes, but when she moved, he grasped her fingers and opened his pale blue eyes. "I am frightened."

Wande wanted to reassure him, but they both knew better. She could not, would not, lie to her brother in what could be his final hours. "The Lord is with you."

"Yea, though I walk through the valley of the shadow of death . . ." His hand trembled. "Please pray that the Lord takes me quickly, if this is my time."

She drew back, but his grasp on her hand strengthened.

"Promise me."

"Ja, Ich verspreche."

Jud patted JM's head as he galloped back through the gate to the Running M. He needed to do some work around the ranch—he'd gotten further and further behind since dismissing Georg. Other business kept interfering with ranch work.

Now he could scratch off one worry, the nagging need to find another parcel of land for Tom and Marion. One of the German families had pulled up stakes and headed on for Neu-Braunfels. Jud snatched up their land, glad to see Texas land return to true Texans. Land bought with the blood of Texans and now bought back with their money.

Jud brushed his hand against his forehead. He could hear his mother's voice quoting Scripture—and at the moment he didn't welcome any spiritual reminders. He had things lined up just fine until the Fleischers made a mess of everything.

The new parcel wasn't ideal—farther removed from town and not as big as the Walford farm. But many couples started with less, including Ma and Pa on their arrival in Texas. He clung to that hope as JM stopped in front of the ranch house.

Jud jumped off the horse and dropped the reins to ground tie him. Through an open window, he heard music—piano music—and laughter. He caught sight of a blond head and his step hesitated. *Billie*. He dashed up the steps before his head caught up with his heart. *Not* Billie. It couldn't be. Billie was dead and gone. Besides, that girl looked nothing like Billie, not really.

Clenching his teeth, he opened the door and marched into the parlor. The quilt they kept over the upright had been folded and placed on the end of the sofa. A book of music was propped against the stand. Marion stood behind the bench, her hands guiding Alvie Fleischer in a scale. "This note is middle C, and the key of C doesn't have any sharps or flats."

"The black keys," Alvie said. "Is C always to the left of two black keys?"

"Yes."

Jud found his voice. "What are you doing?"

Two faces turned in his direction, one smiling, the other puzzled. "I am teaching Alvie how to play the piano."

"The lesson has come to an end."

Alvie jumped up. "That is all right. I will water the garden."

Jud pulled the cover back over the keys and reached for the quilt.

Marion snatched it. "What's wrong with you?" Her glare could have burned a hole in the quilt.

"No one has touched that piano since Billie disappeared."

"Then don't you think it's about time? I know you miss Billie. I do too. But she's gone, and we're still here. And music has been gone from this household for too long." Marion settled the quilt in her arms. "I'll put this in the guest bedroom. The days of its use as a piano shroud are over."

Jud glared at the piano. Memories swirled in his brain, memories he had pushed aside for too long. He opened the key cover and plunked a chord, wincing at the out-of-tune sound. He opened the piano seat and looked at the music waiting there, the same songs he had played years ago. When he was a child, Ma forced him to stay at the piano when he wanted to be outside riding with Pa. But Billie never needed any encouragement. She tackled complicated pieces with ease. His fingers grazed over the thin black case that held a flute—Billie's flute. She loved music. They all did, once. Before the reality of life in Texas. Life anywhere, Jud supposed, although he knew only the Texas version.

He opened the flute case and ran his fingers over the instrument, imagining how Billie's fingers flew over the keys—and the light that danced in her eyes as she played a lively melody. Perhaps it was time for music to return to the Morgan household, but not with this flute. The flute was uniquely Billie's, and Jud would hold it for her in hope, however foolish, that someday she would return home and claim it. Closing the case, he tucked it under his arm, carried it to his room, and buried it at the bottom of his wardrobe.

CHAPTER TWENTY-THREE

Marion joined Alvie in the garden. "How does it look today?"

"These weeds grow overnight, faster than the plants do. Why do you suppose God made them work that way?"

Wande had worked so hard on that little patch of Texas dirt, both Marion and Alvie wanted to protect her investment. Marion joined Alvie on her knees. As she pulled weeds, she prayed for Drud and the others in town struck by cholera. So far God had spared the people at the ranch. The sooner the Fleischers could move to the Walfords' farm, the better it would be for all of them. Then maybe Jud wouldn't be so grumpy.

Ma rang the bell for dinner. Tom sprinted from the barn. Marion joined him at the pump, where they washed up. She waited for his kiss, but he brushed past her and headed for the house. She looked at her dirt-spattered skirt. Of course he didn't want to kiss her when she looked like this. But that didn't explain his attitude yesterday—or the day before. She had gone to the Fourth of July picnic with one Tom and had come back a Tom who was entirely different.

The tension at the dinner table was thick enough to spread across a cake. Only Alvie seemed unaffected, chattering about playing the piano. "Marion taught me a silly song about three blind mice." She hummed the first three notes then put her hand over her mouth. "Mama does not want me to sing at the table."

Marion giggled. "Ma used to tell me the same thing. But I like it." She winked at Alvie.

"I heard you." Ma set down her plate. "It was good to hear music in the house again. Wasn't it, Jud?"

Jud took his time chewing his food. "Yes." He smiled, a watered-down version of this usual grin. "It was good to hear music."

The icy temperature warmed a little.

Jud started to take a bite, then paused. "I have some good news today."

"Do tell. Good news is always welcome at this table."

"I wanted to make this a surprise for the wedding, but Tom already knows some of this."

Marion set down her forkful of potato salad. Anything about the wedding captured her attention.

"Them Fleischers already bought the Walfords' farm." Tom's scowl matched his tone.

"True." Jud drew in a deep breath. "But they're not the only ones looking to sell. I've found another place. It's a little smaller, but it's got everything you need to make a go of it."

Tom settled back in his chair. "Which one is it?"

"The Eggers'. They're going on to Neu-Braunfels."

"The folks that built one of them half wood, half rock houses? Out on the north side of town?"

"The very ones."

"The Eggers are moving?" Marion didn't understand the importance.

"Yup. And I've bought their land." Jud grinned. "As a wedding present for you and Tom." He leaned across the table and clasped her hand. "Congratulations, Marion."

"I don't know what to say." Heat flooded her cheeks and she turned to her fiancé. "Isn't that wonderful?" It was more than most couples had when they got married.

Tom didn't look pleased. In fact, a scowl marred his face. "I thought the Walford farm was a done deal."

"I thought so too. I was going to add some money of my own to what you had saved, but the Fleischers got there first." Jud looked like he was going to say more, but he glanced at Alvie and stopped.

"I've seen the Eggers' place," Marion said. "It's a fine gift, Tom." She glanced at Ma, whose lips had thinned into a tight line, and at Jud, who clenched his fists.

"It's not what was promised," Tom stated.

At that moment, Marion didn't care that the Bible said wives should be submissive to their husbands. Besides, they weren't married yet.

"Now, Tom." Ma spoke first. "I've thought of myself as your Ma since you came here to the Running M, and I can't abide you talking like that."

Marion had to speak up. "Jud's been generous, Tom. I'm ashamed of the way you're acting."

Tom glowered. "I won't mention it again."

Marion had heard enough. "You should at least say thank-you."

Tom stood. "I can tell I'm not welcome here today." He plunked his hat on his head and headed out the door.

Marion jumped to her feet, but Ma stopped her. "Let the

boy simmer down. And give yourself some time."

"My little sister. The spitfire." Jud smiled.

Alvie looked at them with wide eyes. Arguing in front of the child might make her think it was her family's fault. Marion felt ashamed. "I'm sorry."

"I'm not." Ma snorted. "You said what needed saying. And Tom doesn't look good for not listening."

Marion forced herself to finish her meal and clean up afterward. She went outside to look for Tom, but he had gone with Jud on some errand. She didn't get another chance to speak with him until evening.

The men returned just before sundown. They halted outside the barn. Marion waited beneath the acacia trees, listening for what kind of mood Tom was in—hoping he was ready to listen.

"Sure you won't change your mind?" Jud said.

"I already waited too long." Tom didn't sound so much angry as resigned. "I'll talk with Marion tonight."

"Come by before you bed down, and I'll give you your wages."

Marion stepped forward, then paused. Tom might not want her to overhear the conversation.

Jud led the horses to the barn, and Tom headed in Marion's direction. "Good evening, Marion."

He had known she was there.

"Hello." Her voice stuck in her throat.

"Let's take a walk." Unlike earlier times, he didn't reach for her hand. They walked a respectable ruler length apart. "I'm sorry I upset you so at dinner."

"I spoke out of hand, too," Marion said.

"No, you didn't. But this whole business with the land set me to thinking."

Marion wanted to stop her ears. "Thinking about what? About us?"

"Not so much about us as about *me*. Jud was right, Marion. I'm not ready to be anybody's husband. Least of all yours. I'm leaving the ranch in the morning before I make things worse by marrying you."

"What? But Tom . . . I love you." Tears formed in her eyes.

"Would you still feel that way if I said part of the reason I wanted to marry you was to get my hands on that land?"

Shock dried her tears. "What?"

"That's why I didn't say anything before now." His face looked as if he had swallowed sour milk. "'Cause I knew Jud planned on buying us that farm. That's a poor excuse to marry a woman."

"I don't believe it." A part of Marion's mind insisted she did believe it. "Please don't do this."

"It's already done." Tom tugged at the brim of his hat. "I'm heading out of here as soon as the sun comes up." He reached out to touch her, but let his hand fall back. "I'm sorry, Marion. You deserve better."

I do not welcome this answer to prayer. Less than two days had passed since Drud took sick on Saturday evening.

All day Saturday and Sunday, Wande held Drud's hand, willing him to hold to life. At one point during the night, when Mama and Papa were out of the room, Drud begged, "Let me go. I am ready to see my Savior."

Wande bit back a cry. *I'm not ready.* She hadn't been ready to say good-bye to Ulla, and she wasn't ready to lose her brother. But Drud needed his big sister to make this easy for him. "*Ja,* Drud. You will tell our Ulla all about this Texas." She blinked back tears, and did not speak of it again when their parents returned.

The three of them sat by Drud's bed as he passed away

quietly on Monday morning. The other family members had scattered, away from the house of sickness, taken in by people willing to accept the risk.

"God is asking a high price from us in this new land." Mama's words sounded strangled. "First Ulla, now Drud." Tears streamed down her face.

Mama's tears broke the grief in Wande's heart, and she sobbed as well. Papa pulled both women against him and held them until his shirt was soaked. "We must remember that even though we grieve, we still have hope. We will see our loved ones again."

"A mother should not outlive her children."

Mama's words shredded Wande's heart.

"Now, *Liebchen*, we have three other children who need us. Although our Wande is hardly a child anymore." Kindness shone through his tears. "We must be strong."

"As I must be strong for you." Wande's promise rang false in her own ears.

Papa held the two women a few minutes longer before he stirred. "We cannot leave him here in this heat. I must ask Pastor Bader about burial arrangements. I will ask him . . ." He allowed his tears to flow.

When at last Papa pulled himself together enough to speak with the pastor, Mama also stirred. "I will prepare his body."

"Of course." Wande stood, preparing to gather the materials.

"Please. I want to do this alone." Mama blinked back tears, but her gaze remained resolute.

Wande hesitated. Mama should not have to do this alone, but if it was what she wanted . . . "I will be in the parlor."

The door opened as she left the bedroom and Georg entered. "I saw Papa on the way here. I have heard the news." Georg pressed his lips together and blinked.

"He will always live in our hearts." The words sounded hollow even as Wande spoke them. "What of Ertha's family? Are they well?"

He nodded. "Thank the good Lord. But that is not why I came. I went to the ranch last night, to see if they wanted me to come to work or if I could stay in town and see how Drud fared." His voice caught.

During the hours tending to Drud, Wande had all but forgotten about her job. "That was wise."

Georg frowned. "Jud said we did not need to come back."

"That is thoughtful. We can take care of . . . things . . . before we go back."

He shook his head. "You do not understand. He does not want us to come back . . . ever! He says we will be needed on our farm."

CHAPTER TWENTY-FOUR

The following morning, Marion didn't so much wake as give up her battle for sleep. She pulled herself to the window and sat in a chair overlooking the bunkhouse. A light was lit, earlier than the ranch hands got up for the day's work.

A figure she instantly recognized as Tom left the building, a bedroll in one arm, his saddle in the other. He headed for the barn and came out leading his usual working horse, the only one he had ever successfully broken on the ranch. Every moment drew out in agonizing slowness as he saddled the horse, tied down his bedroll, and swung into the seat. Would he look at her window? See her light and change his mind?

His head turned halfway, then he reined the horse toward the gate. Each soft *clip clop* of the mare's hooves drove another nail into Marion's soul. Her heart cried out in pain to the Lord.

⟵ ★ ⟶

Wande clung to the seat as Georg ran their wagon over the ruts created by the winter rains. "Do you think we do the right thing, bringing Alvie back into town?"

Georg flicked the reins over the oxen, and they lurched forward. "She will want to know what happened."

"She's only a child." If only Wande could protect her little sister from the latest grief to overtake their family. She sighed. "But old enough to understand. She will want to be at the funeral, but I worry that she may get sick."

"We are all at risk." Shadows haunted Georg's face. Since Saturday, he had slept only in snatches, alternating his time between their home and the Schumanns'. Ertha's youngest sister had also sickened with cholera, and Georg worried as much as if Alvie were threatened.

"I know." The wind swallowed Wande's words.

They passed through the gate to the ranch. The air felt hollow, empty of sounds. Perhaps it was the early hour—they wanted to fetch Alvie in time for the noon burial. Or maybe pain had dulled Wande's senses.

The yard was as quiet as the road. A chill shivered down Wande's spine. Had the Morgans brought the illness back to the ranch? She ran toward the house. "Marion? Alvie? Frau Morgan? Jud?"

Alvie opened the door and put a finger to her lips.

Wande sagged against Georg in relief.

"Marion does not feel well today," Alvie said. "Mrs. Morgan asked me to be quiet."

"Is she . . ." Wande couldn't bring herself to voice her concern.

"No. I think she is heartsick about Tom, but no one tells me anything." Alvie brightened. "How is Drud? Have you come to bring me home?"

Alvie's words brought tears to Wande's eyes. "Let us go inside and see if Frau Morgan will fix us some of her sweet tea."

"And give us some molasses cookies," Alvie said. "I helped her bake them yesterday."

Wande's laugh sounded hollow. Cookies and tea couldn't protect Alvie from the bad news she brought. But she pasted on a smile and put her arm around Alvie as they walked into the house. Georg headed for the bunkhouse to collect his possessions.

"Marion gave me a piano lesson yesterday." Alvie pointed to the instrument, now uncovered, in the far corner of the room. "She said she would give me another lesson today, but I do not think it will happen."

Wande hesitated at the door to the kitchen. Marion sat at the table, her face between her arms. Her shoulders shook. Frau Morgan sat next to her, rubbing her back.

"Should we go away?" Alvie whispered.

Marion and her mother looked up. "No, come in." Marion sat up and wiped her eyes with a handkerchief. "What news from town?" Her voice trembled.

Wande shook her head and headed for the shelf that held the cups. Alvie went into the pantry and returned with the cookie jar.

"It's not good news, is it?" Marion's voice was clear in spite of the tears clouding her eyes. She stood and took Wande in her arms. "Oh, Wande."

Wande shook herself free. "Alvie—" Her voice broke, and she held her sister and started again. "Alvie, Drud . . . did not get better. He is . . .with Ulla, in heaven, with Jesus, now."

The cookie crumbled in Alvie's hand, and her mouth formed a small O. "But I prayed . . ."

"We all did. But God did not give us what we asked for this time."

"He should. I promised to be a good girl and not argue with Drud or tease him because he does not know English very well."

"Oh, Alvie." Wande's hold on her sister tightened. "You were a good sister to Drud. He loved you." She looked over Alvie's head at Frau Morgan. "The funeral will be at noon today. We came to take Alvie home."

"Of course. And we'll come with you. I'll call Jud." Mrs. Morgan grabbed the dinner bell and walked to the porch. A minute later, Wande heard the clamor.

"And what has happened to you, Marion? No one is sick?"

"No. And I know I should be thankful that God has spared us." Marion's voice shook. "Tom told me he doesn't want to marry me."

Alvie stirred in the circle of Wande's arms. "That is mean."

"But . . . why . . ." Wande's voice trailed off. The pain of being jilted by Konrad was too recent. Tom and Marion seemed so very much in love. Her mind screamed for explanations, but no excuse would ease the pain in Marion's heart. Only the Lord could, and even that took time. "I am sorry. I did not expect this news."

"He was angry last night." Alvie frowned. "But I never thought he would change his mind about you."

Heavy footsteps announced Jud and Georg's arrival.

"He was mad about Jud not getting the Walfords' farm," Alvie said.

"Do not spread gossip." Wande hushed Alvie, but her mind raced. Seconds later, she looked at Jud for the first time since Papa had announced the purchase of the farm. The man she thought she knew had gone into hiding—masked by an expression of disdain.

The hard lump in Jud's heart softened when he saw the hollowness in Wande's cheeks and the circles under her eyes. She probably hadn't left Drud's side since Saturday. "Georg told me the news. I'm so sorry for your loss. Ma said the funeral will be today."

"We cannot wait any longer. We will bury him in the community cemetery."

"We need to go." Georg looked at the sun. "If we are to make it in time."

"You folks go ahead. Won't take us longer than a minute to get our wagon hitched." Ma turned to Marion. "Why don't you travel with them and sit with Alvie in the back?"

Trust Ma to think of the neighborly thing to do.

"Of course."

Jud helped Marion into the back of the wagon, where she sat with her arms entwined about Alvie. Tears would flow aplenty today. But he wouldn't allow himself to cry. He hadn't lost his fiancé or a sibling. Not lately, anyhow. He watched the Fleischers' wagon rattle down the road, Wande's back ramrod straight in defiance of the burdens placed on her. He found himself wanting to comfort her much as Marion was comforting Alvie. Shaking his head, he went to the barn and led out the team.

By the time he had the wagon ready, Ma came out of the house with a basket of food for the Fleischers. At least she found something practical to do. The hole would have been dug, the coffin prepared. The only thing left to do now was to help them move to the farm. Jud scowled. Was that another sign of God's sense of humor, to make him help the Fleischers do the one thing he resented most? He lifted Ma onto the seat beside him and headed down the road.

A wheel bounced in a rut and shocked Jud out of his brooding. If the horses hadn't known the way into town, they'd be headed to Carlshafen by now. Ma would never forgive Jud if they missed the funeral.

"Your face looks as stormy as a thundercloud." Ma held the

basket, probably full of ham, cornbread, and beans, securely in her arms. "Whatever is troubling you, Son, let it go, for the Fleischers' sake. I can't imagine losing two children so close together."

If only it was that easy. "I don't know if I can."

She snorted. "It's not can or can't. The Lord can do it even if you can't by yourself."

Hide it, stuff it down. Jud had done so much of that, he didn't know if he could anymore. He tilted his hat back and looked up at the sky. *Lord, like Ma says, You'll have to do it for me.*

"And if you and the Lord don't work things out, one of these days you're going to tell me whatever has your tail feathers all riled up. You can't carry this burden all by yourself."

Jud guided the horses away from another deep rut. The town came into view, and the hoof beats sounded on empty streets, emptier than Sunday mornings during church. The sole person Jud saw on his way to the cemetery, Dr. Treviño, waved them down.

"Are you well out your way?"

"So far," Ma said.

"You must be on your way to the funeral for young Drud." The doctor shook his head. "Such a shame."

"How many dead does that make now, Doc?" Jud said.

A faraway look came into the doctor's eyes. "Too many. And we haven't seen the end of it yet. Get your family back home as soon as you say good-bye—and stay there." He paused. "Unless one of you gets sick."

Jud nodded. "If you're headed for the funeral, climb on board."

The doctor's shoulders slumped. "I wish I could, but duty calls me elsewhere. Give the Fleischers my condolences."

The doctor trudged toward the center of town while Jud turned aside for the cemetery. Every here and there he spotted fresh mounds with crude wooden crosses.

Death had come calling on the people of Victoria.

CHAPTER TWENTY-FIVE

"Is there anything else?" Jud dusted his hands after he loaded the last chair onto the wagon. He shaded his eyes and peered into the parsonage.

"That is all." Meino tipped his head back and studied the belongings piled onto the two wagons. "I do not know how we carried everything from Carlshafen on a single wagon."

Jud chuckled. "It was piled pretty high." He jumped off the back of the wagon. "And you've acquired more furnishings, it looks like." Everything pointed to the Fleischers' industry.

Fleischer managed a smile. "God has been good." His voice broke, and he cleared his throat. "He has provided for all our needs. And now we get to be neighbors. That is another of God's good gifts."

Jud forced a smile, although he didn't entirely agree. When he'd offered to help them move, Fleischer had asked if he could make it on Thursday. "We want to get out of the city as soon as possible."

Ma offered to keep Alvie at the ranch until they settled in

their new house— maybe to keep Marion's mind off Tom.

"Ma said she'd have dinner waiting for us, so let's get going. Pastor Bader, you're welcome to join us . . . if you want to," Jud said.

"*Danke,* Jud. But I offered to take Wande and some of the smaller packages in my buggy," the pastor said.

Fleischer helped his wife onto the wagon beside Georg, then surprised Jud by climbing onto the wagon beside him. "I will ride with you."

Jud motioned for Georg to go first. The cow, Elsie, and her calf were tied to the back of Jud's wagon, so their trip might take longer.

The streets of Victoria remained deserted, with the exception of a procession headed to the cemetery. Fleischer turned his head and didn't speak until they left the outskirts of town.

"I have something I wish to speak with you about." Fleischer turned his hands over. "Wande tells me you intended to buy the Walford farm for your sister and her betrothed. And this caused hard feelings when we bought the land instead."

"Wande talks a lot."

"She spoke only because she wants us to be good neighbors. And she feels terrible that Tom has broken his promise with Marion. You understand."

Jud did. He remembered how hard Wande had taken the news that her Konrad had married someone else. She knew from personal experience how Marion's heart had scattered in pieces around the ranch.

"I don't blame you," Jud said, "for what Tom did."

"I did not know you wanted to buy the land. Herr Walford mentioned another interested buyer, but never mentioned your name. I thought he was bargaining with me. That he wanted me to pay more money. It is often done that way in Germany."

The reins pulled on Jud's gloved hands, and he adjusted

them. The team wanted to move a little too fast for the calf. What Meino said made sense. He grunted an acknowledgment, not quite ready to release his resentment.

"The Verein promised us land. It is far away, farther even than Neu-Braunfels. But I would like to sell you that land since you did not get the farm." Fleischer chuckled. "I would give you the land, but my wife says you have pride and will refuse a gift. That all men have pride, even *Amerikaners*."

That caught Jud's fancy. He threw back his head and laughed. "Ma would say *especially* American men. She fusses at me for being stubborn."

"It is the way the good Lord made us, is it not? We must be stubborn to make the crops grow out of the soil that would rather grow weeds." Fleischer smiled. "But when we are stubborn with our women, it is not always good."

"No . . . it's not. So, what price are you asking?"

Fleischer mentioned a fair price. Jud knew of some early German settlers who had given away their land for a milk cow. Here Meino offered to give him land for no other reason than he'd bought the land that Jud wanted for his family. The temptation to gain a threshold in the New Germany appealed to Jud. He looked to either side of the road. This place, with its gently rolling hills and dark clay, had been his home for as long as he could remember. He worked the ranch to support the family, but also because he loved horses. Calder couldn't wait to get away, but Jud never felt the desire to roam.

Jud no longer had a reason to give Tom any land. He closed his mind to the curses he wanted to rage against the man who had hurt Marion.

And if Jud left Victoria . . . and the Fleischers stayed here . . .

"I appreciate your offer," Jud said, "but I'm not interested. Keep the land for yourself. Who knows, Georg and Ertha might want to move there one day."

"Very well. So there are no hard feelings?"

Jud slammed the door against his mixed feelings. Germans were Germans, but the Fleischers were a different matter. "No hard feelings." Reluctantly, he stuck out his right hand and they shook on it.

"This house is smaller than the parsonage. The Walfords had only the one boy. Don't you think you'll feel cramped?" Marion fluffed pillows on the bed Wande would share with Alvie. For the time being, Georg would sleep in the barn.

Wande laughed. "At least it is *our* house. And we will add to it. We will have to, before Georg and Ertha get married this fall."

Marion's hand stopped in midair. "They'll need a place other than the barn."

Wande put a hand over her mouth. "I am sorry. I did not mean to make you feel sad."

Marion plumped down on the bed. "It happens." She plucked at some threads dangling from the cuff of her brown calico dress. She didn't think she'd ever again want to wear either of her yellow dresses or her new buttercream dress. Every time she saw them in the closet, she thought of Tom. Maybe she could give them to Wande.

Wande sat and hugged her. "I know how much it hurts. You try to act brave and pretend it does not matter, but inside you wonder what is wrong with you—that he chooses not to marry you."

Marion sniffed. "I feel silly crying about Tom when you just lost your brother."

"It is not silly. In some ways it is harder. Drud did not choose to die, but Tom made a choice. He is the silly one." Wande reached into the pillowcase and pulled out a handkerchief. "Use this. It has seen many tears."

Marion hiccuped and blew her nose. "How do you stay so . . . happy . . . all the time? You have been through so much."

"So many good-byes." Wande ran her hand over the quilt. "My Oma made this for me. I do not expect to see her again before we get to heaven, with Ulla, and Drud, and Opa." She leaned toward Marion. "But I have many new friends. I have met you, and Georg has met Ertha, and Papa is happier than he ever was in Offenbach. And Alvie loves Texas."

Marion saw the flaw in Wande's argument. "But that's everyone else. How has Victoria been good to *you*, Wande?"

Wande looked out the window over the land that stretched ahead, already turned over and ready for planting the fall crop. "I have learned that God goes with me everywhere I go. And that is enough."

"Though I walk through the valley of the shadow of death . . ." The words came automatically to Marion's lips.

"'I will fear no evil, for Thou art with me.'" Wande finished and leaned back. "But that does not mean it is easy. We will not get the house ready by sitting here."

"No, we won't." Marion sneezed into the hankie and crumpled it into a ball, looking for a place to put it. Wande wouldn't want it back in her pillowcase. She dropped it into the box carrying the dirty linens from the old house.

Marion followed Wande into the kitchen, where they helped Mrs. Fleischer organize her things. Her face brightened with each item she uncovered. Wande wiped down the china before placing it in the cabinet, together with a few figurines they had brought from Germany. She cradled one in her hands, a gentle shepherdess carrying a lamb. "This one was Ulla's favorite." She sighed. "The lamb's ear has broken off." She kissed the broken spot. "But I still love it." She set it on the shelf.

"I have a teapot one of my ancestors brought from England." Ma was in the kitchen filling the vegetable bins with corn and sweet potatoes raided from their kitchen. "It's cracked from top to bottom, but I treasure it."

Mrs. Fleischer rummaged through the box of china. "Here it is." She held up the ear and set it next to the lamb. "Everything will be all right. We will get the right glue to fix it." She ran a hand over it, then returned to setting the kitchen to rights.

Things were important, Marion knew. Think of Jud's fuss last week when she played the piano. Things reminded you of people and places and memories.

Grunts reached them from the living room. The four men had to work hard to find a place for all the furniture. Jud, Mr. Fleischer, and Georg did most of the heavy lifting while the pastor gave directions.

"I will see what is the problem," Wande said. Marion followed.

The men squeezed Mr. Fleischer's desk into the corner, behind one of those comfy chairs Marion loved to sit in. "I have room for a chair in my bedroom," Wande said. "It will not be so crowded in here." She grabbed the chair. Pastor Bader reached out to help her.

"Stop a moment, *Liebchen*. Herr Morgan wants to speak with you."

Marion looked from Jud to Wande to Pastor Bader and couldn't decide whose face was turning a brighter red.

"I, uh, spoke too soon when I said we didn't need your help any longer at the ranch. The truth is, I'd be right happy if you'd come back to work. Georg has already agreed." Jud hurried ahead, as if afraid Wande would refuse. "We'll adjust your hours, of course. You'll be needed at your home as well. But I'd welcome any help you can give us."

The color slowly faded from Wande's cheeks. "*Danke*, Jud. I will be glad to work for you."

CHAPTER TWENTY-SIX

When Wande returned to work at the Morgan house on Monday, she felt as if a month had passed, not just a week. How lives could turn upside-down in such a short time.

Wande turned aside to see the garden, and Alvie skipped along beside her. Someone had tended it well in her absence. She bent and checked the plants. A few cucumbers and okra plants still showed promise, but the tomato vines had withered. She had not gathered anything for last Saturday's market. The people of Victoria would not stir out of doors until cholera loosened its grip on the city.

"I took good care of the garden, did I not?" Alvie pointed to the thriving plants. "Mrs. Morgan cooked some of the okra. I told her you would not mind. She cut it into tiny pieces and stirred it in cornmeal and fried it. I liked it."

This okra was one of the new vegetables Mrs. Morgan had recommended for the garden. "I will remember that so I can tell our German friends how to eat it." She straightened her back. "Now remember. I am here to work, so I cannot play with you."

"I know." Alvie drooped. "But Marion promised me another piano lesson."

"We will see how the work goes. I will tell you if you may ask her." She hoped Alvie could play the piano. Her sister had talked of little else—when she spoke at all. She had been quiet, as if afraid her cheer might make everyone around her feel sadder.

"Drud will never get to hear me play."

"I imagine in heaven he and Ulla will sit down to listen every time you play."

"Do you really think so?" Alvie grabbed the valise Wande had packed for their overnight stay and went inside. "No one is here."

"Take our bag upstairs while I look for Mrs. Morgan and Marion. They must be out back doing the laundry."

As she rounded the corner, Wande heard Marion singing one of her favorite hymns, "Amazing Grace." She rejoiced that her friend felt whole enough to sing. A man's voice joined Marion's, a pleasant baritone singing in harmony. It could only be Jud. She waited, out of sight, and listened to the harmonies. "Through many dangers, toils, and snares, I have already come. 'Tis grace hath brought me safe thus far, and grace will lead me home."

Tears sprang to Wande's eyes. "Thank You, heavenly Father, that Your grace has seen Drud safely home. And You have brought me safe so that I did not catch the illness." She whispered the words with thanksgiving and gathered herself before going around the corner.

Jud saw her first. "I've put what you taught me about washing clothes to good use." He lowered his voice. "Ma's back went out last night, and she wasn't up to hanging the laundry today." His mouth lifted at one corner.

"I am sure she appreciates your help. But you do not need to stay now that I am here."

"Chasing me away from my own house, are you?" He picked up a tub of wet clothes as if they weighed no more than a towel and brought it to the clothesline. "That should keep the two of you busy. Did Georg go to the bunkhouse?"

Wande nodded, and he walked away, whistling the melody they had been singing.

"That is such a beautiful song," Wande said.

Marion nodded. "It's as old as the hills, but I still love it. You can't help but praise God when you sing it." She burst into song. "When we've been there ten thousand years, bright shining as the sun, we've no less days to sing God's praise than when we've first begun."

"Amen." Wande's heart began to feel lighter. "It is good to remember heaven. It helps me when I think of Drud and Ulla." She and Marion took a sheet and flung it over the line. "But it did not help me when I learned Konrad had married someone else. I could only think I would have to share heaven with Konrad and his wife. That did not make me happy."

Marion laughed. "You're so funny. I confess I've pondered how I could make Tom suffer. Send a bee his way or something." She shook her head. "Then I remember I'm supposed to forgive him. Ma keeps reminding me, but it's so hard. As for Jud . . ."

"He says nothing, but looks like he wants to send the entire hive after Tom."

Marion laughed. "Yes, something like that. I think he's fighting a bad case of the 'I told you so's.' So he holds his tongue instead of saying anything."

"Papa was the same way. 'I never thought Konrad was good enough for you.' As if that made me love him any less." Wande slipped a couple of clothespins over the sheet and grabbed a pillowcase. She glanced up and saw Jud at the door to the barn, staring in her direction.

Jud whirled and headed back into the darkness of the barn, angry with himself for staring at Wande like an addlepated boy in love. Love. That wasn't possible.

Georg had slipped back into their routine as if he had never been gone. He took on extra chores, the few Tom used to do, without needing direction. He was a keeper.

But something had changed in the quiet young man. In a word: Ertha. Georg couldn't stop talking about her. "I am glad you let me go home in the afternoon. I want to make a room where we can live. I do not wish to have to wait until next year." The boy blushed, from the straggly hairs on his chin to the roots of his hair.

"I don't blame you." Not that Jud knew what it was like. The closest he had come to finding a gal was giving Betsy Jones a peck on the cheek behind the schoolhouse on his fourteenth birthday. "There's more than one way to get that done. Ma could whip together a house-raising faster than she could churn butter." There was no reason those two should have to wait any longer than necessary to get married. Of course, they didn't need a whole new house, just another room.

Georg continued in much the same vein, punctuating his work with sentences beginning with "Ertha did this" or "after I am married." The chatter kept Jud from having to contribute much to the conversation.

"Do you think that is a good idea?" Georg leaned on the rake and looked at Jud. He must have asked a question.

Jud dug through the bits of dialogue he had heard. Something about fall crops?

"I'm not much of a farmer." Jud pointed around the barn. "Horses are my world."

"But you and Marion, you taught Wande what to plant. Papa has a book that the Verein gives to everyone who comes here. It says what to plant and when and every single step." Georg shook his head. "But Papa says it sounds like the same way he farmed in Germany, and he wonders if there is a better way to plant here in Texas."

Too bad he didn't ask the Walfords when he had a chance. "A lot of people hereabouts plant cotton. It makes good money and grows pretty good."

"But those people often have slaves to help them pick the cotton, *ja*? We did not own slaves in Germany."

Jud nodded. "A lot of them do, yes."

"So Papa wonders if it is a good crop for a single family to grow. We know nothing about it."

Jud shifted from cleaning the stalls to rubbing down JM. The horse hadn't had a thorough grooming in days. "Maybe that agricultural society you belong to can give you information on crops." Still, he wished he knew more about farming. Georg made him feel pretty special, asking him all these questions.

Ma rang the bell for dinner. As Jud passed the parlor window, he could hear someone stumbling through a simple piano melody.

"Is that Alvie?" Georg said.

Jud nodded glumly. "Think so."

The two men washed at the pump before going in. Alvie jumped up from the piano bench when she saw Jud.

"He won't hurt you. I told him you were going to take lessons. Didn't I?" Marion dared Jud to protest. And yes, she had told him.

"I like to hear you play." Georg hugged his little sister. They walked into the kitchen, chattering.

"I like having her play also," Marion said. "It's—I don't know—a little like having our Billie back with us. I'm glad Wande lets me borrow her little sister."

Marion leveled her eyes on her brother. "Having Alvie around the house is a comfort to me. I pray you can feel the same way." She followed Georg and Alvie into the kitchen.

The back of Jud's neck tickled. He knew before he turned that he would see Wande.

"Do you not want Alvie to play the piano?" Her face paled under the color the Texas sun had added to her skin.

"It is hard," he said. "No one has played the piano since . . . Billie." He drew out a long sigh. "But I am sorry I scared Alvie. What good is a piano if no one plays it? Marion was brave enough to take the first step."

Ma poked her head out the door. "Are you two coming to eat or not? Your food is getting cold."

Alvie went home with Georg after the noon meal, sparing Jud an afternoon full of wedding plans. Somehow throughout the evening he kept bumping into Wande. When he went back for a second piece of pie, she was washing the dishes. When he retired to his desk to balance the books, she was thumbing through an English Bible. Even when he went to his room, he found Wande changing the bed linens. He stood in the doorway.

"I can make my own bed." His voice sounded crosser than he intended.

"I only want to help. I just finished ironing the sheets. I love clean sheets. They smell like fresh air and sunshine."

He lifted his pillow to his nose. "Too bad we can't bottle that and spray it around the barn."

She giggled. "There, I am done." She brushed past him to get to the door, then turned. "And Jud?" She had almost conquered the *J* sound in his name. "Thank you for inviting us back to work." She walked out the door and disappeared in the direction of Marion's room.

Jud wished she hadn't left so abruptly.

A screech like a wild animal pierced the air in front of the Fleischers' barn on Friday morning. Wande ran from the house and arrived at the same time as Papa and Georg.

Mama stood in the middle of the chicken pen, an empty basket dangling from one arm. Wande pinched her nose against the stench. When she approached the fence, she could see the cause. Bloody feathers and bones lay scattered across the pen.

"What is this?" Papa took Mama in his arms.

"Some kind of animal, it must have been."

"But if a coyote got in, surely we would have heard something." Georg walked the fence. "There is no break. It is as if a person did this."

Wande shivered. "Are they all gone?"

Mama could only nod. "Every one of our laying hens is eaten."

In big ways and small, Texas demanded a lot from them. Wande lifted her chin. She was ready to fight back.

CHAPTER TWENTY-SEVEN

The sun had not yet risen. Last night Mama asked Wande to accompany her to market Saturday morning, though she only had a small bin of okra and cucumbers to sell. Mama would look for more hens when she was in town. She carried a handful of the beautiful purple flowers that grew everywhere to lay at Drud's grave.

Wande's heart tightened. "Do you think the illness has passed?"

Mama shook her head. "We hear nothing out here. I am not used to country life. Always I have lived in the city." Tears crept into her eyes. This first year in the new land was wearing her mother down.

"Come, Georg is ready to leave. He wants to see his Ertha." Wande hoped the trip would encourage her mother. As for Georg, nothing bothered him much, not when thoughts of his beloved filled his mind. Though still weak, the youngest Schumann girl had survived the cholera. "We want to get there before the sun is too high and the best chickens are gone."

"Mrs. Gruber should have some chickens I can buy. But I do not know if I wish to pay what she will charge."

"I would not worry about the price. She will be reasonable." Wande hooked her arm with her mother's and led her to the wagon, where Georg helped them onto the seat. Alvie waved from her bedroom window.

They traveled west in the pearly dark, the light behind them not quite illuminating the road ahead. Still, Georg handled the oxen expertly and avoided most of the ruts.

Georg set up the stall in their favorite spot in front of the store. Mrs. Grenville waved to them from the door. "I didn't know you were coming to town today, Mrs. Fleischer. How good to see you too, Wande. I was so sorry to hear about Drud."

Georg made sure they were settled before he took off, whistling, toward Ertha's house.

"It's good to hear someone whistling," Mrs. Grenville said. "It's been all doom and gloom around here." She remained on the porch to chat.

"Is the sickness still bad?" Mama said.

Wande stayed busy, arranging her vegetables. To encourage people to buy the okra, she had written down a couple of recipes from Mrs. Morgan, one for frying, one for soup.

"Ten more died this week. Poor Doc Treviño looks like a ghost. He's hardly eating or sleeping." Mrs. Grenville lifted the edge of her apron to her eyes. "That, and we received word this week of more casualties from the war."

"I am sorry to hear that." Mama spread a bright tablecloth over the stall. "Maybe people will want to come out and meet with others. Our fresh vegetables will help those who are ill."

"No disrespect, Mrs. Fleischer, but I'm afraid it's going to take more than a few garden vegetables to cure this cholera." She smiled. "If there's any you don't sell, I'll take 'em for you."

"Are you and Mr. Grenville well?"

"So far, praise the Lord." Mrs. Grenville went back into the store.

The sun had not fully risen, yet the air was already sweltering. Wande did not like this Texas summer. Even the plants protested. At least the covering over the stall provided some shelter. A few more people set up stalls along the street, about half the usual number.

"There is Mrs. Gruber. I will ask about chickens." Mama left. She stopped at a number of stalls and chatted with the women.

Frau Decker—a regular customer as well as the lead soprano in the chorale society—stopped by and turned over the okra. "I tried frying these. They were okay. Not as good as sautéed mushrooms."

"If you want to try the okra again," Wande said, "I have a soup recipe you can make."

"Who wants soup in this heat?" Frau Decker thought about it.

Wande gave her the recipe anyway. When they came to Texas, she did not know she would have to learn a whole new way of cooking.

"So you still have vegetables to sell."

Wande turned her head at the familiar voice. "Jud, I did not expect to see you here."

"Marion insisted she had to do some shopping." He lounged against the railing in front of the store. He nodded down the street, where Marion chatted with Miss Potson. "And Ma thought it would be good for her to get out of the house."

"Your mother is a wise woman. Marion should not hide away at the house as if she has done something wrong." Mama had insisted Wande join the chorale society in spite of the rumors about her and Konrad. Wande was glad she did. "Do you have business in town yourself?"

Jud's nearness made her feel crowded.

"Do you have any tomatoes?" a customer asked.

Wande shook her head. "The heat has killed them all."

The woman passed on.

Jud hadn't moved. He stood there, as if he belonged.

"Marion asked me, if I ran into you, to tell you Alvie's welcome any time she wants to come play the piano." Jud swiveled his head around. Georg was with Ertha, but no sign of the girl. "Where is Alvie? I expected to find her here."

"She stayed home this morning. Papa made her a special chest for her things, and she is busy arranging everything. She is making a doll out of a corncob."

Billie had one special doll, one that still waited for her to return. If he told Ma about Alvie's corncob, she'd want to give her Billie's doll. He might ask her about it. Or he might not. "If you don't mind, I'll wait here until Marion and Ma finish shopping."

"You do not wish to join the game of checkers?" Wande nodded to the men across the street.

Jud was reluctant to leave with Tom around. "I'll hang out here."

"Then sit down." Wande shifted a few crates under the stall and pulled out a low stool.

He eyed it. "I think I'll stand. My knees would hit my chin if I took that seat."

"I am sorry."

"You have nothing to be sorry for." Marion had insisted he keep Wande company. He wondered if Wande was aware of Marion's machinations. Her own disappointment with Tom had driven her to help Jud—at least that's how it appeared to him. She found opportunities to throw them together several times every day. Only yesterday, on Wande's day off, she sent him to the Fleischers' farm to "borrow" some butter.

Wande listened to a customer explain how to make sweet pickles from cucumbers, her face intent in concentration. No, Jud thought. Such an idea would cause Wande as much consternation as it caused him.

Marion and Ma left the dry goods store and meandered down the street. Wande waved at them. Marion smiled and walked in their direction while Ma stayed behind at a stall to haggle over the price of some seeds.

"I've just heard good news," Marion said. "Our church is going to have a picnic social after the services tomorrow. The pastor just told me." She nudged Jud in the back, where Wande couldn't see. "You will come, of course. And your family is also welcome. No need to bring any food. Ma is already planning enough food to feed General Scott and the army."

Wande agreed quickly enough, Jud thought as he got dressed on Sunday morning. She checked with her parents, and soon the event became a joint venture between the German Lutheran church and their congregation. He tucked in his shirt, buttoned his trousers, and opened the door.

Marion stood at the door to her bedroom wearing her new spring dress. That was a change. She had worn only the darkest colors she owned since Tom broke their engagement, as if she had gone into mourning. "You're wearing that?" she said.

"What's wrong with it? It's clean."

"But we're going to a party." Marion shook her head with a gesture that said "men." The clock chimed eight. "We have time. Come on." She led him back into his room. "You have a vest in here somewhere." She opened his dresser drawers.

"Wait a minute. I don't want you going through my things."

Jud frowned. "And I'm not wearing a vest. It's the middle of July, and it's only a church social."

Marion kept searching.

He stretched his arm in front of the drawer, keeping her from digging any further. "I'm serious. Even if you find it, I won't wear it."

Marion pouted for a second. "Then at least wear a different shirt. That one's been washed so many times, it's the color of soap. " She stopped rustling among the clothes. "How about this one?" She handed him a blue and red plaid shirt that always reminded Jud of the flag.

"Not that one. This one." Ma stood at the door, holding a fine linen shirt that had belonged to Pa.

"I can't . . ."

"You can—and you will. You are much the same size as your pa. And you'll do us proud."

"Since when are you both so concerned about how I look?" Jud felt like he was ten years old, when Ma forced his head under the pump and made him clean up.

Ma looked at him from head to toe, concentration forming wrinkles around her eyes. "Too bad I don't have time to trim your hair."

"Longer hair is in fashion, Ma." Marion patted the back of Jud's head. "Just be sure you brush it."

Jud had enough. "I can't change if you don't leave."

Marion grinned and shut the door behind her.

When they arrived at church—a little late, thanks to all the attention to his attire—wagons lined the lawn. He helped Marion and Ma from the wagon, and they hustled inside. Rather than the sparse attendance Jud had expected due to the cholera epidemic, everyone who could stand had come out—including some people he hadn't seen in church for years.

On the left side of the aisle, in the fourth row where his

family normally sat, the Fleischers waited for them. Alvie spotted them and tugged at Wande's sleeve.

When Jud saw Wande in her mauve dress, he was glad he had taken the time to change. Marion nudged him forward and first into the pew, so he ended up sitting next to Wande. Her eyes swept over him swiftly, but he knew she had noticed his fancier-than-usual shirt and the extra attention he had paid to his hair.

The pew was so crowded, there was barely space to slip a thin Bible between him and Wande. He was aware of her every movement, the way she explained the differences in the service to her family, and her sweet soprano voice ringing out with the English hymns she had come to know and love.

Jud allowed himself to get lost in the music, in worship of the God worthy of all praise, his voice harmonizing with Wande's.

When the last amen sounded, Alvie darted out through the open doors with the other children, searching for the promised game of town ball. Their mothers bustled after them, ready to spread food across the plank tables assembled on the lawn. Mrs. Fleischer followed Ma.

"I should go." Wande fidgeted at his side.

"No, they have plenty of help." Marion patted her hand and followed their mothers out the door. "You stay and keep Jud company."

"Don't feel like you have to keep me company. I am old enough to take care of myself. But if you insist . . ." Jud extended his arm to Wande.

Wande accepted and they walked down the aisle. "I am certain you can do anything you want to."

Jud's heart warmed as if he had just been given a Christmas orange.

The sanctuary had almost emptied. Jud saw the gleam of

the worn wooden pews, the white walls in need of fresh paint, the piano even more out of tune than theirs at home. The church had taught him about the Lord—and so much else—since he was a young boy. He wondered if the Fleischers felt the same way about their place of worship. He held the door for Wande, and they stepped into the sunshine.

Marion waved to them, then froze in place. She stared at something behind them.

Jud turned his head.

Tom came around the corner of the church with a redhead by his side. Their laughter said it all.

CHAPTER TWENTY-EIGHT

Marion forced herself to stop staring, to turn away and walk toward Jud and Wande. "I began to think you got lost inside the church." She managed a chuckle.

"Do you want me to punch Tom in the nose?" Jud asked in a soft voice.

This time Marion's chuckle was genuine. "I'd love to see it, but it wouldn't change anything. It wouldn't even make me feel any better. And Ma would tan our hides for sure."

"Why would I need to tan your hides?" Ma said. Then she glanced up and saw Tom with his new girl. "Oh. I can guess." She leaned across the table until she was less than a foot from Marion's face. "You listen to me. You will smile and have fun—or at least pretend you're having fun—and don't let that man think you give a grain of salt about his goings on."

"Come for a walk with me." Wande took Marion's arm and they strolled down the street in the direction of the parsonage. "I did not think things could get any worse when

Konrad married another. Now I realize how blessed I was. But I did not have to watch it happen. I am sorry." They reached the corner and turned back.

"Ma is right. I'll pretend I don't care. And I don't want you feeling sorry for me. You go spend time with Jud. I insist." Marion's voice wobbled, but her eyes remained dry. "I'll be all right."

"Tell me more about this game of town ball."

Jud let Wande draw him away from Marion toward the area where two captains were choosing sides. Alvie jumped up and down with the others. "Pick me! Pick me!"

Wande stopped where the numerous conversations around them made it unlikely anyone would overhear. "Marion does not want you to charge after Tom like an angry bear. It only makes it harder."

"I'll take your word for it." Jud started to stick his hands in his pockets, then remembered these trousers didn't have pockets. Instead he ran his hand through his hair. "May I ask you a personal question?"

She turned those blue eyes on him, ones that remained icy calm whatever the circumstances. "You are my friend. You may ask." She smiled. "But I may not answer."

"Fair enough." Jud faced the town ball field. Alvie cheered when she was called to join one of the teams. Billie had never enjoyed the game. "Does what happened with Schuster still trouble you?"

When Wande looked at him, relief had melted the ice blue of her eyes. "I do not regret not marrying Konrad."

"But . . ." Jud studied her face. Something else still troubled her.

"Some things a girl does not discuss even with her good

friends." She gave him a gentle smile. "Let us watch the game until the food is ready."

A little stung that Wande wouldn't share her troubles, Jud did his best to explain the systems of balls and strikes, bases and home runs. Wande made intelligent comments that indicated she heard what he said, but her interest flagged until Alvie came to bat. She flinched at how close the ball came to Alvie's elbow. "This game is dangerous. If that ball hits her . . ."

"It could break her arm. I know. Some mothers tried to talk Doc Treviño into campaigning against allowing children to play." The memory made him smile.

"But he did not succeed."

"Instead, he played with them. He said the exercise was good for children. His biggest concern was that their skirts might trip the girls when they ran the bases."

"Then the girls should not play." Wande took a hesitant step forward as if to remove Alvie.

"What upset the mothers most was when he said maybe the girls should wear trousers when they played."

"I do not believe you."

"It's the truth. He didn't get his way, as you can see. By the time the girls start wearing long dresses, most of them stop playing."

Wande looked down at her dress to where the hem hung over her shoes. She shook her head. "I would not choose to run for play."

The dinner bell sounded, and the game broke up.

Wande woke up early to join Georg on his morning trek to the Morgan Ranch. She had discovered the Morgans had a passion equal to her own for making pickles, but they used a different recipe. Frau Morgan begged her to come work an additional day to help put up the last of the cucumber harvest. They had split the vegetables between them. Mama had enlisted Alvie in the pickle-making process at home, and the whole family looked forward to crunchy, zesty treats through the winter months when fresh produce wasn't available.

Wande gathered six eggs, a good number, from the hens they had purchased for the reinforced chicken coop. She paused by the cattle pen to pet Karlina. Georg's baby calf was growing into a pretty little heifer. Karlina bumped her hand in welcome. Wande enjoyed the calf, but she preferred spending time with the foals at the ranch. Someday they might have horses to call their own. Imagine. A family like the Fleischers back in Germany would never have dreamed of owning horses. Here in Texas, several of the German families who had lived for some time in Victoria had one, even two, horses. Some displayed the distinctive features of the Morgan horses—their proud carriage and upright neck—that Wande had come to recognize. Products, no doubt, of the Running M Ranch.

By the time Wande took the eggs into the house and ate a simple breakfast of toast with peach preserves, Georg was ready to leave. Mornings like this, Wande wished they *did* have a horse. Walking to the ranch house took an hour or more. Driving their wagon took almost as long, since they had to go by way of the road and not straight as the crow flies.

This early, the temperature hovered at a comfortable mark, and Wande enjoyed the exercise. A rain shower had fallen the night before, and the air smelled as fresh as a field of daisies. A jackrabbit froze beside a crape myrtle, then hopped away. Her sturdy walking shoes cushioned the pebbles and occasional twigs beneath her feet. Passing beneath an acacia tree, she heard the rambling song of a goldfinch. A year ago, in Offenbach, she could never have imagined a place like this. Texas was not like the land she pictured from the Verein's descriptions. Honey did not run like sap from trees. But it was a new land, a good land—a land so big, so full of possibilities, she felt free to dream big enough to fill the space. She hummed "Amazing Grace."

"You sound happy this morning." Georg swung a water bag in one hand and a rifle in the other.

"I am. God is good, and I think . . . I'm beginning to like this Texas."

"I like Texas too." Georg smiled. "I met my Ertha here."

Ertha. Of course. Texas had given things to them as well as taken them away. So far she had lost Ulla, Konrad, and Drud. This land was demanding of her. Perhaps this was what Jud felt about Texas. The country had demanded his father's blood. He belonged. Now she could say the same.

She stopped at the creek that divided their two properties and reached into the water for a drink. Refreshing, even if a little warm—and cleaner than the water in town. If people had good, fresh food and cool creek water, maybe they would not get sick so easily. None of the families out this way had taken ill.

They arrived at the ranch house, and Jud rode up on his horse at the same time. Wande wondered where he had been so early.

"There you are," he said. "Ma is eager to start on the pickles."

"I am here, ready to work." Wande smoothed the skirt of her dress, aware of how worn and dusty the blue calico must appear. Not that it should matter. She was there to work, not to make an impression on Jud. She ran her hands under the pump.

"I will see you at dinner." Georg headed for the barn.

"Make that late this afternoon. We're going up-country today." Jud patted his saddlebag. "Ma's fixed us a meal. She wants us out of the kitchen today." He tipped his hat. "Good day to you, Wande." The slow smile that lit his face warmed her insides like oatmeal on a cold morning. She watched as he mounted JM and headed out with Georg.

The ladies finished pickling all twelve dozen cucumbers before Jud and Georg returned. Wande's muscles ached, and she felt drained from every pore, not to mention coated with a salty layer. Honest labor.

"You look tired," Mrs. Morgan said. "You're welcome to stay for supper. Or spend the night."

Wande closed her eyes, imagining the pillows on Marion's bed and the always plentiful fare that Frau Morgan cooked. But Mama and Papa were expecting her and Georg—and would worry if they did not come home. "I appreciate the offer, but I must go home. I will take a glass of tea first." Through the window, she saw Jud and Georg had returned. Jud swung down from the horse, his legs bowed but a smile on his face. Georg said something to him, then started across the yard toward the Fleischer farm.

"What is he doing?" Wande jumped to her feet and ran to the door. "Georg!"

Her brother turned and waved, then continued walking. Wande put her hands on her hips. She did not wish to walk home by herself.

Water ran from the pump, and she heard a garbled voice from beneath the gushing water. "Don't blame your brother. It was my idea." Jud lifted a dripping head. "I offered to escort you home. I figured you'd be pretty tired after today."

"You do not need to do that."

"It's my pleasure. How would you like to ride Apple?"

"But I do not know how to ride a horse." Perhaps she would have to ride double with Jud.

CHAPTER TWENTY-NINE

"You don't ride?" Jud scratched his head. "I should have expected that. I forgot I had to teach Georg. Are you willing to ride behind me? Georg has already headed home."

Color flowed into Wande's cheeks. Jud couldn't tell if the thought of riding behind him embarrassed her, pleased her, or just left her confused. Although he hadn't planned on it, he liked the idea.

Wande looked back at the house, at Ma and Marion on the porch.

"Go ahead," Marion said. "All you have to do is hold on to Jud."

Ma leaned over the railing. "You're welcome to spend another night with us, but I know you're aching to get home."

Wande nodded, descended the steps, and stopped in front of JM. The horse snuffled his lips across her hand, seeking a treat. She stroked his head. "When I was Alvie's age, I dreamed of owning a beautiful horse like you. I will not let you scare me now." She looked up at Jud.

Looking down into her trusting face, Jud realized how high the horse must seem to her.

He lifted his left foot out of the stirrup. Marian helped Wande get her foot into the stirrup and gave her a boost onto the back of the horse. Jud felt her settling behind the saddle and slid his foot back in the stirrup. Marion helped her arrange her skirts.

"As soon as you're ready," Jud said, "put your arms around me, and I'll get you home." He'd see Wande home safely. That was all that he cared about at the moment.

Wande's arms sneaked around his waist, but she held herself rigid, keeping distance between them. He could tell her it would go easier if she leaned against him, but she'd figure that out as they rode. He didn't want to make her feel any more uncomfortable than she already did. "Are you ready?"

"Yes." He felt her breath on his ear.

Jud squeezed JM, and the horse ambled in the direction of the field. But he turned the horse around and headed for the road. There he could see upcoming difficulties more clearly and make the ride as easy as possible on Wande.

He urged JM into a slow jog. Although JM had a smooth trot, the movement caused small jolts each time the horse's body dropped away. Jud didn't notice it until Wande cried out.

Her hold on him tightened. "I am afraid I will fall off."

Jud slowed JM to a walk. "Slide in closer to me. You'll be safer."

Wande adjusted her position, and Jud's back felt like fire where she touched him. "Better?"

"Yes." The word came out in a gasp. Jud knew conversation was pointless as long as they were riding.

They passed under the Running M sign and turned north for the Fleischer farm. "Do you know the boundaries for your farm?"

"The fence," Wande said.

Jud started to shake his head, then stopped. He didn't want to knock Wande in the head with his hat. "That's just the part that's fenced in. See that stand of trees up yonder?" He pointed to a line of acacias. "That's your southern boundary."

A jackrabbit ran in front of JM, and he shied to the left, causing Wande to lurch into Jud and hang on tighter.

"We almost had rabbit for some of that stew your mother likes to fix," Jud said when the horse settled into his walk again.

"Hasenpfeffer."

"Strange how some of your German words are almost the same as English and some are so different."

They passed the tree line. "Now we're on your land." He couldn't wish for a prettier day, the sky unmarred by a single cloud. They passed a field dotted with flowers, a calf gamboling and bawling.

"Stop." Wande's arm tightened. "That is Karlina."

Jud turned JM in the direction of the field and urged him to a trot. The heifer had the distinctive white streak down her back that Jud remembered, and she was bawling at the top of her lungs. Where was Elsie, the calf's mother? Jud stopped beside the calf, and she bolted a few yards.

Jud stood in the stirrups and looked in each direction. No sign of the mother cow. "What is she doing out here, alone?"

"I do not know." Wande sounded worried. "During the day we put them in the pasture near the house. But it is fenced."

"We'll get her home." He reached for the rope on the front of the saddle and circled it over his head as he rode near the calf.

Karlina bolted, but he let out the rope and it landed perfectly around the calf's neck. She bawled as it tightened and prevented her from running.

"I'm going to have to get down. You'll have to let go." Jud waited until Wande straightened and released her hold on him, then jumped down. He knelt beside the frightened heifer. "You've had a hard day, haven't you?" He ran his hands down her back and spoke softly. Karlina didn't stop calling for her mother, but she did stop shivering. When she quit shaking her head to rid herself of the rope, he adjusted it so it wouldn't harm her.

Back in the saddle, he said, "We'll take it slow and easy from here. Karlina will follow along behind."

The calf trotted after the horse while Jud worried on the problem. It would be hard for the Fleischers to make a go of it in Texas if they couldn't even manage to keep their animals penned up.

Wande worried about Karlina. After the coyotes had gotten into the chicken coop, Papa and Georg had spent days checking all the fences. They were good and strong, although Papa wanted to build stone walls later. No animal could break through a stone wall, and only a few could jump over one.

Wande's legs ached, and she suspected they would be chafed raw in places. Even so, she had enjoyed the ride. She hadn't realized how strong Jud must be, how easy he made it seem to handle the horses, when she could feel the strain in his side to control JM.

Karlina bawled behind her. Wande wanted to look over her shoulder but didn't dare, afraid any movement would upset her balance and she would fall.

They rounded the final bend, and the farmhouse came in sight. Karlina let out another blat. From the direction of the yard came an answering bellow, a belligerent sound nothing like Elsie's usual greeting.

Karlina answered, and Wande heard the faster plodding of feet. Something—the calf—bumped into the side of the horse and jostled Wande. She clutched a handful of Jud's shirt.

JM spurted forward and raced the last few yards to the house. Wande held on to Jud and closed her eyes, certain they would fall at any minute. They stopped as suddenly as they had started running.

"We're here," Jud said. "You can let go."

Wande opened her eyes and saw Mama and Papa and Alvie—Georg must not have made it home yet—staring at her with wide eyes. A flush spread across her cheeks. She released Jud and sat back. She looked down at the ground. A long way down. Jud held her arm and she slid down JM's side.

Papa undid the loop around Karlina's neck, and the calf rushed to reach her mother.

Mama hurried to Wande's side. "*Liebchen,* are you all right? The way that horse was running . . ."

"I am fine. How is Karlina?"

Back safe in the cattle pen, the calf was busy nursing and comforting herself. Papa ran hands along her legs, nodding. "She has not come to any harm. We must thank you, Herr Morgan."

"Couldn't leave the little thing all alone out there in the pasture, could I?" Jud grinned. He walked toward the enclosure. "This must be where you keep them during the day." He walked along the rails, bending here and there to check.

Wande took a step forward, but her legs would not support her. She had not felt this unsteady since landing in Carlshafen after months at sea.

Jud grunted, stooped, and checked something. He straightened and moved on. "How'd she get out? The fence seems secure."

"The door was open." Papa spread his hands. "We do not

know how. Just enough for the little one to get out."

Georg jogged into the yard and heard the story.

"I am remiss." Ma carried a pitcher of water from the house. "You must be thirsty after your ride, Herr Morgan. Here is some water, or I can fix you some coffee."

"I'll be fine. But I'd better get home." He swatted Karlina playfully on the back. "She's growing into a fine little heifer. Next time, be sure you keep the door latched. No telling what animal might have attacked her out there in the fields." Tipping his hat, he climbed on JM and headed back down the road.

Wande took a step and paused. Her muscles didn't want to move.

"Wande, come inside. You must be tired." Mama took her arm and helped her across the yard.

"You rode his horse." Alvie pouted. "I want to ride a horse." She grinned. "Was it fun?"

"Until JM started running." In fact, Wande had enjoyed the ride until she had to get off the horse's back. Maybe her muscles would adjust to riding if she practiced. "Marion says they must give us all lessons, that a good horse is as important as a milk cow here in Texas."

"They sell horses," Mama said.

"Because it is too far to walk from one place to another." Wande lifted her foot to climb the porch steps. "I will need some of your ointment, Mama," she whispered.

Mama led Wande through the house, redolent with the scent of pickles, to her bedroom. She brought fresh water and her ointment. "Do you want my help?" Wande shook her head, and Mama left her to repair the damage.

The bed beckoned, but Wande had promised to help Mama finish with the pickles. She freshened up as best as she could, dabbed some ointment on the sore spots, and headed back to the kitchen.

". . . why didn't he say so this morning?" Papa held a cup of coffee. "Wande, come in. We are discussing what happened with the cows."

She slid onto her usual chair, careful not to wince. Mama handed her a cup of coffee and brought out cream and sugar. Wande added a bit of both.

"We were wondering why Herr Morgan did not say he would bring you home tonight when he was here this morning." Papa's eyes had flecks of iron, as they did when he was angry.

"He was not here this morning." Wande put down her cup. "Was he?"

Papa looked at Georg, and he nodded. "I saw one of the Morgan horses. It must have been Jud."

"You were so happy to see him, you forgot all about closing the gate." Alvie giggled.

CHAPTER THIRTY

Wande's face heated faster than if she had been stuck in the oven. "But I did not see Jud this morning until I arrived at the ranch."

"It is all right, *Liebchen*." Papa patted her shoulder. "You do not have to hide the truth. We are happy that you have found another man."

"But I have not . . . he is not . . ."

"Your head has not caught up with your heart yet," Mama said. "But in your heart, you know. Such good news for you."

"He did ask to bring you home today." Georg shuffled his feet. "I am happy for you."

"You rode behind him on his horse." Alvie sighed. "Like a knight rescuing his lady from danger."

Wande stared at them all. "You think . . . Jud is courting me?"

Mama and Papa exchanged a look. "I do not know how *Amerikaners* arrange such things, but it seems that way to us."

Wande sank onto the Biedermeier chair and shook her

head. No. They were wrong. She had known of Konrad's interest, had been expecting it. But she had never expected the gruff *Amerikaner* to be interested in her, not in that way. "You think I forgot to latch the pasture gate because I was thinking about Jud?"

"It all turned out well. I am not worried. Jud had a chance to be a hero." Papa winked. "But do not do it again."

Mama hugged Wande. "And invite him inside for breakfast the next time he comes in the morning."

"But Jud was not here this morning, I am certain." Wande wasn't sure why the thought troubled her so.

Marion heard whistling when Jud came in a little before supper. That silly cat song they learned from the Fleischers. She raced to the door. "How did it go?"

Jud was petting an almost-grown cat, the pick of the litter from Mittens and Marmalade that Alvie named Puddles. The cat purred loudly, squeezing her eyes. Jud had the same look, as if he had just discovered a bowl of fresh cream. "How did what go?"

"Taking Wande home, you silly goose."

Jud began to smile, but the cat jumped out of his arms and he turned serious. "I am concerned about how the Fleischers are going to make a go of the farm. First the coyotes got at the hens, and now someone left the gate to the pasture unlatched. The calf got out."

"Oh no."

"Don't worry." He grinned. "I rescued Karlina—that's the name Georg gave the calf—and we led her home. Everything went well until she heard her mama and tried to run ahead of JM."

Marion pictured a race between the horse and the desperate calf and laughed. "That must have been a sight." She looked at him sideways. "We've all left a gate open a time or two. Don't see why you have yourself in a twist about it."

He shrugged. "He's jumped into farming and hasn't bothered asking anyone a thing about what works in Texas, as far as I can tell."

He led JM to the barn, and she followed. "So your pride is hurt, is that it? What makes you think you know anything about farming?"

He removed the saddle and gave JM a feedbag while he rubbed down the gelding. "As far as I can see, they have this guidebook, and all the German farmers get together in some society that discusses the best methods. But even raising horses took some changes here in Texas. Pa was just learning the ins and outs of it when he died, and I had to learn things the hard way." He huffed. "I'd have welcomed some advice."

"Wande asked for advice about the kitchen garden." Marion combed her fingers through the horse's mane. "Did she enjoy the ride?"

Jud hesitated before continuing to rub down his animal. "I think she did."

Marion saw a gleam in Jud's eye. He was coming around to see what a find Wande Fleischer was—German or not. She'd have to wait for Wande's version of the events until she returned to work Monday.

But when Marion next saw Wande, she didn't waste time discussing the ride with Jud. She brushed it aside, a worried expression on her face that Marion hoped did not reflect her true feelings. She had one question on her mind. "Did anyone from the ranch ride over to our farm Friday morning?"

Marion had to think back. "Like who?" She and Ma rarely went riding, and that day they had spent the early hours preparing for pickling. "Jud and Bert were out early checking on the colts, but as far as I know they didn't head in your direction. Spill the beans, Wande. Did you enjoy your ride?"

Wande brushed her hair back from her face. "I did." She blushed. "Alvie cannot stop talking about it. She thinks she should have been on the horse with Jud. She keeps begging me to ask him to teach her to ride."

"Maybe he can give her some lessons before she goes back to school. Music and horses. She's so much like our Billie, sometimes it hurts. And other times it's a comfort. She's not Billie, but we get to enjoy having a little girl around the house again."

Wande smiled. "And you are like the sister I lost. God did a wonderful thing when He made our wagon break down by the road to your ranch. He gave us each a good friend."

"Yes, He did." And maybe, if Marion's guess was right, more than friends.

Wande tackled the subject of the unidentified Morgan horse with Georg before he went home that afternoon. Normally, after they finished the noon meal, she jumped up and worked on the dishes giving her brother only a quick good-bye. Today she followed him outside. "Let me walk with you a short way."

He looked at her sideways. They walked to the edge of the yard before pausing. "What is troubling you?"

"I wanted to ask you again about the Morgan horse you saw at the house last Friday morning."

A pained expression crossed Georg's face. "I know what I saw."

"Was it a horse you recognized? Like JM or Apple or the stallion Midnight with the mares?"

Georg considered her question. "Not exactly. But you

know that Morgan is a kind of horse. I am certain it was a Morgan. Who else would be riding it but someone from the Running M?"

"But they sell their horses. Other people own Morgan horses."

Georg shrugged. "If someone from town who has a Morgan horse came out this way, why did he not come in?"

"Perhaps he was going to the ranch and passed by our house."

Georg snorted. "They would have to pass the ranch to reach us."

"Oh." Georg was right. She did not have the best sense of direction. "I believe you. But do you believe me? I did not speak to Jud that morning."

Georg considered it. "I believe you did not speak to him. But he could have been at the house even if you did not speak to him." He grinned. "Perhaps he needed to build up courage to speak to you."

"Jud does not lack courage for anything."

Georg stared at her, and Wande's cheeks warmed.

"I must get home. Papa wants to make the stone wall before we add a room to the house." Georg slung his canteen strap over his shoulder. "And we must add the room before my wedding." He walked away quickly, love speeding his steps.

The next morning, Alvie burst into the ranch house with Georg and ran into the kitchen. She danced in front of Jud. "Is it true? You will teach me how to ride a horse?"

"Alvie."

The others' laughter drowned out Wande's reprimand.

"I will, but it won't be today."

Alvie's face fell so far, she almost toppled.

"Georg, Bert, and I will be busy today. Can you come back tomorrow?"

“Yes.” Alvie turned to Georg. “You will bring me again tomorrow?”

“I will.”

“Make that Thursday, and we will go home together,” Wande said.

Alvie scowled, but then her good humor reasserted itself. “May I have a music lesson today?”

Again laughter overrode Wande’s frustration. If Alvie lived in the Morgan house, she would be a spoiled little girl—more than she already was as the youngest in the Fleischer household.

After dinner, when Wande went outside to check the clothes on the line—thanks to the bright sunshine, several items were dry enough for ironing—she heard piano music floating through the open window. Alvie played with confidence pieces she had practiced. She had learned quite a bit over the summer. But she showed some hesitation when she worked on a new piece.

Wande might have objected to Alvie taking music lessons. She might have objected to doing this part of the laundry by herself. But when she saw the smiles on Marion and Mrs. Morgan’s faces as Alvie played, she felt this too was part of her job—allowing the Morgans joy after they had lost their Billie. She finished gathering clothes and carried the basket inside to the kitchen. While she ironed, she hummed along with the simple songs until they stopped. “Alvie?”

Alvie came in. “Mrs. Morgan promised me milk and cookies.”

“Come sit by me a minute.”

With a glance toward the pantry, Alvie complied. “What is it?”

Wande turned the iron on end so it wouldn’t burn through the fabric and studied her sister. When she was Alvie’s age, she had Ulla and their brothers for company. In Offenbach,

Alvie played with the children next door. Out here in the country, she had no one her own age. Mama might not be the only one to get lonely. "I bet you like Karlina."

Alvie blinked. Perhaps she thought Wande wanted to scold her for the music lesson. "I do. She is sweet."

"And you spend time with her each day." Wande remembered a calf she had loved until he grew up and Papa sold him to the butcher. At least that wouldn't happen to Karlina. The family looked forward to having another milk cow.

"When Mama does not need me." Alvie took the pillowcase Wande had just ironed and folded it.

"Were you with Karlina last Friday?"

Alvie glared at Wande. "Do you think I left the gate open? I know better."

"Somebody left the gate open. And I have tried hard to remember. It was not me."

"I didn't do it." Tears pooled in Alvie's eyes.

Wande sighed. "I believe you."

If it wasn't Alvie—or Wande—then who had unlocked the gate so the calf could get out?

Who was the rider on the Morgan horse?

CHAPTER THIRTY-ONE

Your sister will make a fine rider some day," Jud said as he and Georg rode into the ranch's biggest pasture Friday morning.

"Which one?" Georg grinned.

"I was thinking of Alvie. She did well at her lesson yesterday." Jud was glad the brim of his hat shadowed his face.

"For days she has talked of nothing else but riding horses. There are Bert and Tucker." Georg pointed to where the other two cowboys waited.

Jud had sent the two hands out early to bring the stallion and his band of mares and colts in closer. The time had arrived to cull the two-year-olds from Midnight's band to begin their training. The army might come back through at any time, and Jud wanted to have fresh mounts ready to sell them. They had purchased several horses when they passed through Victoria earlier in the year.

"Wande has not said much about her ride," Georg said, "but I believe she enjoyed it."

Jud had wondered, but hadn't dared ask, knowing the ranch hands would tease him for sure.

"She should learn how to ride sidesaddle. Your mother as well. Every woman needs to know how to ride in case of an emergency."

"Even if we do not have a horse?" Georg patted Apple's flanks. "As soon as we have the money, I will get a good horse like this girl here."

Jud took having horses for granted—as much as the air he breathed. He wished he could just give the Fleischers a horse, but most of their good mounts had gone to the army. Even if he offered one, their pride would not allow them to accept such a gift.

"I have a question for you about your horses."

"I'm listening," Jud said.

"Do you remember last Friday? When you brought Wande home and rescued Karlina?"

"Yes." Was Georg about to give him a brotherly warning?

"Did anyone from the ranch come to our house that morning?"

"No, we were waiting for you to show up. Why?"

Georg stared into the distance. "I saw a Morgan horse in the yard that morning. I wondered if it was you."

"No, it wasn't me. Does it matter?"

Georg shrugged. "We wonder, that is all."

"Let's go." Jud clucked his tongue and squeezed JM's side. The horse broke into a gallop. Time to get started.

Bert tipped his hat when they rode up. "We're all set, Boss. Midnight's a little suspicious, and he's got 'em all bunched up yonder."

Jud looked. A quarter mile away, the black Morgan stallion pranced about on a rise. Jud smiled. Midnight was still one of the prettiest horses he'd ever seen, and most of his offspring had his looks, conformation, and bearing.

"Let's take 'em home." Jud urged JM forward.

The four riders galloped over the rise and circled the herd. The mares left off grazing and whinnied to their foals. The older colts leaped and bucked before setting out at full speed for the joy of running.

Jud and his men followed, moving up and swinging their ropes whenever any of the horses veered away. They drove the band across the vast pasture toward home.

When they neared the barn and the corrals, Bert rode ahead and prepared to man the gate. Jud, Georg, and Tucker stayed back, using their presence to guide the horses toward the opening. One of the lead mares ducked through the gate, and the rest of the band followed. Once inside, they circled, snorting and calling to each other.

Midnight drew up and let all his mares and the young stock pass him. He reared and neighed as the riders grew closer. The stallion darted right, then left, as if seeking to bar their access to his band.

"Come on, you've made your point," Jud said. "Either get in there with them or get out of here." He didn't care if Midnight stayed out in the big pasture for the day. He'd soon be letting the mares and the youngest colts out again. Only the two-year-olds held his interest now.

"Shut the gate, Bert!"

The cowboy swung the gate shut with all the horses except Midnight and the men's mounts inside.

Jud eased JM closer to Georg and Apple. "We'll let him get by us. As soon as we let a few mares loose again, he'll settle down."

Midnight ran by, through the gap between him and Tucker, kicking his heels at JM as he passed. In the open pasture he galloped in a big circle, then stopped to snort and paw the ground.

"Good work," Jud called to his men. He studied the horses milling inside the fence. "Start with that one."

An hour later, all the mares and young ones had joined Midnight in the pasture. Only one of the two-year-olds slipped past Bert at the gate. Tucker rode after him, roped him, and brought him back. The colts trotted inside the pen, whinnying to those outside.

Two hundred yards away, Midnight circled his smaller band. He halted and stamped, then let out a challenge.

"You rascal," Jud called.

Midnight pawed the ground and lowered his head.

"You don't scare me. I've known you since you were younger than those colts."

They both knew the dance and went through the moves every time Jud checked on the herd. Midnight ran back and forth, and Jud watched him, grinning. The Running M horses had spirit as well as looks and stamina. Eventually Midnight stopped and hung his head.

"It's okay," Jud shouted. "You were probably about ready to kick the young lads out anyway. They're getting old enough to challenge you."

Midnight tossed his head before running off. The mares and their young ones followed him out of sight toward the farthest reaches of the pasture.

Once the stallion disappeared, the colts settled down. Jud joined his men in watching them and picking the ones that showed the most promise.

One of the colts ran about the pen with extra fire and spirit.

"That is a fine horse," Georg said. "What is his name?"

"Crockett, after a hero of the Alamo." Jud slapped JM's neck. "Well, boy, that one just might let you retire in a few years." JM whinnied as if he disapproved. "Or we might keep him for stud purposes."

His men's teamwork pleased him, even Tucker, who worked only when Jud needed an extra hand. Georg had proven himself adept on the short roundup—perhaps more so than Tom. Jud knew he had made the right decision.

"Let's get something to eat, men. Then we'll start working with the best ones."

A good morning's work done. And tomorrow—well, on Saturday, he could head into town for market day and see Wande again. The thought made him want to move up his weekly bath by a day.

After breakfast, Jud raced through his Saturday morning chores before checking Ma and Marion. "Are you ladies ready to go?"

Marion looked at Ma. "Do you remember when he hated going to market every week?" She winked at her brother. "Give us five more minutes."

Although the garden would not produce any more vegetables until the fall season, Jud knew Wande had butter and eggs to sell. She had said she didn't intend to give up her spot by Grenville's store, so she would bring what little she had.

The day seemed half spent by the time they arrived in town. Jud called a greeting to Wande and scampered up the steps into the store. "Do you have the newspaper?" The *Victoria Advocate* had been in publication only since the war started last May, but already Jud looked forward to his weekly copy. A lot happened in a week's time across the state.

He took a seat beside Wande—she had taken to bringing a tall stool for him. "How's it going today?"

She frowned. "The butter is soft in spite of keeping it in a crock of cold water." She glanced up and down the street.

"More people are out today. They say there are no new cases of cholera this week."

"Praise the Lord." Jud perused the front page for news from the war—no new skirmishes. Again he thanked God he had no family fighting in this war. He turned to the editorial page and read the headline, "Wedded Bliss for Prince Carl?"

Wande glanced over his shoulder. "So Prince Carl has married. He is one of the men who formed the Verein. What does it say?"

So this man was responsible for the tide of German immigrants. Jud scanned the page. "His wife refuses to leave Germany for Texas, even though he built a castle for her." He laughed. "Did he really build a castle? Here in Texas?" He shook his head. "This is America. We don't have lords and castles here."

Prince Carl. Wande loved the romanticism of his story. A soldier as well as a prince, he had been forced to abandon his true love, his first wife Luise, because she was beneath his station. Last December he had married Princess Sophie. He bought the land where Neu-Braunfels was founded. His reports of the fabulous opportunities in New Germany, which trickled back to the homeland in 1844 and 1845, had convinced Papa to try the adventure.

She remembered reading that the prince had built a castle for his bride-to-be. She and Konrad had laughed about it. He said he could not build her a castle, but he would build her a sturdy home.

Apparently Prince Carl's dreams of marital happiness had proved as elusive as hers.

Jud read most of the article aloud, stopping every sentence or two to laugh or comment. "What kind of man lets his wife decide where they will live?"

Wande wanted to grab the paper from Jud. Prince Carl was a brave soldier and a visionary. "How would you feel if I made fun of Sam Houston?"

Frau Decker stopped by the stall, interrupting their debate. "Do you not have more vegetables?"

"Today just eggs and butter. Would you buy pickles if we sell them?"

Pastor Bader came up behind Frau Decker.

"A good *Gewürzgurke*? You have them?"

"I'll bring some next week."

Jud continued to chuckle. The pastor caught sight of the paper. "What is the news of Prince Carl?"

Jud lowered the page.

Wande spoke before Jud said anything. "He may not come back to Texas."

"I will look for your pickles next week." Frau Decker left without buying anything.

"That is sad about Prince Carl." Pastor Bader shook his head. He leaned against the store railing as if waiting for an invitation to join the conversation.

Jud tilted back on the stool. "That gave me a good laugh." He set the stool back on all its legs and looked at her, some of the amusement gone from his face. "You don't think it's funny."

"Do you think it is funny to make fun of someone's dreams? Or when a husband and a wife cannot agree?" She held out her hand for the paper. "Please do not say anything to my customers." She whispered so the pastor would not hear. "We respect Prince Carl, and I for one am sorry that all is not well with his marriage."

Jud shrugged and handed her the paper. "Sorry if I upset you." He clamped his hat on his head and stood. "Looks like Ma and Marion are almost done with their shopping. I'll see you at church tomorrow."

"You are right to be upset with that young man, Wande," the pastor said. "He doesn't have a very Christian view of marriage—or Germans—from what I understand."

"Pardon me, Pastor. You were saying?"

"I was about to ask if you would like to attend church with us tomorrow. I—we would love to hear your beautiful soprano voice in the congregation."

Perhaps she would go to church with her family, back to the familiar German hymns and words of Scripture she did not have to strain to understand. "*Danke* for inviting me. I think I will join you tomorrow."

Jud's actions reminded Wande that he resented most Germans for invading his Texas.

Wande could do many things, but she could not change her place of birth. She was as German as they came.

If Jud did not like Germans, he could not like her.

CHAPTER THIRTY-TWO

"Jud, wait a minute." Marion dashed out of the house toward the paddock where her brother was mounting JM. "Can you wait a few minutes and help us carry the tubs of water?" She was surprised she needed to ask. Since Ma had been burned so badly, he had helped with the Monday morning laundry, and he usually offered to do the heavy lifting.

Jud glanced to where Wande bent over the washtub, scrubbing clothes. He handed JM's reins to Bert and strode across the yard. "Are these ready?" Without waiting for Wande's reply, he picked up the tub and moved it. He looked around for the second tub and moved that as well before returning to Marion. "Anything else?"

Marion lifted her eyebrows. "No, we should be able to handle it from here." Jud was in one of his moods. Puddles, their kitten from Marmalade and Mittens' litter, played with the apron strings dangling from the line. Jud brushed by her and headed out of the yard.

Marion stared at Jud's departing back and shook her head. "Sorry about Jud's foul mood. You know he doesn't mean it."

Wande glanced up, her eyes opaque. "I understand." She returned her attention to the laundry, scrubbing the delicate fabric of Marion's buttercream dress so hard, Marion wondered if it would tear. Wande might understand Jud's attitude, but that didn't mean she didn't resent it. Her behavior was as out of character as Jud's. Something had happened, but neither would talk about it.

Marion refused to let her brother's mood ruin the morning. She looked at the sky, punctuated with puffy white clouds like lace, and sang the first words that came to her mind. "Fairest Lord Jesus."

After she finished the verse, Wande said, " '*Schönster Herr Jesus.*' That is a German hymn. Is it not a good thing that God speaks both English and German?" She smiled, and the ice in her eyes melted.

"Amen to that." Marion sang the second verse. "Fair are the meadows, fairer still the woodlands." Wande joined her in German. Next they sang one of Wande's favorites—she said the melody came from a drinking song—Martin Luther's "A Mighty Fortress Is Our God." They sang their way through half a dozen hymns until the laundry was ready to hang.

The wind whipped the laundry around the line. Puddles leaped for the apron strings and yowled when water from the sheets dripped on her. Wande laughed. "I am glad to sing."

"Me too." They hung the last of the laundry and headed inside for a short break.

"I did not think it was dinner time," Wande pointed to the chestnut Morgan mare grazing on the grass where it was tied to the porch railing.

Marion looked at the sky. "It's not. Someone has come calling." The horse looked familiar.

"We have company." Ma stood at the door, drying her hands on her apron. She added in a lower voice, "It's Tom. He says he needs to talk to you. Should I send him away?"

Marion glanced over Ma's shoulder, but Tom wasn't in sight. Probably he had taken a seat in the parlor, Ma plying him with a cup of coffee. She would offer hospitality to General Santa Anna if he showed up at the door. Marion Morgan was no coward. She lifted her chin and straightened her back. "I'll see him."

Ma nodded. "He's in the parlor."

"I'll go with Mrs. Morgan into the kitchen." Wande slipped through the door behind Ma.

Marion took a deep breath before entering the parlor. Tom stood behind Jud's desk. He had taken care with his attire, the way a man did when he wanted to impress a woman: a crisp, white shirt without a speck of dirt, freshly ironed, as if he had hired a woman to take care of his laundry. He had combed his hair into a high arc over his forehead, giving him a serious, respectable look.

He took two steps toward her.

She remained immobile. "Hello, Tom." She sat in the chair nearest the door, Ma's usual spot so she could slip in and out to take care of supper.

Tom glanced around, as if deciding what to do next, but remained standing. "Thanks for agreeing to see me."

"I expect this will be a short meeting," Marion said. "We don't have anything we need to talk about."

Deep red spread across his cheeks and down his neck, but he didn't drop his gaze. He reached into his pocket and withdrew a small box. "I bought this for you." He took one step forward. "May I?"

Fuming, she gestured for him to approach. Did he think he could appease her with a gift and sweet talk?

Before he handed her the box, he dug into his other pocket

and brought out a small paper sack. "I bought you some lemon drops from the store. I know how you like sweets." He held his hand out.

Automatically she accepted the offering. "I'll give them to Alvie. She adores hard candy."

Tom paused, then said, "I hope you'll keep this." He handed her the box.

This time, she thought before taking it. She opened it—a beautiful filigreed brooch, with hints of blue topaz. Its beauty did nothing to warm her heart. She replaced the lid and handed it back to him. "I don't want it. You should give it to the redhead I saw you with."

Tom fidgeted. He looked for the closest chair and pulled it closer to Marion. He leaned forward, his hands between his legs, looking at her with puppy dog eyes. "I bought it especially for you, to apologize. I wondered if you would give me a second chance."

Marion waited for her heart to melt, the way it used to when he looked at her like that. Instead, her words were sharpened on the stone of her hurt. "What happened, did she refuse your gift?"

His eyes widened. "Molly? You mean that day at church?"

"You didn't waste any time finding someone to take my place."

He stared at his hands before he lifted his head again. "I admit, I escorted Molly to a couple of events. But she's not you. I realized pretty quick I made a big mistake. Please give me another chance. I'll make it up to you, I promise."

Half a second—that was all it took for Marian to reject his apology. "No. It's too late."

"It can't be." He got on one knee. "Give me some reason to hope."

"Be a man," Marion said. "Get up before you embarrass yourself any more than you already have." She stood. "This interview is at an end. If you come back, I won't talk with you."

Tom's puppy dog eyes turned to hard brown dirt, and he slowly lifted himself to his feet. "As you wish." He dropped the box back in his pocket.

Marion opened the door for him. "I wish the best for you, Tom, I surely do. But it won't be with me."

Tom hesitated, one leg over the door sill. "You can't say I didn't give you a chance. Sooner or later, you'll be sorry you turned me down." Settling his hat on his head, he sauntered out to the horse, not looking one whit sorry.

"He's gone." Wande watched Tom ride away.

Mrs. Morgan opened her eyes. She had made no pretense of working while Marion met with Tom. Not that they could hear what either one said, except a word here and there. But Mrs. Morgan sat with her Bible open and her eyes closed. Wande was too restless to follow her example. She was not sure what she would have said if Konrad had begged her forgiveness.

"All is right with the world, then," Mrs. Morgan said. "I keep forgetting Marion's a grown woman. She'll come in here if she wants to talk."

"Mama says I'll always be her *kinder*, and I am her first-born. She says that I will understand when I have children of my own—if I have children of my own."

"You will, my dear Wande. There is a good man out there who will love you." She looked at the door, as if willing Marion to walk in.

"Wande, Marion, I'm here." Alvie bounced into the kitchen.

Wande looked out the window. The day had fled, and now she would have to hurry to complete the laundry. She did not think Marion would venture outside again today. Or maybe she would. Sometimes work provided a balm to a troubled spirit. "How was school today?" Wande went into the pantry and brought out a couple of oatmeal-raisin cookies and a glass of cool milk.

"I had so much fun." Alvie beamed. "Miss Thurston moved me up to fifth-grade English and said if I work very hard, she will put me with sixth grade."

"That's wonderful." Mrs. Morgan smiled as if nothing troubling had happened that day."You must be one smart girl, but we already know that. To get a whole year ahead in English, when you hardly knew any when you came to Victoria last year."

"I don't expect to go ahead in math," Alvie said. "I don't like math."

"Do I hear Alvie?" Marion came in. Aside from a loss of color in her face, she looked composed.

"Marion." Alvie stood and flung her arms around her friend. "I'm ready for my piano lesson."

"Your lesson . . ." Marion swallowed.

Wande recognized the look. Marion's mind was miles away. Any change to her routine could cause her to fall apart. "I will finish the laundry if you wish to give Alvie her lesson now."

"Are you sure?" Marion accepted the cup of tea her mother handed her.

"I will be fine." Wande stood and headed for the door. "Open the window so I can hear your music. Time will go faster."

The clothes had dried except for the men's heavy work pants. Wande made quick work of taking everything else from the line and lugged two full baskets into the kitchen. If only Alvie could play hymns, they would cheer Marion's spirits. But Alvie did not yet play well enough.

Alvie finished practicing her scales by the time Wande had heated the iron. She cocked her head and listened to the music. Humming along, she occasionally added harmony or her own words. Puddles tugged at the strings as Wande ironed the apron, and Wande sang to her. "Puddle-cat, Puddle-cat. See how she plays." She had always done that, making up words to any song she happened to hear.

Alvie hit a grating note in one song, and then in the next, but Marion did not make her correct her mistakes. Alvie stumbled through one piece Wande had not heard before, and then stopped.

Marion came into the kitchen and sat down. "I wasn't much of a teacher today. I let Alvie go early."

"You are a wonderful teacher. She was excited about going back to school today."

"Perhaps." Marion headed out the back door and returned with the trousers. "These will dry when I iron them if I get the iron hot enough."

Yes, and she could take out some of her frustrations on the iron. Wande had done that more than once. She let Marion take over the ironing board and began to put away the dishrags and kitchen towels. She watched Marion push the iron back and forth, steam hissing where the iron hit the damp material.

Marion finished the first pair of trousers and added them to the pile of men's shirts Wande had ironed. She tossed a second pair onto the board. "Did I do the right thing, telling him to go?"

"I cannot decide for you."

"If it had been you, what would you have done?"

Wande had no doubts. "The same thing you did. Tell him to leave and never come back."

Marion managed a smile. "I thought so."

They finished their work in silence.

CHAPTER THIRTY-THREE

"I appreciate you staying until suppertime." Jud caught up with Georg as they herded the horses back to the paddocks from the pasture for the night.

Georg shrugged. "Mama wants someone to walk home with Alvie. We all want to pay Marion for the piano lessons. It is fair." He settled in the saddle like someone who had been riding all his life. In fact, Georg looked about as Texan as they came, with his plaid shirt, sturdy boots, and broad-brimmed hat. Even his skin had darkened with the long hours under the summer sun. He gave away his German roots only when he opened his mouth. He didn't have the ease with English that Alvie or Wande did.

Wande. Whenever she tried to say Jud's name, her mouth twisted like a prune. When she wasn't concentrating on the *U* in Jud, it came out "Jood." Jude. Well, he was a brother of the Lord and wrote a book of the Bible, so Jud could think of worse names.

Instead of the music Jud expected to hear on the days

Alvie took her lessons, only the *clip clop* of the horses' hooves and the clucking of hens greeted them when they entered the yard. Jud opened the paddock gate, and Georg went in first. With one of them on either side, they quickly got the horses settled in.

"Go on ahead. I'll see you bright and early in the morning."

Georg stayed put. "You taught me I must always take care of my horse first, and then she will take care of me." He dismounted and headed for the barn, leading Apple. Jud followed.

Alvie sprang from where she sat on the front steps. "I thought you would never get here."

Georg lifted an eyebrow. "It is my usual time. Last week I had to drag you away from the piano."

Jud removed JM's saddle and listened. Something was off kilter.

Alvie sighed. "I did not play very long today. Marion was so sad, I thought she would cry."

Georg looked at Jud, who shrugged. If Alvie couldn't stir Marion out of the doldrums, something must be truly upsetting her.

"I'm sure she's glad you are here," Jud said. "We look forward to seeing you on Mondays." Jud surprised himself when he discovered the truth of that statement.

George nodded to his little sister. "Go back inside and say good-bye to Wande while I rub down Apple."

Alvie scooped up Puddles, who loved to track the horses' swishing tails, and ran to the house.

"I told Jud that you were sad." Alvie's face was a bright pink.

"Alvie." Wande put the full force of Mama's disapproval behind the word.

Alvie shifted her weight from one foot to the other. "But I didn't tell him anything else. Honest."

"It's all right," Marion said.

Wande breathed a sigh of relief that Marion did not seem upset.

"You be a good girl and study hard," Marion said. "I want to hear all about fifth-grade English when I see you Wednesday night."

"I will. I will bring home *The Sketch Book of Geoffrey Crayon, Gent.* and read it for you."

"That is good. I like a good story." Wande walked outside with Alvie and hugged her good-bye.

Georg looked like he wanted to ask a question, but he simply said, "Good night, Wande." He leaned toward her as if listening to every word of one of Alvie's almost too-tall tales.

Wande rejoined Marion and Ma in the kitchen. "I am glad Tom left before Alvie arrived. That one, she does not know how to keep quiet."

"She's a high-spirited girl." Mrs. Morgan did not appear concerned. "She means no harm."

The door creaked.

"Not like some of the gossips in town who repeat everything they hear." Marion managed a smile. "And so what if they do? They'll be saying how Tom left here with his tail between his legs." In spite of her plucky words, she picked at the strings dangling from her cuff.

"Did I hear Tom's name?" Jud marched into the kitchen. "Did that skunk show his face around here?"

"Now Jud." Mrs. Morgan used a tone that usually poured oil over troubled spirits, but it didn't appear to help Jud.

"He should be ashamed to come here after what he did."

"Judson Morgan, you settle down. Your sister's a grown woman, and it was up to her to decide whether she wanted to speak with that foul-smelling animal." Mrs. Morgan lifted her chin, a gesture Wande had seen repeated by both her children. "And she sent him packing. Didn't need any help from anybody to do that."

Jud stopped inches from Marion, towering over her small form. She matched him glare for glare until he seemed to shrink back to normal size. Wande decided she and Marion were blessed to have brothers who wanted to fight their battles.

"Where did he go while he was here?" Jud's voice had taken on a more normal tone. "Did you leave him alone at all?"

"He was in the parlor a few minutes, but I don't see what difference—"

Jud stormed out of the kitchen. Marion glanced at Wande and her mother before following him. Wande joined them.

Jud slammed the desk drawer shut. "It's gone. I knew we couldn't trust him. He took all the money I had put in there."

Wande blinked. Tom had stolen money?

"So he took the money you said you were saving for him." Marion shrugged. "Wasn't it his money? You did promise him a pay raise."

"I only gave him a raise when he was marrying my sister." Jud's face turned an ugly red. "Ma, go ahead and start supper without me. I'm going into town."

"Jud, stay here before you do something that will bring shame on the Morgan name." Mrs. Morgan's face was turning as dark as her son's. Like Mama, Mrs. Morgan also became the bear protecting her young.

"Tom did that all by himself. The only shame would be if I let it go on any longer." Jud lunged for the door, brushing past Wande. "Alvie told me Marion was sad. He upset you. I can't let him get away with hurting my family."

Wande laid a steadying hand on Jud's arm. She thought she understood some of what drove him, but he would only endanger them if he acted in haste. “Do not make this harder for Marion by getting hurt.”

“Don’t worry.” His smile twisted Wande’s heart. “I’m not the one who’ll be crying when this is over.” He slammed the door behind him.

The three women looked at each other and went out to the porch. Mrs. Morgan peered at the sky. “The moon’s near three-quarters full tonight. He should have plenty of light, if it doesn’t cloud over.”

“Maybe he’ll have the good sense to stay in town instead of riding back in the dark,” Marion said. “But he’s not showing much sense at the moment.”

Wande did not like fights, but Jud’s attitude did not surprise her. Men always fought to defend their honor. A soldier himself, Prince Carl represented that ideal to the Verein. Perhaps she could tell Jud some time when he was not so angry.

The barn door opened, and JM flew down the road as if the entire Mexican army nipped at his heels. *God protect both Jud and Tom. They’re going to need it.*

There was nothing like riding at full gallop to clear one’s head. Jud hovered over JM’s neck, but the gelding needed no encouragement. With each stride, the wind stripped away some of the raw emotion.

When all that remained of Jud’s fury was iron-hard purpose, he slowed JM. “That probably wasn’t very wise at this time of night, but we had fun, didn’t we, boy?”

JM snorted. Two miles of fierce riding and the horse wasn’t even breathing hard.

“Maybe I should have put you to stud instead of Midnight, huh, fella?”

JM’s head jerked against the reins.

"I might let young Crockett take over some of that pretty soon. It's time we had two stallions."

Ma would probably say he should ask God to take care of Tom and not go after him. But Jud figured God worked through people most of the time. If a man didn't protect his own sister, when would he act? Who else would God send to do the job?

A quiet conversation, that's all they needed—provided Tom would return the money and promise never to return to the ranch. They could act like reasonable men. No matter how tempting the idea, Jud wouldn't challenge Tom to a duel at dawn.

Unless Tom refused to act like a reasonable man. Jud almost hoped he didn't.

Where had Tom holed up? The joke would be on Jud if Tom had taken a position at another farm and wasn't staying in town.

No, Jud decided. Tom couldn't have gone to see Marion in the middle of the afternoon if he was working. The most likely place he'd taken lodging was Miss Nellie's boardinghouse. He'd start there. They headed to the left, into one of the older sections of town.

A rambling, ramshackle house came into view. At least once a year a storm broke through the roof, and the repairs never seemed to last. Jud dismounted and tied JM to the hitching post and knocked on the door.

A plump matron with graying hair answered. "Well, Jud Morgan, as I live and breathe. What brings you here on a Monday night?" What Miss Nellie's house lacked in amenities, she made up for with a cheerful spirit, ample food, and perhaps most important to Jud, an adequate barn for horses. She was a good Christian woman who wouldn't stand any fuss, and single men found her place the best choice of lodging in town.

"I won't keep you long. I'm looking for one of your boarders, Tom Cotton."

"He's not here. He went out for a piece of pie and to chat up young Molly Spencer, I expect."

Tom hadn't wasted any time on regret about Marion's decision.

Something in Jud's face must have given his thoughts away. Miss Nellie put her hand over her mouth. "I shouldn't have said anything. Me and my big mouth. What a shame things didn't work out with your sister."

"I won't take any more of your time, Miss Nellie. Good evening."

"You won't cause any trouble, will you?"

"Nothing like that." *Not unless Tom insists.* Jud untied JM and walked down the street. He wanted to talk to Tom man to man, and he could manage that better standing.

He made it most of the way to the restaurant when he spotted Tom coming out the door. He hung back to see if Tom had any company. He did: she of the curly red locks, Miss Molly Spencer. Her laughter rang like chimes.

Jud waited until the door closed and Tom stepped away before he showed himself.

"Hello, Tom. I've been looking for you."

CHAPTER THIRTY-FOUR

Tom stood his ground. Jud gave him credit for that. He stood solid, a cocky grin evidence that he felt no shame over his actions. "I was wondering how long it would take you to show up."

"Do you want to take our conversation somewhere more private?"

"Right here is fine," Tom said.

"Very well." Jud might as well be blunt. "I want the money back."

Tom raised an eyebrow. "The money you were saving for me? I reckoned that belonged to me." He smiled, that same insufferable grin. "I thought it just slipped your mind. I knew you wasn't eager to talk with me."

"I gave you that raise with the understanding you would use it to take care of my sister. When you broke your engagement, you forfeited the money." Jud cracked a smile of his own. "Call it a dowry."

Tom's hands formed fists, and he shifted his legs a few

inches apart. "I earned that money fair and square. It's mine."

"There's also the little matter that you took more money than what I'd set aside for you. That's theft, no matter how you look at it." Jud drew in a breath. He didn't want to lose control. "Look, you took your horse Princess when you left. I didn't speak against it, although she belonged to me. I'll give you a choice. Give me back the horse or the money." He grinned. "If you still have the money, that is, and haven't spent it all already."

Tom moved one foot forward.

Maybe Jud would get his fight after all.

Tom rocked back, fists still clenched at his sides. "You can't take my horse. How can I get around?"

"Fine. I'll take the money, then."

Tom slowly uncurled his fist and reached into his pocket for a wad of banknotes. He handed them to Jud. "That's all I got."

Even without counting, Jud knew Tom had spent a chunk. The stack was too thin. He had come to the ranch, tried to sweet talk Marion into doing something foolish, then come back to town and spent a bundle on his current lady-love.

"Don't ever come near my sister again." Jud's right arm swung, making contact with Tom's jaw.

If Wande stayed still, perhaps Marion could sleep. Wande had taken the prime place by the window. She loved to look at the shifting shadows, the moonlight transformation of familiar objects. To listen to the rhythms of the night sounds: the hoot of an owl, the purr of cicadas—some sounds familiar, others new since she came to Texas. Including Marion's gentle, slowed breathing—which was missing tonight. Nightly worship of the God of creation had lulled Wande to sleep on more than one occasion. But not this time.

"Are you awake?" Marion whispered.

"I cannot stop thinking about Jud and Tom."

As usual, the women had retired to bed shortly after complete dark. In the hour or so since, Wande knew Jud had not returned. Her ears had strained for any sound.

"Me too."

Both turned over so they lay flat on their backs, staring at the ceiling.

"I think it is sweet that Jud wants to protect your honor," Wande said. "He is like a knight. He should live in a castle." Like Prince Carl wanted to live in a castle with his bride. Jud would not like the comparison. Wande laughed.

"What's funny? I could use a laugh." Marion's voice was like a thundercloud heavy with rain.

"It was not funny when it happened. Jud read in the newspaper about Prince Carl. He made fun of him."

"I'm sorry. So why is it funny?"

Wande explained about the castle, and she received the best reward she could have hoped for.

Marion laughed. "I never thought of Jud being anything like a knight."

"It has nothing to do with where you live or what work you do. It is who a man is inside. Jud is that kind of man."

"You like him, don't you?"

Wande gave the only answer she could. "What woman would not like a knight?"

"Yeah. Too bad some turn out to be villains."

Their laughter didn't quite cover the sound of hooves. Wande slipped out of bed and knelt by the window. A giggling Marion joined her. They lifted their heads so they could see into the yard.

Jud slid from JM's back, his left arm cradled against his chest.

"He's hurt." Wande grabbed her dressing gown and raced downstairs.

Mrs. Morgan sat in the parlor, eyes closed and snoring gently. She was still dressed in her day clothes.

By the time Wande buttoned her dressing gown, Marion had thundered down the stairs. Mrs. Morgan's eyes flew open. "Is he here?"

"Outside."

The front door opened and Jud stumbled in. His left eye had swollen, and he lurched on his feet, but he smiled as wide as the Atlantic. "I wasn't expecting a welcoming party. If I had known about it, I'd have tried to get home sooner." His laughter doubled him over in pain.

Wande did not know if she wanted to yell or laugh. He looked like a little boy coming home from the schoolyard after his first fight. Some shame, some swagger—and the biggest grin this side of Christmas.

She wanted to give him the same treatment Mama gave Georg and Drud after their first fight. But the reprimand wouldn't come. Turning on her heel, she went upstairs and rummaged through her bag for Mama's ointment. She went back down and found them in the kitchen. Mrs. Morgan eased Jud's shirt open and exposed a portion of his chest. Blushing, Wande retreated up a couple of steps and made more noise on the stairs. "Is he dressed?"

A cough cut short Jud's laugh. "All except for a bit of missing skin."

"I brought my ointment." Wande leaned forward enough to see the kitchen. Mrs. Morgan was dabbing with a rag at an ugly patch of scraped skin down his left side. Wande winced. Mama's ointment would surely ease the pain.

She checked that her dressing gown was closed and walked into the kitchen.

Jud held a piece of steak to his eye. "If you think I look bad, you should see Tom."

"And Tom won't get any of your special ointment." Marion sounded pleased.

Wande offered the jar. "It has helped Georg more than once." She sneaked a look at Jud's bare skin and glanced away.

Mrs. Morgan took the jar and dabbed some on her fingers. "Does it sting?"

"Yes," Wande said.

"No," Jud countered. "I used it when I got blisters on my hands. Go ahead. I'm a big boy."

Mrs. Morgan coated the wound. Jud's gaze didn't flicker from where he watched Wande. Marion took boiling water from the stove and poured it over tea leaves.

Even when his mother probed the sensitive skin, Jud didn't blink. He smiled, a half-smile somewhere between grimace and a grin. "So even German boys get into fights?"

Wande giggled. "Yes." She accepted a cup of tea from Marion.

By Tuesday morning, Jud's fight-induced euphoria had faded, replaced by a pounding head and aching muscles up and down his side. He felt every bit of his twenty-six years, not to mention foolish. And not regretting a minute of it.

After Jud swung the first punch, Tom wasted no time. He was a scrappy fighter, but it was an uneven match. Jud had several inches and maybe thirty pounds of work-hardened muscle on the kid. The fight didn't last long, only two or three punches each. Jud came to his senses first and pulled back. Tom wiped the blood from his lip and raised his fists to take another swing.

"No more." Jud was sorry he had started it—a little. "But don't come back to the ranch again—ever. Not without a printed invitation." He climbed on JM's back and let the gelding find his way home.

Jud touched the bruised area on his side. It did feel better this morning. Wande's ointment worked miracles.

Below he heard voices—Bert had come up to the house for breakfast. Time for rehashing the previous night's events had come and gone. He finished dressing and ignored the twinge in his side as he went downstairs.

Georg arrived about the time they finished breakfast. He took one look at Jud and raised his eyebrows. Bert shook his head.

Here might be a good reason not to get involved in fisticuffs. He didn't want his ranch hands getting into scuffles. But Jud saw no point in lying. These men knew a black eye when they saw one. "I ran into something."

"A fist." Bert curled the fingers of his right hand and grinned.

Jud grinned back. "Tom's fist."

"Ah." Georg nodded. "Alvie told me some of what occurred. But more must have happened. You would not fight over something . . ." Georg moved his hands together. ". . . so small."

Jud frowned. His men didn't need to know that Tom had robbed him. Or perhaps they did. They could keep an eye on the house when they were close by. "He took something that didn't belong to him. I went to get it back."

A smile flickered on Georg's face. "We will make certain he does not have another opportunity."

"Of course you can count on me, Boss." Bert tipped his hat.

"I doubt he'll show his face here again." Jud hoped Tom had learned his lesson. "Let's get to work."

They spent the week working with the colts a few at a time, and Georg proved a fast learner. He had picked up riding in a flash, as did Alvie, the couple of times he had put her on the back of a horse.

As Jud dressed on Thursday morning, he mused on Georg's skill with horses. Maybe all the Fleischers would do as well, if given the chance. Only they had never had the opportunity to own any horses.

Jud tried to imagine a life without horses. *Impossible*. His clothes suited his occupation, from his hat to his spurs. Maybe if he hadn't been able to raise Morgan horses here in Texas, he would have wanted to move somewhere else. Like the Germans pursuing whatever dreams they held.

If the Fleischers were born horsemen, he wanted to get Wande on the back of another horse as soon as possible. The thought brought a smile.

Georg knocked on the kitchen door during the middle of breakfast. "Boss." Georg called Jud "Boss" during their working hours. He said he wanted to show Jud the proper respect. "A colt is missing . . ."

Jud hurried out to the corral. He could see over the backs of the horses to the far side of the corral. "One, two . . . ten, eleven . . . You're right." Which one? He opened the gate and walked in. Georg followed and latched the gate behind them.

He counted seven fillies—they were all accounted for. So which of the five colts was gone? There was Shadow, a close replica of his dear old dad. Hercules, who would some day make someone a good, solid workhorse. Twilight, Moonshine . . .

The colt that was missing was the cream of the crop. The one he wanted to succeed Midnight as stallion. Crockett.

CHAPTER THIRTY-FIVE

Tom again.

If Jud were a cursing man, he'd have let out a string to turn his tongue blue. How could one man create so much trouble? Jud reined in his anger. He had no proof Tom had taken the colt. Maybe Crockett had spent the night up in the pasture—he hadn't come in with the others, and they missed him last night when they brought in the horses.

Jud turned to Georg and Bert. "What do you think happened?"

Georg cocked his head and thought about it. "I am certain he was here last night." He blushed. "I gave him an extra treat."

Jud smiled.

"And if we had left the gate open, all the horses would leave."

So far Georg was echoing his thoughts. Jud turned to Bert.

"The dogs would have kicked up a ruckus if someone came in the yard last night. And they was quiet." Bert took off his hat and scratched his head. "I don't know what could have happened."

The dogs wouldn't bark at Tom. They considered him family. But Jud wouldn't confront him, not without proof. And once he had proof, he'd go straight to the sheriff. "Until we figure it out, we'll stand watch over them." He turned to Georg. "Can you stay tonight?"

Georg gazed in the direction of his family's farm. "I will go home and tell Papa I will spend tonight. I am a soldier in your army. I must stand guard over the horses. He will understand."

"Good. That's settled."

Wande was glad the whole family came to market on Saturday. Next week none of them might be able to come; they expected to be planting the first crop on their farm.

Mama missed Georg, Wande knew, with all the extra hours he was putting in at the ranch. With their work hours, and Alvie's lessons, they spent almost as much time with the Morgans as at home.

Now with autumn approaching, the temperatures had dropped to a bearable level. Or perhaps Wande had grown accustomed to the heat. Whether due to the milder weather or the easing of cholera cases, people flocked into town. Wande was glad she brought jars of pickles, as well as squash, for sale. Housewives without their own kitchen gardens wanted to buy ahead.

Frau Decker stopped by the stall as usual. "You never told me. Did you get any white potatoes?"

Wande shook her head. "None that you would wish to eat. But I do have sweet potatoes, if you want them."

Her nose wrinkled at the thought. "I hope to buy German food from you, *fraulein*."

“Then buy a jar of my pickles, made from my mother’s favorite recipe.”

Frau Decker smiled and handed over the cash readily enough.

“Good morning, Fraulein Fleischer.” Pastor Bader approached the stall. “I see you have pickles today.” He bought a jar.

Alvie came out of the store with the lemon drop she usually convinced Mr. Grenville to give to her. If he gave candy away to every child, did he ever sell any? “I do not understand why Mr. Grenville gives away candy. No child ever pays.”

“That’s easy.” Alvie plopped on the low stool beside her sister. “I bring Mama to the store so I can get candy, and she buys things. She buys more because he gives me candy.”

“When did you get so smart?” Wande tugged at her sister’s hair, braided in the Texas style.

“There’s Georg, down by the livery. May I go?”

Wande was about to say no, but the look in Alvie’s eyes changed her mind. Every girl should have the opportunity to fall in love with horses. Here in Texas, Alvie might even get her own horse one day. “Go ahead.”

Alvie skipped down the street as if she was rolling a hoop—not quite ladylike, but not an outright run, either. Wande sighed. She had been so much more grown up when she was ten, but by then she had four younger brothers and sisters and was Mama’s helper. Alvie was their baby. She did her share of the work, but Mama seemed willing to let her remain a child. Perhaps Wande would feel the same way about her youngest.

Mama searched the stalls, looking for a bargain on wheat flour and sugar, as well as special items dear to a German cook’s heart. She promised to come back to the stall in time for Wande to shop for seeds. Next week Wande would plant her winter garden. This time she would grow cabbage. Her mouth watered. They would eat sauerkraut sparingly until they had a fresh supply.

An *Amerikaner* stopped by the stall, interested in Wande's butter. By the time she finished the sale, Alvie and Georg were almost upon her. Jud was with them. "Good morning, Jud."

"Morning." He tipped his hat, his eyes gleaming at her.

Her cheeks warmed and she glanced toward Pastor Bader, who stood by the booth.

"I told Alvie she must stay with you," Georg said.

Alvie pouted.

"Oh?" Wande said.

"Jud and I have business we must do."

"What business in town?"

Jud mouthed the word "Tom," and she went still. "Be careful."

"Don't worry." Jud winked. The two men walked away. Georg had filled out, almost as wide across his shoulders as Jud.

"What did you mean, be careful? Where are they going?" Alvie stuck out her tongue, examined her lemon drop, and popped it back in her mouth. "I bet they're going somewhere Mama would disapprove of. Don't you think so, Pastor Bader?"

"Indeed, I do." The pastor's eyes followed as Jud rounded the corner.

Wande turned her attention on Alvie. "You should not stick out your tongue like that." Wande handed Alvie a washrag and made her wipe her face. She hoped that would take care of the stickiness.

"People always talk as if they think I can't hear what they're saying," Alvie said. "Papa says Georg is a man, and Mama must let him follow his own conscience."

"*Nein,* child," Pastor Bader said. "We need to follow the Word of God and not lean on our own understanding."

A customer approached, and Alvie dropped the subject. After Georg had told their family about the theft of the horse, Papa worried. First their chickens, then their cows, now this. Wande knew he planned to ask at the agricultural society if anyone had experienced similar problems. Or was someone targeting their two families? Wande sent up a prayer for wisdom and protection. Men had the hard work of being courageous and fighting battles, while women needed as much strength to stay at home and pray. God knew that.

The discoveries Jud and Georg made that afternoon led to a lively discussion over the Fleischers' evening meal.

"So you did not see this Morgan colt at the boardinghouse." Wande hoped, for Marion's sake, that Tom was not to blame for the theft.

"No," Georg said. "But Frau Nellie said Tom left only yesterday—that he was taking a trip, but would return. And she thought she saw a colt with him."

"That is not proof." Papa scowled. "Herr Morgan should act only if he has evidence."

Alvie shoveled peaches into her mouth, listening to every word. Wande stifled a laugh.

"I spoke with the society." Papa laid down his knife and fork. "We are the only ones who have had these kind of problems. Still, it may be nothing more than forgetfulness."

Protests erupted around the table.

"I know. We do not believe we forgot. I know Herr Morgan is not a careless man. But as long as we are human, we can make mistakes." He picked up his utensils and bit into a sausage. "Mama, you make a fine sausage chowder." The discussion had come to an end.

They ate a few minutes without conversation. Mama broke the silence, pointing out the window at the ground broken in preparation for the winter crop. "People have been very kind to us since we came to Victoria. Some of them are even coming to help us plant our first crop. I want to do something to thank them."

Alvie raised her head from her plate. "That's what the Pilgrims did their first year here."

"Pil-grims?" Papa said. "Are they Texans?"

"No, Papa. They came from England to America—to Massachusetts, that's far away from here, almost as far as Germany—so they could worship God the way they thought was right. But they did not know how to make a living from the land. Indians taught them what to grow and how to plant crops." She grinned. "The way the *Amerikaners* give us advice."

"That is interesting. Did they do something special to thank the Indians?" Mama handed the dish of beans to Wande to pass.

"They did. After the harvest, they held a feast and invited the Indians to attend."

Mama looked at Papa. "We could hold a feast. A thank-you feast for helping us plant the crop." She nodded at Georg. "I do not wish to wait until after harvest. Then we will be holding a wedding."

"If that is what you wish to do," Papa said.

Everyone had someone they wanted to invite. The Morgans and the Schumanns, of course. Alvie wanted to ask her teachers, and Papa suggested Pastor Bader. When the number grew to thirty, Mama said to stop thinking of people to invite. They set the date for next Saturday.

Jud gained a new respect for farmers as he helped the Fleischers plant their crop. To make up for some of the extra hours Georg had put in at the ranch, he volunteered for two days of farm duty, but he hadn't expected his back to ache or his hands to get so sore.

The women kept the men supplied with cool water. Wande brought out a fresh bucket and handed him the ladle. He dipped it into the water, poured a little over his head and hands, and winced. She laughed and dug in her apron pocket for her jar of ointment. "I thought this might come in handy."

"Thanks." He wiped his hands dry on his trousers and rubbed in some of the ointment. "It does help." He nodded at Bert. "He might need some too. Tell him I said so."

"I will do that."

Jud was no farmer, but even with his limited experience, some of the things Meino did seemed strange. Whenever he had a question, he consulted his Verein guidebook and talked with the others. Jud didn't say a word. Along this part of the field, the Fleischers had torn down the old rail fence and begun a low-lying stone wall. Jud decided a short break wouldn't hurt, and he sat on it, his fingers running along the fitted rocks. What a lot of work. He wondered if they meant to extend it around the entire field.

Meino spotted him and came over. "I hope we are not making you work too hard."

"Nothing like that." Jud gestured at the wall. "This is built to last."

"Of course." Meino's shoulders straightened.

"So you intend to stay in Victoria? You won't go up to the land grant you own from the Verein?"

"I do not think so. Georg may want to go with Ertha. We have discussed this possibility. But my wife and I do not wish to move again." He faced Jud. "And what of you, Herr Morgan? Alvie tells stories about your family. That you started in Vermont and went to Kentucky and then here. Do you plan to move as your parents did?"

"I don't think so. Not if I find the right woman to stay by my side and share my dream of having the best horse ranch in all of Texas." His eyes drifted to Wande.

CHAPTER THIRTY-SIX

In bed that night, Wande's thoughts kept returning to Jud and Papa's conversation as they sat on the wall. They looked so cozy, like two old men discussing the day's work and ruminating about life. At one point both looked up from their work and stared at her with sheepish smiles. When Papa returned to the field, he winked at Wande and nodded at Jud. She could not figure out what that meant. She wanted to beg Papa to tell her, but was not sure she wanted to hear the answer.

Alvie lay curled next to Wande, a hand held over her doll, the one that used to belong to Billie Morgan. At times like this, Alvie still looked like a child. Wande brushed her hair back from her cheek. Alvie stirred and turned over.

Mittens jumped up beside Wande, crowding the side of the bed. She meowed softly, asking for attention. She was taking a break from her new litter of kittens, safe in a box in the corner of their bedroom. "You've had a hard few days, haven't you?" Wande murmured, running her hand down her back and scratching her under her chin. Mittens purred and bumped her head against Wande's hand. Wande stroked her a few times, and her eyes drifted shut.

Mittens climbed onto Wande's chest, giving full voice to her complaint.

"Go take care of your kittens and let me sleep." Wande brushed her hand at Mittens, but her fingers met a claw.

"Meow," she repeated, louder.

"What's wrong, Mittens? Did we forget to feed you?"

Alvie sat up, rubbing her eyes. "Is there something wrong with the kittens?" The cat paraded on the bed, continuing her complaint.

"I might as well see what is troubling her." As Wande stood, Mittens ran for the door. In the new silence, Wande heard other sounds. The chickens were cackling, and even the rooster was crowing as if daybreak had come. Elsie's lowing could be heard in brief seconds of silence, and the calf hurled herself against the pasture fence hard enough to break it. "Alvie, go wake Mama and Papa. Something is wrong."

As soon as Alvie opened the door, Mittens ran out. Wande grabbed her dressing gown and headed downstairs.

Georg raced behind her. "What is happening?"

"I do not know. But all the animals are making noise. There might be an intruder."

Georg headed for the parlor, where a rifle hung over the mantle. "I hoped I would never have to use this."

Wande held her breath. They had never faced such danger in Germany. They had never owned a gun until the Verein guidebook said a gun was necessary for life in Texas.

Papa and Mama came down the stairs, followed by Alvie. As if satisfied she had done her duty, Mittens reappeared with a black-and-orange kitten in her mouth. She demanded that Papa open the door. Papa glanced at Georg, who pointed his rifle at the arch, and Papa opened the door. The cat streaked into the darkness. With the door open, the cacophony of the yard tripled.

"Meino!" Mama called from the kitchen, terror in her voice. Georg pointed the rifle toward the kitchen door, but Papa waved him back and plunged into the kitchen, a pistol ready in his hand.

Georg glanced at Wande, and she nodded. They headed for the kitchen—and stopped as soon as they crossed the threshold. Alvie squeezed between them.

"*Gutte Gott im Himmel,* what do we do?" Papa voiced the prayer that was on all their hearts.

No shadowy intruder had captured Mama. She had seen something more sinister, more implacable—*fire*. Seeing it in the distance beyond the farmyard through the kitchen window, Wande recognized the scent that had troubled her earlier.

They remained frozen in place for what felt like an eternity. Then Papa began calling out orders. "Wande, move the cows. Georg, start hauling water from the well. Alvie, collect all the buckets you can find in the house."

"I will look after the chickens." Mama darted out the door, the others following.

The cows. Wande focused on the task Papa had given her. She headed for the pen, grateful the fence held in spite of Karlina's knocking. She could see a fire roaring to the southeast, in the direction of open pastures on the Morgan Ranch, with only dry grassland standing between the flames and their house. Close, too close. The road might stop the fire if they could not put it out before it reached their buildings. It was the best she could think of. She led the oxen out first. Next she tied Karlina to her mother. Elsie planted her feet and refused to move. "Do not worry. I am taking you to a place of safety." Elsie didn't budge.

She thought back to the commands she gave the oxen "*Hu*. Go, Elsie. Take Karlina to safety." The cow retreated a few steps.

In the coop, the chickens squawked even louder as Mama started grabbing one hen, then another. One in each hand, she looked to grab another, only to have the first hen scramble out of her arms.

Alvie dashed across the yard to the well, carrying three buckets. Only three buckets to pass water all the way to the end of the field. It would never work. They would also need to soak blankets to beat at the flames.

"God in heaven, help us," Wande said. "Let this cow come with me like the animals boarded the ark for Noah." The secret to controlling an animal, Jud had said in her one riding lesson, was to exercise authority without frightening the animal.

Wande could do nothing about the fright. The cows were terrified. So was she, but she could think and pray and trust. Poor Elsie had only the instincts God had given her—that fire was the enemy.

But Wande could command authority. For Elsie's sake, for the sake of her family, she must. "Come." She used her sternest, do-not-tell-me-no voice. *"Hu."* She tugged Elsie's lead, and the cow followed her, step by halting step. *"Gutte kuh."*

Only the first miracle of many needed.

The barking awakened Jud. Then he heard the horses' frightened neighing. He grabbed his rifle and dashed into the yard, then moved more calmly toward the corral. The horses rolled wild eyes, tossing their necks and kicking against the fence. "Come out, wherever you're hiding. You won't get away with it this time." Jud held his rifle to his shoulder, his finger itching to pull the trigger.

"Jud, put that thing down." Ma appeared beside him. "If you'd use your nose and your eyes, you'd know what the problem is. Look toward the Fleischers'." She pointed north. A red glow sparked where there should be only darkness. *Fire.*

Marion stumbled into the yard before Jud could collect his thoughts. Bert wasn't here. He had decided to spend his night off in town. One less person to fight the fire. Jud wet his finger and held it in the air. The wind was blowing north—blowing the fire away from the ranch . . . toward the Fleischer farm. His heart jumped into his throat and urged him to act.

"Marion. Go into town for help. Send them to the Fleischers' unless the wind changes direction. Get dressed, grab JM, and ride like the wind."

She nodded and disappeared inside the house.

He turned to Ma. "We're not in any immediate danger, so I'm going to leave the animals where they are. Let's saddle up and head to the Fleischers'."

Jud helped Ma into the saddle, then mounted up on Adara. Ma was the least accomplished rider of all the Morgans. They had to take the road; the route across the pasture would lead them into the heart of the fire. Every delay made Jud's nerves scream. He wanted JM beneath him and a clear path for him to fly. Every second's delay could spell disaster for the Fleischers.

Even without much moonlight, he could see the road almost as clear as day. Shapes danced and shifted as the flames pressed forward. He hoped, he prayed, that they could get through to the Fleischer farm. That the fire would not bar their way. That the buildings were still standing—at least that the family was safe. He scanned the horizon, checking for signs of the fire spreading in a new direction.

"Do you see that?" Ma pointed ahead, to a lone figure on horseback on the road to town. "That's one of our horses, isn't it? But it can't be. It's not Marion. It's a man. Could it be Bert?"

Jud slowed Adara and looked. If he stopped, the rider would know he was being watched. It was a Morgan horse all right, but it wasn't Bert. Not heavy enough to be his ranch hand.

The man turned his face—only for a second, but long enough for the fire to illuminate his pale skin. His identity seemed of a piece with the night.

"It's Tom. Tom Cotton."

CHAPTER THIRTY-SEVEN

Wande sent up a prayer that the cows wouldn't wander too far and that they wouldn't trample the chickens. She ran back to the well, expecting their bucket brigade to have started. Instead, Georg knotted a rope to the bar over the well and tied it to a bucket. "Someone cut the rope."

Wande gasped. She had hauled water only hours ago, before supper. Someone had come onto their property and cut the rope.

Someone started the fire.

"Do we have the bucket?"

Georg shook his head. "Only the three Alvie found. I do not know if we can stop the fire, but we have to try." Determination lined his face. "Alvie is our fastest runner, but she cannot carry full buckets."

"I will do it. You go down the way."

They turned and watched in horror as the fire licked the pasturage to the west of the fenced-in cultivation. "Go. Hurry."

They formed a team that worked without stop, without speaking. Alvie stayed at the well, drawing bucket after bucket. Mama toted quilts out of the house, drenching each spread and carrying them to Papa to beat at the approaching line of fire. Slowly the fire pushed him back, ever nearer to the house. Wande ran with full buckets to Georg and returned at a faster trot to the well. Near the fire, she could see Papa, his figure black against the flames.

The crackling drowned out all other sound. Wande did not know anyone had arrived until Marion tapped her on the shoulder. A dozen men from town joined the fire line, the one nearest the well laden with enough buckets to water the cavalry. Others beat at the flames with drenched blankets. Most of the men she recognized from church, including Pastor Bader. "How did you know of our plight?"

"Miss Morgan rode into town and woke me up with such sharp knocks, I came fully awake. I sounded the alarm bell, and men gathered within minutes. But did we get here in time?" A burning tree crashed, and flames raced in the direction of the barn.

"Your animals." Marion took a step toward the barn.

"Safe." Wande nodded across the road. As one flame flickered in the advancing line, another rushed to take its place. Sparks and smoke turned and came at them. The line of men fighting the blaze moved closer to the house, prepared to use every drop of water in the well to protect it. They began throwing water on the wood-shingled roof. But Wande did not think they would succeed. The fire was too massive, their resources too few.

Wande joined her mother with the men in the fire line.

Marion scanned the fire crew, but saw no sign of Jud or Ma. They should have arrived first. *Go to the Fleischers' first unless*

the wind changes direction. She hadn't checked for that. Panicked, she wet her finger and held it to the sky. The wind had shifted, to a southwesterly blow that could send the fire toward her ranch, her family.

Before she could act, Alvie ran up to her. "Have you seen Mittens?"

"Mittens, the cat? No. But I'm sure she's safe." She ran to the end of the line, anchored by Pastor Bader, who was hauling water as fast as he could pull the rope. His fair hair flopped over his forehead, and sweat glistened on his face. "Pastor, have you seen my brother?"

"Nein." He didn't stop pouring the water into waiting buckets and dropping the pail back into the well. "Is there a problem?"

"The fire is also threatening our ranch. I'm afraid something has happened."

Pastor Bader hesitated a fraction of a second. "Herr Decker." His pulpit voice carried above the roar of the fire.

A middle-aged man ran from his place in line, and the others adjusted to cover the gap. *"Ja."*

"Take over here at the well. I must help Fraulein Morgan's family." The pastor hurried with Marion to the waiting horses. He boosted her onto JM's back and swung into the saddle of his own mount.

"Should I call on some of the men to come with us?"

"I don't know," Marion said. "They're needed here."

"But they might be needed at your home as well. If we meet anyone else coming from town, we will ask them to come with us." He clicked his tongue, and his horse moved quickly. JM kept pace.

"There he is." Marion pointed to the crossroads, where their farm road joined the main road from Carlshafen to Victoria.

⟵ ★ ⟶

Tom must have recognized Jud at the same time Jud spotted him. Tom turned his horse and galloped down the road toward Carlshafen. Jud's mount snorted, ready to take up the chase, but Jud reined him in.

"Don't waste your energy chasing him," Ma shouted. "You can go after him later."

Jud wasn't so sure. Texas was full of crannies for someone who wanted to hide. But Ma was right. He envisioned Wande silhouetted against the fire, and he urged Adara forward.

Wind brushed under his shirt, coming from the side. His horse carried him several yards before the significance registered. The wind had changed direction. He reined in Adara and tested the wind. It was blowing west-southwest, toward to the ranch. He brought his horse parallel with Ma's. "The wind's changed direction. We need to go back and check on the ranch."

Ma's lips compressed, but she nodded. They reversed direction and galloped back to the ranch.

Jud sniffed the air, but the smoke didn't smell any stronger. He trotted into the yard. The line of flames still stretched across the horizon, but no closer to the ranch than before. He could stay in case the fire attacked his land—or he could go help the Fleischers. There was no question of what he needed to do.

Again they headed down the road. Jud prayed it wasn't too late. When they reached the crossroads, he saw Marion and the German pastor headed their direction.

"Is the fire threatening the ranch?" Marion's cheeks were smudged with soot.

"We rode back to check, but it doesn't seem to be." He nodded to Pastor Bader. "I see you got help. Let's not lose any more time." He would tell Marion about Tom later.

Jud's horse pulled back when he turned toward the Fleischer household. The fire must be close for the horse to refuse an order. Jud patted his neck and soothed him, and he responded to the reins. They arrived at the farmhouse minutes later.

Two lines of firefighters scrabbled between the well and the house, and also the barn. Two dozen men—Germans, Americans, even Dr. Treviño—stood shoulder to shoulder fighting the fire. But they had already lost the battle. As Jud jumped down from his horse, flames licked the back of the house.

Jud looked for Wande, but the only woman he spotted was Mrs. Fleischer. Then he saw a slim figure dash into the house. Wande.

"Herr Morgan. You are here." Mrs. Fleischer clutched his sleeve. "You must help. Wande has gone inside to find Alvie."

Jud stared at the wooden structure, fire racing up its side. A black-and-white cat plunged out the door, a kitten in her mouth. But Alvie and Wande did not appear. Mrs. Fleischer thrust a wet towel into his hands, and he raced toward the building.

CHAPTER THIRTY-EIGHT

Smoke billowed around Wande as she opened the door. Even with a wet towel pressed against her nose, she could scarcely breathe. She had to find Alvie quickly.

She lifted the corner of the towel so she could be heard. "Alvie!" She could hear no reply over the roar of the fire. A plank fell at her feet and she jumped, almost tripping over Mittens, who ran to the door with a kitten in her mouth. "Alvie?"

". . . upstairs." Alvie's shout came no louder than a whisper.

"I'm coming." Leaving only the smallest slit so she could see, Wande felt her way to the stairs. She raced up the stairs, blinded by the smoke. "Where are you?"

"Our room."

The kittens, of course. Mittens wanted to save her kittens, and Alvie wanted to save Mittens.

The fire wasn't so bad upstairs, but the smoke made it impossible to see. Wande moved by instinct to her bedroom.

Alvie rocked on all fours on the threshold, clutching one last kitten against her nightgown. Her chest was heaving.

Wande knelt next to her sister, ignoring the heat scorching her knees, and gave the towel to Alvie. "Hold this against your nose. Can you stand?"

Alvie nodded, and Wande stood, half carrying Alvie. They lurched for the stairs. She heard a crash. A section of the stair railing had fallen. "Step down." Wande closed her eyes against the flames that would engulf them when they reached the bottom step. One step at a time, she told Alvie when to move her feet. When at last she thought she reached the bottom, she opened one eye. Two steps to go. Flames stood between them and the front door.

Alvie shrank back. "I can't go through that."

"You must. Mittens is counting on you to save her kitten." The cat would give Alvie courage she didn't have on her own.

Alvie tucked the kitten under her nightgown. They took the final two steps, then heard a man's voice. "Wande! Alvie!"

Wande almost collapsed. "Stairs!"

"Stay!"

Wande didn't move. She was afraid she would fall if she tried.

Jud walked through the flames like the angel in the fiery furnace, scooped Alvie in his arms, and held Wande against his side. "One, two, three." He raced for the door, half dragging Wande as the fire lapped at her nightgown.

Seconds later, blessed air. She gulped big breaths and coughed, expelling smoke from her lungs.

Mr. Fleischer took Alvie from Jud.

Wande collapsed against Jud's chest, sobs racking her body. She clung to him, not caring what he thought or who saw her. "You are my Prince Carl."

"Shh." Jud stroked her hair. "Don't try to speak."

Wande was happy to oblige.

⟵ ★ ⟶

Jud grieved at the sight of Wande. Her hair lay in blackened strands down her back. Fire had eaten away the bottom of her dressing gown so high he could see red welts on her feet and ankles. She couldn't stop coughing.

The line of firefighters had fallen back from the house. Mr. Fleischer stood halfway across the road with Alvie. Jud and Wande needed to move, now. "Can you walk?"

Wande tried to move her foot, then sobbed.

Jud swept his arms under her and carried her to the others. "Doc!"

Treviño was checking Alvie, holding his head to her chest and listening as she coughed. He held up a hand to let Jud know he had heard. "Find some place she can lie down," he told Meino Fleischer, "but keep her head up."

Jud approached him with Wande in his arms.

"Her feet," Jud said, "they're burned." As bad as he remembered Ma's burns looking. Wande lay motionless in his arms.

Mrs. Fleischer laid out two quilts—two of the dampened quilts—and Jud placed Wande on one. The doctor knelt and examined her.

"How is she?" Jud said.

Doc ran his finger over Wande's parched lips. He stood and turned to the waiting group. Jud had nearly forgotten about everyone else. "Both girls have sustained severe burns, and they have inhaled a lot of smoke. But they are young and healthy. They will be fine, given time, as long as we prevent infection from setting in." Relief swept across the crowd.

"Are they strong enough to ride in a wagon?" Ma said. "They can't stay out in the elements all night."

The men looked for the Fleischers' wagon, but it had gone up in flames. They would have to go all the way to the ranch for one. Jud stood over Wande staring, praying, beseeching God for the lives of these two girls.

Ma came beside him and put her arm around his waist. "We'll take good care of them. You've done all you can."

He shrugged. It hadn't been enough.

"This is a good time for you to go hunting Tom, if you still are of a mind."

Jud had forgotten about Tom while fighting the fire. Purpose surged through him to go after the man who had endangered so many lives and cost the Fleischers everything they owned. "I'll go find the sheriff, and we'll track him down."

Sheriff Gutierrez wasn't at the jail, so Jud tracked him down at home. He explained about Tom—what he knew and what he suspected.

Gutierrez rubbed his chin, bristling with whiskers he would shave in the morning. "I'm sorry about the fire. Glad your place was spared, though. Let's go round him up. I hear he's staying at Miss Nellie's."

But Tom wasn't at the boardinghouse. On a hunch, Jud checked the stable and found Crockett eating oats in a corner. "This is the colt I told you about. Tom must have brought him back."

"Good thing. We won't have to beat it out of him."

Jud wasn't sure if Gutierrez was joking. He had a reputation for making criminals pay.

"That's if we can find him," the sheriff said. "Any ideas? He was closer to your family than anyone else in Victoria, at least until this happened."

Jud considered it. "He's been stepping out with Molly Spencer. Maybe he's hiding at her place."

They rode close to the Spencer home, dismounted, and snuck up to the house.

"You go around back in case he tries to leave," Gutierrez said.

As Jud reached it, the back door flew open. Tom practically fell into his arms. He came up swinging, landing one on Jud's jaw. Both fought with the fury of men who had no choice.

The door opened again, and Molly stood in the doorway. The sheriff joined her but stood with his arms crossed, awaiting the outcome of the fight.

Jud thought Tom might give up when he saw the sheriff, but his presence seemed only to increase his desperation. In the end, Jud's strength and experience won out. He flipped Tom onto his belly, tying his hands behind him with the rope Gutierrez tossed him. He jerked him to a sitting position.

"I suppose you're going to lynch me." Tom spit blood.

"You deserve it, between the destruction at the Fleischers' farm, stealing my colt, then setting the fire." Jud smiled and let Tom panic a few seconds. "But I'm going to do something worse. I'm going to take away what you value most." He held up one finger. "I already have the money that you stole." He added a second finger. "I found Crockett in Miss Nellie's stable." Then a third finger. "And now I'll have Princess back. Humiliating you in the process is the icing on the cake."

Tom struggled against the ropes but didn't speak.

Jud turned to the sheriff. "Why didn't you stop the fight?"

"I thought you'd appreciate a chance to give the pup a good whuppin'."

He was right.

CHAPTER THIRTY-NINE

Marion and Ma insisted on providing food for the workers who assembled to rebuild the Fleischer house and barn. Everyone from St. John's Lutheran and their own church had volunteered, as well as a number of townspeople. Those not involved with putting up the buildings set themselves to the task of fashioning basic furniture. The Fleischers had escaped with their lives and livestock—and the clothes on their back.

The women insisted on bringing food, so they had enough to feed the whole town of Victoria. Spicy Mexican dishes, savory German dishes, an abundance of Southern specialties, and peach desserts of every description promised enough for every volunteer. Everyone seemed happy. Georg and Ertha walked along the outline of the house, so clearly a couple, so glad to have a new place to start their married life together. Alvie dashed about with the other schoolchildren, healed from the burns the fire had inflicted. Even Mittens lay content under a spreading acacia, nuzzling her kittens as they gamboled about her. Every one of the miracle kittens would find a home. Alvie's heroic rescue of them had been the talk of the town.

"May I have some tea?" Pastor Bader stopped in front of Marion.

She poured him a glass. "We have a good turnout." She sighed with satisfaction.

"It is. And it is good to see our *Amerikaner* and German brethren working hand in hand."

Marion nodded. She expected the preacher to return to work, but he lingered.

"Miss Morgan. I want to express my admiration for your bravery on the night of the fire."

Marion blinked. What bravery? She hadn't dashed into any burning buildings, hadn't even come close to the fire.

"You rode into town in the black of night all alone. You trusted God to protect you, and He did." The pastor smiled in a way that expressed an abundance of appreciation. Even admiration.

"I only did what anyone would do." Still, his compliment warmed her down to her toes.

He bowed in her honor and returned to work.

Wande and Mama had been given strict orders to let others do the work. The burns on Wande's legs, from knees to toes, were still tender, and Dr. Treviño warned her to stay off her feet and let God finish the job of healing.

Mama did not like sitting still. She wanted to oversee every aspect of the adventure. "A new house. A house that we can build any way that I want. I never thought to have such a thing."

Wande almost laughed. "And all new furniture, as well." And quilts, pots, dishes, clothes—anything they might need.

Marion had insisted on giving Wande the buttercream-colored dress that reminded her of Tom, as well as a couple of older garments.

Jud's work crew, responsible for the newlyweds' wing, took a break. Most of them headed for the food, but Jud joined Wande. "Mrs. Fleischer, do you mind if I whisk your daughter away for a few minutes?"

Mama beamed. "Of course. But do not bother leaving—Wande should not walk. I will go get something to eat."

"Jud, you have not eaten," Wande said. All morning she had not been able to tear her eyes away from him. Over and over she relived the moment he carried her from the burning house.

"Food can wait. This is more important." He took the seat Mama had vacated but didn't speak. Wande did not mind. As long as she was in his company, she was content. She could not have predicted his first words.

"I know I'm not perfect . . . I've been angry about a lot of things since Pa died, and it got worse when Texas joined the Union and Germans started arriving."

"Not this again." Wande had seen that side of Jud, but she thought he had changed.

He held a finger against her lips. "I know I was rude the first time we met. I didn't want you here. I thought the Lone Star State should be for Texans only." He stopped again, gazing in the direction of the road so many had traveled in hope of finding a new life in Texas.

"But then I met you and your family. Good people. Hard workers. A family who had suffered loss, as ours had. I couldn't hate you. It took me long enough to figure out I was also wrong about the other Germans. You were just people who came to Texas, wanting to start over. Ma and Pa did the same thing when I was a boy."

"I know," she whispered.

"When I almost lost you in the fire, I finally figured out that *you* are the most important person in my life. You fill my thoughts. You've taught me things about God I didn't think I needed to learn."

Wande's heart raced.

Jud leaned forward, tracing her chin with his fingers. "I'm not perfect, and I can't promise I'll always say the right thing or do the right thing. But I can promise you that I will always love you . . . with all my heart. What do you say, Wande Fleischer?" He pronounced her name perfectly. "If you are willing, make me the happiest man on earth and say you will be my bride. Do you think Georg and Ertha will agree to a double wedding?"

Wande could hardly form the words. "I will insist."

He leaned in close and claimed her lips with a kiss, as sweet as the scent from the acacia trees.

EPILOGUE

VICTORIA, TEXAS, 1850

Wande peeked into the sanctuary, trying to settle her fussy baby. The combined Morgan and Fleischer clans took up almost half the seats. Tears tickled her eyes.

"Why the tears?" Jud tipped her chin to look at him.

"I am happy."

"Women." He shook his head and grinned.

Through the door, the pastor beckoned them to come forward. "It's that time."

As the congregation sang "Faith of Our Fathers," a new hymn introduced by recent German settlers, Jud held Wande's arm as they walked down the aisle. Will, their first son, toddled out to greet them with a shout. "Mama!"

Laughter rippled across the congregation. Calder winked at Wande and Jud from his seat next to their mother.

From the far end of the pew, Marion stood with her husband, Peter Bader, pastor of the German Lutheran church. The Baders made ready to dedicate their infant daughter. Joining them were Georg and Ertha with their firstborn, Heinrich.

Pastor Bennett, new to the church since the Fleischers' arrival in Victoria four years ago, welcomed the three families with a smile. He led the parents and church members in a simple service, dedicating themselves to nurturing the three babies to faith in Christ. After the dedication, Wande found herself back in the pew wedged between Jud and a squirming Will. She didn't hear much of the sermon, but contentment over having her family gathered around her flooded her soul.

After the service, the congregation headed outside. The ground had dried enough from recent rains to allow a meal out of doors. "You must try some of our cheese," Papa urged Dr. Treviño. "Our cows give us good milk."

"You'll have half of Victoria lined up to buy your cheese next Saturday," Jud said.

"That will be good."

Again tears gathered in Wande's eyes, and she blinked them back. She wanted nothing to interfere with the happiness of this occasion.

"What's troubling you?" Jud tugged baby Drew out of her arms.

"I am thinking we may not ever all be together like this again."

"Wherever we spread across the state of Texas, we'll always be together in spirit. And Billie, wherever she may be." As always, Jud choked a bit when he said Billie's name. His hopes that his sister would return from captivity diminished with each passing year.

"I know. I wish we didn't have to scatter. Georg and Ertha are going off to Mason County to claim the land promised us by the Verein. Calder and Emily are heading home. Marion will leave when Peter is called to another church. And even Alvie is growing up so fast."

She glanced at her sister, now wearing long skirts, carrying on a sedate conversation with a serious young man. "To think they used to play town ball together."

A smile sneaked around Jud's mouth. "We can challenge them to a game now."

"Oh no. We will wait until our boys are old enough to play."

"Soon our families will have enough children for a team all our own. That's how God means it to be. Our family roots sink deep in the Texas soil. Only God knows where new growth will appear next."

Wande leaned against her husband, as strong and steady as the acacia trees she had come to love, and looked into the distance. God was faithful, no matter what the future brought to their families.

Will toddled toward them, carrying a ball. "Daddy play ball."

Jud handed baby Drew back to Wande. The Morgan family would face the future—together.

Excerpt from *Captive Trail*

PROLOGUE

1845

Taabe Waipu huddled against the outside wall of the tepee and wept. The wind swept over the plains, and she shivered uncontrollably. After a long time, the stars came out and shone coldly on her. Where her tears had fallen, her dress was wet and clammy.

At last her sobs subsided. The girl called Pia came out of the lodge. She stood before Taabe and scowled down at her.

Taabe hugged herself and peered up at Pia. "Why did she slap me?"

Pia shook her head and let out a stream of words in the Comanche language. Taabe had been with them several weeks, but she caught only a few words. The one Pia spat out most vehemently was "English."

"English? She hit me because I am English?"

Pia shook her head and said in the Comanche's tongue, "You are Numinu now. No English."

Taabe's stomach tightened. "But I'm hungry."

Pia again shook her head. "You talk English. Talk Numinu."

So much Taabe understood. She sniffed. "Can I come in now?"

"No," Pia said in Comanche.

"Why?"

Pia stroked her fingers down her cheeks, saying another word in Comanche.

Taabe stared at her. They would starve her and make her stay outside in winter because she had cried. What kind of people were these? Tears flooded her eyes again. Horrified, she rubbed them away.

"Please." She bit her lip. How could she talk in their language when she didn't know the words?

She rubbed her belly, then cupped her hand and raised it to her mouth.

Pia stared at her with hard eyes. She couldn't be more than seven or eight years old, but she seemed to have mastered the art of disdain.

She spoke again, and this time she moved her hands as she talked in the strange language. Taabe watched and listened. The impression she got was, "Wait."

Taabe repeated the Comanche words.

Pia nodded.

Taabe leaned back against the buffalo-hide wall and hugged herself, rubbing her arms through the leather dress they'd given her.

Pia nodded and spoke. She made the "wait" motion and repeated the word, then made a "walking" sign with her fingers. Wait. Then walk. She ducked inside the tepee and closed the flap.

Taabe shivered. Her breath came in short gasps. She would not cry. She would not. She wiped her cheeks, hoping to remove all sign of tears. How long must she wait? Her teeth chattered. *It is enough*, she thought. *I will not cry. I will not ask for food. I will not speak at all. Especially not English. English is bad. I must forget English.*

She looked to the sky. "Jesus, help me learn their language. And help me not to cry." She thought of her mother praying at her bedside when she tucked her in at night. What was Ma doing now? Maybe Ma was crying too.

Stop it, Taabe told herself. Until they come for you, you must live the way the Comanche do. No, the Numinu. They call themselves Numinu. For now, that is what you are. You are Taabe Waipu, and you will not speak English. You will learn to speak Numinu, so you can eat and stay strong.

She hauled in a deep breath and rose. She tiptoed to the lodge entrance and lifted the edge of the flap. Inside she could see the glowing embers of the fire. The air was smoky, but it smelled good, like cooked food. She opened the flap just enough to let herself squeeze through. She crouched at the wall, as far from Pia's mother as she could. The tepee was blessedly warm. If they didn't give her food, she would just curl up and sleep. Since she had come here, she had often gone to bed hungry.

Pia didn't look at her. Pia's mother didn't look at her. Taabe lay down with her cheek on the cool grass. After a while it would feel warm.

She woke sometime later, shivering. Pia and her mother were rolled in their bedding on the other side of the fire pit. The coals still glowed faintly. Taabe sat up. Someone had dropped a buffalo robe beside her. She pulled it about her. No cooking pot remained near the fire. No food had been left for her.

At least she had the robe. She curled up in it and closed her eyes, trying to think of the Comanche words for "thank you." She wasn't sure there were any. But she would not say it in English. Ever.

A Morgan Family Series

paperback 978-0-8024-0584-5

eBook 978-0-8024-7852-8

CAPTIVE TRAIL

Taabe Waipu has run away from her Comanche village and is fleeing south in Texas on a horse she stole from a dowry left outside her family's teepee. The horse has an accident and she is left on foot, injured and exhausted. She staggers onto a road near Fort Chadbourne and collapses.

On one of the first runs through Texas, Butterfield Overland Mail Company driver Ned Bright carries two Ursuline nuns returning to their mission station. They come across a woman who is nearly dead from exposure and dehydration and take her to the mission. With some detective work, Ned discovers Taabe Waipu's identity.

paperback 978-0-8024-0585-2

eBook 978-0-8024-7876-4

THE LONG TRAIL HOME

When Riley Morgan returns home after fighting in the War Between the States, he is excited to see his parents and fiancée again. But he soon learns that his parents are dead and the woman he loved is married. He takes a job at the Wilcox School for the Blind just to get by. He keeps his heart closed off but a pretty blind woman, Annie, threatens to steal it. When a greedy man tries to close the school, Riley and Annie band together to fight him and fall in love.

But when Riley learns the truth about Annie, he packs and prepares to leave the school that has become his home.